THE WAY TO ....

SEAN ASHTON was born in Harlow. A former editor of MAP *Magazine* and writer for *Art Review*, his books include *Living in a Land* (Ma Bibliothèque, 2017), a memoir of a hypothetical citizen written in sentences constructed in the negative; and *Sampler* (Valley Press, 2020), a selection of pieces from an imaginary encyclopaedia written by poets. He teaches at the Royal College of Art and Leeds Beckett University.

SEAN ASHTON

THE WAY
TO WORK

SALT

CROMER

PUBLISHED BY SALT PUBLISHING 2023

2 4 6 8 10 9 7 5 3 1

First published in Great Britain in 2023 by
Salt Publishing Ltd
12 Norwich Road, Cromer, Norfolk NR27 0AX United Kingdom

www.saltpublishing.com

Salt Publishing Limited Reg. No. 5293401

A CIP catalogue record for this book is available from the British Library

ISBN 978 1 78463 292 2 (Paperback edition)
ISBN 978 1 78463 293 9 (Electronic edition)

Typeset in Neacademia by Salt Publishing

Printed and bound in Great Britain by Clays Ltd, Elcograf S.p.A

For Anat

'The madman's exclusion must enclose him; if he cannot and must not have another prison but the threshold itself, he is kept at the point of passage.'
MICHEL FOUCAULT, *Madness and Civilisation*

```
K E E P G O I N G J C N B S Q I E T Y C
I P L K D N D H E T M J I D J I E W Q
N C X U T O J F X A V Y T H I W O C H
L S T E H F Q W P L M C H V Z I S J G
D D F L P E I V B N M C W Q I R C V I
M P P N T Y U Y W W T Q Z V S D K G
J F E Q D C H J S K T Y W V N T I E W
Q Z X G T N B J D U C P L S H D I J C
H T U N V M C Z L H E G Y Y J U Y T
C L E W Q S F H G J O P C X M B Z L E
E U J L K G O P C V N X U S Y E W V L
```

I
BOARDING

1

IT WAS TUESDAY when I set out, and I hurried for the train as usual, keen to secure my favourite seat, the one at the rear of Coach B, the designated quiet coach. The quiet coach was barely half full, and it looked like it was going to be a tolerable, perhaps even a pleasant journey. As we left the station and accelerated through the suburbs, past the football stadium and industrial estates, I noticed there were no announcements. Usually, there's a constant sizzle of electricity coming from the speakers, that threatens to bloom into a long-winded enumeration of station stops, reminders to keep one's personal possessions alongside one at all times, warnings not to smoke anywhere on board, including the toilets and vestibule areas, or to knowingly permit smoking anywhere on board; but the public address system didn't seem to be working, and not without relief did I reflect that we wouldn't have to endure the Guard's party piece, which he always seemed to enjoy more than he should.

I'd nearly run into Mark Ramsden on the way to the station. He lived barely a mile from me. Our routes converged in the market square and that morning I'd only just managed to avoid him. For a long time it wasn't clear if I was avoiding Ramsden or Ramsden was avoiding me. It took us a while to work out that we were both avoiding each other. If I spotted him first, I'd duck down a side street and sprint to the rear of the station while he continued to the main entrance. Ramsden favoured a similar method. If I thought he'd seen me first, I'd linger under an awning pretending to check my phone: a clear signal to Ramsden that he should take the initiative. But sometimes we'd see each other at the same moment, and it was unclear who should hang back and who should proceed to the station. Sometimes I'd stop and rummage through my bag to make it look like I'd forgotten something – anything to prevent us running into each other. It was just two men trying to get to work, but we seemed to resent the similarity of our routines.

That morning, I'd outmanoeuvred Ramsden, spotting him through a side street before the market square and sprinting to the station. I'm pretty quick for a 45-year-old. There was plenty of time to get my ticket and pastry prior to boarding, and I still had a minute or two to get comfortable before my colleague came through the sliding door.

There was an awkward moment when, having taken his own seat halfway down Coach B, Ramsden had to go into the vestibule to take a phone call. He really ought to have chosen the front vestibule at the other end, but his path was blocked by passengers still boarding, so he was forced into the rear one where I was sat, and as he went past he shot me a lugubrious look. Despite our reluctance to interact at that time of the morning, we both favoured the same coach. In point of fact, we coveted the same seat: the one at the back, on the right, with the extra leg room: 77a. You would think that, if we had to sit in the same coach, we would have nominated a favourite seat as far as possible from the other man. But we seemed to need this tension, it seemed to serve some purpose.

I wasn't looking forward to the conversation we'd have to have once Ramsden had completed his call. Because once we'd boarded the train, different rules applied. It was childish to

4

ignore each other for the whole journey, so at some point – usually on my way to the buffet car – I would nod at Ramsden, or Ramsden would nod at me. It depended on who'd got seat 77a. It was understood that some concession was expected of the victor. A smile was usually enough to defuse the awkwardness, at most a remark about nothing in particular: as long as you kept moving as you talked and said something utterly banal, the emptiness of the gesture was clear. There always was a danger, of course, that your remark would be more interesting than you intended or – worse still – misheard and you'd have to repeat it, accidentally initiating a longer conversation when the real purpose of your exchange had been to eliminate the need for conversation altogether. I'd seen this happen to other work colleagues, who clearly would have preferred to sit apart but felt compelled to sit together for no other reason than that they were colleagues. Ramsden and I were above all that. We had an understanding.

Anyway, there we were, in Coach B, each in his bubble of pre-work freedom. I'd turned my phone off, fearing a call from Dan Coleman, who regarded the journey as company time. This was a legacy of his predecessor, the late Fred Teesdale, who hadn't cared when we came in as long as we did our jobs. It was always understood that we could catch the later 8:08 train, rather than the 7:08. Dan had continued to allow this on the understanding that we made ourselves available for consultation, but I always turned my phone off. Inevitably, when I went through the ticket barrier at the other end, I'd find a text message from my line manager: I TRIED TO CALL BUT YOU'RE NOT PICKING UP?!?! Or something like that. Now, I have to confess that Mark Ramsden had stolen a march on me here. He was able to give the impression to Dan Coleman that *his* working day began on that 8:08 train, simply because he always answered his calls. And his geniality was very convincing when he picked up. I'd watched him nodding and smiling, nodding and smiling, as though our line manager were right there with him in the carriage, before giving his phone the finger the very second he hung up. It was true that Mark Ramsden was able to sustain the illusion of being more conscientious than me, but at what cost to his personal wellbeing?

Where were we? Yes, we had just pulled out of the station. We're just going past the football ground, and it's starting to rain. Mark Ramsden is there in the vestibule, taking his call, possibly discussing strategy with Dan Coleman for the meeting later that morning. It was an important day: some prospective new clients were coming over from Germany. There was to be a briefing at 11:30 to discuss strategy. The plan was that I was to meet them in the foyer after lunch and take them on a tour of the facilities. I had misgivings about this arrangement. I'd go so far as to say that our prospective German clients had been enticed over to England on false pretences. I knew for a fact that the price we had quoted them was lower than that which Dan Coleman would later write on a piece of paper and push across the boardroom table, and my role, as I led the German delegation around, would be to prepare them for this surprise by dropping hints about our rising production costs. The majority of our clients had no idea how many stages were involved in our manufacturing process, and Dan Coleman's thinking was that they would be less likely to baulk at our final figure if we showed them the full scope of our operation. After the tour of the facilities, this hospitality was to be extended into the evening. Everyone had been asked to prepare for an overnight stay, Dan Coleman having arranged to take our guests out to dinner. Hence my overnight bag. I noticed that Ramsden had his too.

Ten minutes passed before I realised Ramsden was no longer in the vestibule behind me, that he had managed to end his call and creep back to his seat without my noticing. I felt a surge of admiration for my colleague here: just when you thought you'd set new levels of detachment and aloofness, Ramsden upped the ante. But no: he was not in his seat. He wasn't anywhere in Coach B. I thought maybe he'd gone to the buffet car or the toilet, but the 'engaged' light wasn't on and he never went to the buffet car this early. I've watched Ramsden closely over the years and am wise to his routine: a brief look at the newspaper on boarding, a quick scroll down his emails. But that morning he'd given me the slip, and it bothered me not knowing where he was. I knew I wouldn't be able to eat my pastry and enjoy my crossword, not till he was back in his seat where he belonged, not till we'd got the formalities out the way.

2

BEFORE GOING ANY further, I suppose I should tell you something about cat litter. It's not strictly germane to the rest of my account, but it is my vocation, after all. The first recorded use of cat litter is during the reign of Neferirkare II in ancient Egypt c. 2040 BC. This is not surprising given that cats were venerated in that region. We know from the hieroglyphs found in his tomb that Neferirkare's cats were not suffered to bury their waste in ordinary desert sand – that mud was transported from the Nile delta to produce a blended compound. Archaeologists have recreated this compound and found it to be only 26% less efficient at neutralising odour than modern-day equivalents. I don't go so far as to call him the sole pioneer in this area, but we may speculate that Neferirkare was more discerning than most in his quest for a satisfactory formula. The hieroglyphs tell a story of constant experimentation with different proportions of dry and wet material, organic and inorganic, granular and smooth, the aggregate refined with crushed rock, shredded palm leaves, sawdust and bone meal, all in honour of his prize puss Imhotep, whose mummified remains are exhibited alongside Neferirkare's own at the Egyptian Museum in Cairo.

I quote from Fred Teesdale, who made me learn all this by heart on my first day at work nearly fifteen years ago. I once heard him tell a more nuanced version to some Belgian clients, which had it that Neferirkare was also the first to coin the term 'clumping', and which everyone agreed was a more effective sales pitch than the truth. Things were different then. I'd go so far as to call it a golden era.

I should really say a bit more about what I'm leaving behind. Or rather, who. I loved Fred, and Bob Buchanan was entertaining in doses, but Mick Leadbetter? Don Drinkwater? Les Cundy, Jack Meanwell and all the rest of them? I don't think I'll miss them, nor they me. And as for Dan Coleman, I should really have left when he took over.

Mark Ramsden was the only other exception. Despite everything, I have always respected Mark Ramsden. I have always admired his approach. In some ways it resembles my own approach – in some ways we are similar. There are few people with whom one can have a completely tacit understanding, but Ramsden is just such a man. He understands that he must not try to understand me, just as I understand that I must not try to understand him. Ramsden might put it differently, but that is my reading of the situation.

As colleagues, naturally we have often been required to operate *in concert*, but always preferred to do so at a distance. We shared an employer but saw no reason why the right hand had always to know what the left was doing. Our ability to predict what each other would do was far from telepathic, but I wouldn't have dreamt of phoning Ramsden to check whether the thing to be done had in fact been done by him, nor he me. We preferred to rely on instinct, and on those occasions when instinct led to our replicating a task, the results were not uninteresting – I go so far as to call them enlightening.

I'm not sure Dan Coleman saw it that way. But give him his due, it was not long before he managed to exploit this synchronicity. It's worth my fleshing this out, I think; I can see that an example is called for.

'What does a cat like to do in the bathroom?' he asked us one afternoon.

This was more than five years ago now. He hadn't been with us long, Dan – a few months at most – but he'd changed the way we did things already, substituting a more aspirational mindset for the easy-going complacency of Fred Teesdale. This euphemism said it all. What was wrong with 'litter tray'?

'I ask you again,' he said, when no replies were forthcoming: 'What does a cat like to do in the bathroom?'

'As in . . . ?' This was Mark Ramsden.

'As in: besides the obvious.'

'What else is there to do?' asked Don Drinkwater.

'What are the options?' said Les Cundy.

'I want *you* to give *me* options,' said Dan. 'Throw something at me.'

'Dig?' offered Jack Meanwell.

Dan Coleman got as far as the upstroke of the *d* then recapped his marker pen: no, digging was a related activity.

'Bury?' And this – this was Bob Buchanan.

Dan's head shook vigorously. Had Bob even been listening?

'Think laterally,' he said, rejoining us at the table. 'Laterally.'

Dan explained that he wasn't talking about what cats really did, he was talking about what their owners could be persuaded to think possible. His eagerness to distance himself from the basic function of the litter tray was a hallmark of his first days in office. Despite the seniority of his position, he was palpably ashamed of the nature of our business: not a little mortified by the staple product that had served us well for more than forty years. While it was true that we had already begun to manufacture plenty of other things under his leadership, cat litter still accounted for 70% percent of our profit. Some of us were openly nostalgic for the days when that figure had been 100%, when there was nothing but sacks of Premium Grey stacked up on the pallets in Despatch, but the monumental chastity of that enterprise had long gone, our single-product stance having given way to a plethora of sundries: scratch poles, cat flaps, play tunnels, activity towers, all sorts of injection-moulded knick-knacks. Much had been gained, I suppose, in terms of revenue and job security, but was I alone in thinking that something had been lost?

I had managed to remain in my job without contributing a great deal to Dan's programme of diversification, so I surprised myself when, a few days later, I approached him in private with an answer to the question he'd put to us in that meeting. We were not on good terms, but I was due for my appraisal and needed something I could take into my PDR. That, in truth, was my sole motivation.

He seemed to like my idea:

'Make it happen,' he said, slapping the desk in his dismal mock-American way. 'You have two weeks. The workshop will give you carte blanche.'

As I left his office, I noticed that the certificates, the many industry awards we'd garnered during Fred's long tenure, had been taken down. I also noticed that the glass case containing a sample of the very first batch of cat litter we'd ever manufactured – also installed by Fred Teesdale, four decades ago, long before I joined the company – was now covered with a sheet. I wondered whether the display was still intact: the bags of Premium Grey arranged in a pyramid; the black and white photo of Fred in a warehouse coat, flanked by his Brylcreemed staff; the brass plaque on its miniature easel bearing the company motto 'Do What You Do Do Well'; the silver cup from the European Guild of Cat Litter Manufacturers that we won three times in the mid-1970s. As I went towards the door I lifted the corner of the sheet, but Dan Coleman intervened:

'I think we're done here,' he snapped, 'I think we're through.'

This was odd. If he was so bothered by the lowly status of our staple product, why had he given up his position with a leading office supplies manufacturer to come and work for us? His defection from that sanitary world bordered on the neurotic.

A fortnight later, we presented our designs. For it turned out that I was not the only candidate, Mark Ramsden and Bob Buchanan also having thrown their hats into the ring. When Dan Coleman had given me 'carte blanche', I'd assumed that mine would be the only project under discussion, but it was not the case.

There was nothing from Mick Leadbetter, Jack Meanwell, Les Cundy or Don Drinkwater, and Bob Buchanan's pitch fell apart quicker than a circus clown's automobile, leaving myself and Mark Ramsden in a face-off. We'd both elected to work with the hooded model, the litter tray that comes with a detachable roof. I'd had someone in the workshop cut a hole into the end of an existing litter tray, opposite the entrance flap. Then I'd gaffered a second tray onto the back of the first, filling the first with litter and leaving the second empty. There was also a join of cardboard between them, a walkway of sorts that I'd had to improvise to cover up the gap, the curved walls of the two facing lids not being flush. I hadn't factored this into my calculations – hence the makeshift solution. It was all a bit last-minute, and it didn't help that I was late for the presentations. Ideally, I would have got there early and thrown a sheet over it. Whenever possible, it is always better to unveil things. The unveiler is always granted a five-second window of positivity, is he not, regardless of what he unveils?

As it was, I shuffled in halfway through Bob's meltdown, the object naked under my arm.

'I thought you'd do it like that,' said Mark Ramsden, as I placed it on the table.

'Do what like what?'

'The annexe.' He nodded at my assemblage. 'You've stuck an annexe on. So have I. Look.'

Ramsden hit the space bar on his laptop, and there was his design on the projection screen. He hit another key and we had a cat's view of the interior. Like me, he'd got the technicians to help him, but hadn't made the mistake of physically manifesting his idea; he'd done it all on computer, producing a slick animation that took you through the first litter tray and on into the second, which in Ramsden's version was placed on the left-hand side. As well as being aesthetically more radical than my end-on solution, this also had technical advantages. With my design we would've had to recalibrate our machinery, buy in new parts, but with Ramsden's no changes were necessary. Note, also, how Ramsden used my entrance as a springboard for his presentation, gaining rhetorical momentum directly from the inertia of my own failure – precisely what I would have done in his position.

It was a classic case of 'after the lord mayor's show' when it came to my pitch, but Dan was surprisingly upbeat, nodding and laughing all the way through. I had provided the *counter*-example, said our line manager, the option that needed ruling out. Despite its obvious shortcomings, my design had played its part, the cardboard walkway alerting us to the drawback of an end-on solution. Good feedback, on the face of it. And I achieved my main objective: I had something I could take into my PDR.

I later learned the whole thing was a sham. The only reason

Dan Coleman set us this challenge was to provide him with something he could take into *his* PDR. This accounted for the hurriedness of the whole affair, the kneejerk meeting he'd called at the beginning of PDR month. A few weeks later, I found out that Mark Ramsden had already tabled his design in private with Dan Coleman before the day of the pitch. In other words, he let Bob Buchanan and I toil over our offerings for no other reason than to cement his own position with senior management. Our respective travesties, in conjunction with Ramsden's sexier submission, were evidence of the competitive spirit he fostered among his team. But it was total fiction, a story cooked up after the fact.

I can't complain. I got through my own PDR with no probationary measures. There was no beef between me and Ramsden. Had Dan come to me instead, I would've had no compunction about keeping Ramsden in the dark. Like I say, in many ways we are similar. As for Ramsden's design, it is still manufactured to this day. Quite what the cat's supposed to do in the annexe – Ramsden's animation was so slick no one thought to ask. Whatever, there are now trays with annexes, or 'Powder Rooms', as our marketing men prefer. Whether that's a good or bad thing, I don't know, but they are out there, alongside all the other paraphernalia. For better or worse, more world has been added to the world.

3

IT WAS DIFFICULT to pinpoint the precise moment when I noticed something different about my journey. I'd been making this commute for a decade now and was sensitive to any deviation from the norm, so when, after ten minutes, we failed to pull in to our first scheduled stop, I assumed the timetable had changed. When the second stop was also missed, I looked out on unfamiliar terrain, the buildings sparser than usual, the arable fields replaced by common land strewn with dead silver birch trees. In the distance was . . . nothing. No gentle moors disappearing in mist, no cooling towers up ahead on the horizon, none of the usual landmarks. The horizon was not visible at all; the track, usually raised up over the marshland that began just after the suburbs, was instead following a cutting that only allowed you to see fifty metres or so either side. I did not recognise anything. There could be no doubt about it, I was on the wrong train.

I had to be: the sun was breaking over the left-hand side of the track when it should have been on our right at this time of the year. We were on a branch line, peeling away in a gentle south-easterly curve that had continued, it seemed to me, ever since we'd left the station. I checked the reservation stub on the seat in front to see where we were headed, but it was blank. I scanned the carriage again for Mark Ramsden. At least we were both on the wrong train. And by the way, what were the chances of that, two experienced commuters like us? Occasionally there was a late platform alteration, but I remembered checking before boarding. Tempting though it was to go automatically to the platform from which the 8:08 usually departed, I always checked the screen, because the one day you didn't, that would be the day it left from another platform.

I didn't see how I could have made this error. That I had followed due procedure, doing everything I normally do, everything a passenger needs to do to put himself on the right train, bothered me more than the fact of my being on the wrong one, and I took a few minutes to compose myself before trying to find my colleague. I was known for my calmness at work, a meticulous deception on my part, and I didn't want to spoil that illusion by making an exhibition of myself in front of Mark Ramsden. But where was Ramsden? Making his way to the buffet car, as yet unaware of our predicament? Or had he stepped out onto the platform before we left, realising his error at the last moment without bothering to alert me? He'd taken his bag into the vestibule when he'd answered that call, and I was sure I hadn't seen him return to his seat.

I reviewed my options. If I could get off at the next stop, I could catch a connecting train from there or go back and get the 09:08 service. The worse case scenario was the 10:08, which would get me to work around 12:30, and even if I took the 11:08 I'd still be there to greet our German clients and lead the tour of the facilities. But would there be any trains going back the other way? We'd been on a single-track branch line for a while now, and it stood to reason that no trains could come from the opposite direction till we vacated it. Clearly, I needed to find the Guard. He usually began the journey in a small office at the front, just beyond First Class, where he made his preliminary announcements and prepared for his routine ticket inspection, so I decided to take a stroll down-train and intercept him on the way.

Coach C was sparsely populated, and when I asked where we were going no one responded. Now this sometimes happens when you direct a question at everyone, especially in England, so I did not find the silence of the passengers all that strange, to be honest. Neither did I find it odd when I bent down and directed the question at a woman in a rain mac sitting just by the door, and she shrugged and smiled, shaking her head quickly in the way people do when they don't speak your language. Even when I asked a young student on the other side of the aisle, and he didn't respond either, this was fair enough; I could see he was in the middle of some difficult calculation, a ring binder open across his lap, the pages full of equations and complicated-looking flow-charts. I apologised for disturbing him and continued through the carriage.

'Excuse me,' I said to an elderly lady at the far end; but before I could complete my sentence she disappeared into the vestibule, locking herself in the toilet.

'Excuse me,' I repeated, turning to the woman on the other side. But I was already talking to an empty seat. She too had just got up, scampering down the aisle to the rear of the carriage while my back was turned.

In Coach D I approached a man at a table, sliding in opposite and confronting him directly. Possibly I was a bit short with him. And he was busy, flicking through documents in his briefcase with one hand while scrolling down a page on his laptop with the other, a half-eaten pain au chocolat balanced on the edge of the keyboard. On reflection, he was the worst person to ask for he was already doing three things at once.

'Where's this train going?' I nevertheless demanded, angered now by my failure to obtain this basic piece of information. But he didn't seem to hear. When I repeated the question, he simply reached for his pain au chocolat, nibbled at the corner, and set it down again on the edge of his laptop, continuing to ignore me.

It was the same in the rest of the carriage: everyone looked straight through me. There were still no announcements from the Guard, no information about our scheduled stops or final destination, no reminders to keep one's personal possessions beside one at all times, none of the usual stuff.

I proceeded on to Coach E, usually one of the busier coaches, but this morning there were nothing but bald men in suits hunched over laptops, each at his own separate table seat, not a single one of whom stirred as I put the question. I had no joy in Coach F either. The heating had failed here and it was deserted, the only occupant a young man in a blue shell suit with red hair and a silver crucifix dangling from his ear, who scowled at me as I passed, sipping from a tin of cider. I checked the reservation stubs, but again they were blank.

Coach G was packed, probably due to the fault with the heating in the previous coach, and the atmosphere seemed friendlier here, so I stopped in the middle of the aisle and made a formal announcement, a plea I suppose you'd call it, addressing the passengers as one:

'Excuse me,' I said, 'I'm sorry to bother you but . . .'

I stopped, realising that this was just how the homeless guy begins his spiel before holding out the paper cup, and I sensed the passengers stiffening in their seats, just waiting for me to leave. Better to single someone out. I chose the fat gentleman in the green mohair suit with a carnation in the buttonhole and a bright yellow bowtie. His outfit suggested a certain approachability, but he dismissed me with a ruffle of his newspaper, so I turned to the woman in the headscarf behind him who was knitting. I felt sure she'd respond, but she cursed me for making her drop a stitch, even though it happened a split-second before and I wasn't really to blame.

Finally, I approached the man in the wheelchair at the front end of the carriage. I was relieved to see it was the same man I saw every day on the 8:08, and I was certain he'd put me at my ease, inform me that we were simply going via a different route. I regarded him as one of the stalwarts of the 8:08 service. Usually he smiled whenever I passed him on my way to the buffet car. He smiled at everyone, as well he might, for he had a special area of the train all to himself the size of a small studio flat. We'd never actually exchanged words before, but there was an unspoken solidarity, an understanding of sorts, built up over years of eye contact. This morning, however, he was silent in a more morose way as I came alongside, shoulders hunched, head bowed, hands steepled on his lap. He looked like he was praying. At least the other two had acknowledged me, but the man in the wheelchair seemed unaware of my presence, screwing his eyes shut when I put the question and murmuring under his breath.

It was time to put a stop to this. I stood, turned round, addressing the whole carriage once more:

'Look,' I shouted, in a voice I hardly recognised as my own, 'won't someone help me? Where's the Guard? Has anyone seen the Guard? Won't someone tell me where we're headed?'

4

To put all this in context, I should really describe a typical morning on the 8:08. Usually, about half an hour into my journey, I would rise from my place in the quiet coach at the rear of the train to visit the buffet car in the middle, located in Coach H. Now, you could wait for the trolley service to come round if you preferred, but any experienced commuter will tell you that the water dispensed from a trolley is not nearly as hot as that dispensed in the buffet car. And there was entertainment to be had, was there not, from passing through the intermediate coaches, each with its distinct atmospheric register. Coach C was regarded as an auxiliary quiet coach by some in the designated quiet coach, a refuge for those who had given up policing the behaviour of other passengers. For some reason Coach D always had a high percentage of corporate types hammering away on laptops, each commandeering an entire table seat to him or herself, a peripatetic extension of the office desk. This was in contrast to Coach E, the most eclectic carriage, full of senior citizens on day trips, backpackers, screaming kids, families on holiday, folk on their way to weddings, yacking 'creatives' with loud electronic devices. Coach F was characterised by a slightly sinister compliance, to my mind, everyone here berthed in their allotted seat, preferring to sit next to a stranger when there were plenty of double seats elsewhere. Coach G was full of people who had clearly sprinted for the train and just decided to stay put, thankful to have made it at all and lacking the motivation to find a better seat. And then there was Coach H, the buffet car itself, with its deafening extractor fan and humid gust of pastry aromas, marking the end of Standard Class. Just a little further was a vestibule where I sometimes liked to loiter after getting my coffee, peering through the sliding door at the First Class passengers, with their complimentary newspapers and at-seat restaurant service, for no other reason than that my ticket entitled me to do so.

This, then, was the normal order of things. But that morning everything already seemed out of tune as I took my seat in Coach B. The subsequent behaviour of the passengers – their silence when I asked them where we were going, their refusal to acknowledge me – was foreshadowed by an intuitive sense that all was not as it should be. Only a little later did I perceive its root cause, which became more noticeable the further I advanced. As I got up and passed along the aisle, several faces were well known to me from my daily commute. Naturally, the presence of these regulars didn't strike me as odd when I believed I was on the right train. But it became very odd indeed when I realised I was on the wrong train. It took a while to realise that what was most unsettling was that we were *all* on the wrong train. Everyone should have been just as anxious as me, up on their feet, looking for the Guard, asking each other what was going on, but there was nothing in their faces to suggest that the scenery rushing past the window as we continued to bear south-east was anything but familiar.

After Coach G, the next vestibule should have led directly to the buffet car in Coach H, but there were no pastry aromas, no food smells of any kind, and I could see from here that there was no counter at the far end of that carriage, just further ranks of passengers canted over to one side as we continued to bear left. As I approached the door, I assumed this was a new train recently brought into service - the newer models have an extra coach before the buffet car, and the livery looked slightly different, a bluer shade of grey with a glossier finish.

It was then that I thought it might be a better idea to go back. I thought I remembered seeing the Guard at the rear of the train, just before pulling out, and it seemed more sensible to eliminate that possibility before heading to his office at the front. There was another coach right at the back, not accessible to the public, between Coach B and the rear engine, that the trolley operators sometimes went into after they'd completed their first leg of Standard. Sometimes the Guard began his routine ticket inspection from there, emerging from behind you and taking you by surprise.

When I went back into Coach G, the man in the wheel-chair had moved from his special area on the left, positioning himself in the middle of the aisle. I assumed he was about to visit the disabled toilet, so I stood aside, waiting for him to go past. But he stayed where he was, head bowed, hands clasped together in that same gesture of supplication as before, the tips of his fingers going red, his forearms shaking from the pressure. He held this posture for a few seconds, then his hands parted theatrically and he came closer, forcing me towards the vestibule.

'Excuse me,' I said.

It was now that this hitherto jaunty commuter, for so long a talismanic presence on the 8:08, was transformed into what I must now call the Harbinger. I call him that because he seemed to mark the boundary between things as they were and things as they are now.

'And what can I do for you?' he asked.

I was wrong-footed by the Scottish accent – I'd always assumed he was English.

'I need to find the Guard.'

'The *Guard?*'

He was in much better shape than I remembered. His upper body development was impressive, enhanced by the lumberjack shirt he was wearing, which was cut off at the shoulders, revealing his huge biceps. His wrists were thicker than my forearms, massive trapezoids joining his neck halfway up, a tiny head that he kept low, like a ram getting ready to butt you, and a face that seemed too big for it, top lip curling up over his teeth, which were whiter, much whiter than I remembered. I didn't recall him having such good teeth and such fine arms, or such a small head. Not till he became the Harbinger.

'He needs the Guard,' he shouted over his shoulder. 'He's asking about the Guard. Has anyone seen the Guard?'

There was a howl of laughter from the whole of Coach G.

'No Guard hereabouts,' said the Harbinger. 'Not for a while now.'

'But I saw him,' I said. 'I saw him at the back.'

'The *back?* He says he saw him at the back.'

More laughter.

'Yes. Near Coach B.'

'Coach B?' The Harbinger grinned, his huge hands caressing his wheels, fingernails running along the treads of the tyres. 'B, you say? Which one?'

'What do mean which one?'

'*Which* B?'

'*Coach* B.'

'Yes, but which Coach B are you talking about?'

'I don't understand.'

'Let me put it this way.' The Harbinger rolled closer, pinning my shoe under his wheel, pressing me against the vestibule door, which slid open, leaving me on the threshold. 'How many coaches did you come through? Just now?'

I counted them on my fingers: 'B, C, D, E, F, and this one, G.'

'Six coaches? That's all? And you say you saw the Guard?'

'I think so.'

'You think so. He thinks so. Tell me, which direction was he going in?'

'This way, I assume.'

The passengers were whispering now, some of them pointing to their temples, making 'mad-person' gestures to each other.

'Quiet!' yelled the Harbinger. 'There must be some mistake, some personal oversight on your part. The Guard has never been seen in these parts.'

'What do you mean, these parts? I saw him at the rear of the train.'

There was further laughter here, more muted than before. 'No Guard hereabouts,' said the Harbinger. 'Hereabouts or thereabouts.'

'Hereabouts or thereabouts,' murmured the other passengers moronically, 'hereabouts or thereabouts.'

'Look, I need to get back to my seat.'

'Inadvisable,' said the Harbinger.

'Let me past.'

'I strongly advise against it at this time.'

'Let me through. My stuff's there.'

'Your what?'

'His stuff!' It was a child's voice, coming from the rear of the carriage.

A thin man in tweed with a greasy comb-over got up from a table seat, and the boy handed him a bag: my overnight bag.

'There you go, sir,' he said, when he'd come back up to our end of the carriage. 'I'm afraid we had to look inside to establish the identity of the owner. Oh, and this is yours too, I believe.' He handed me a ticket.

'I already have a ticket.'

'With respect, sir, I think it's yours.'

I checked my pockets. There was nothing there.

'Thanks. Thank you.'

'No problem, sir. We found it in your wallet.'

'My wallet?'

He was already handing it to me. Then he bowed and returned to his seat.

'Hang on a minute. My jacket. What about my jacket?'

Here it came, passed up the carriage by the other passengers, the arms dragging over the tops of the seats like the wings of a dead bird.

'There,' said the Harbinger. 'You have all you need. And now you must go.' I thought he was going to shake my hand as he leaned forward and caught hold of my wrist, but he gave me a massive Chinese burn and pushed me in the chest as hard as he could, sending me flying into the vestibule. 'Go!' he repeated, as the door slid shut. 'Go, and do not come back!'

Have you ever walked into a patio door you thought was open? Or thrown your whisky onto the backgammon board when you meant to reach for the dice shaker? Or stood in a bar and stared at your dead father for ages before realising the far wall is mirrored, the bar half as big as you'd thought, your face no longer as young as you'd imagined? Or fallen ill on holiday and asked a local to direct you to a doctor, and he has pointed to a plausible facade in a side street, with a clean reception staffed by refreshingly informal women, where you have waited for five minutes before realising it's a brothel?

All these things have happened to me, but I began to think, as I lay there in the vestibule, smarting from the Harbinger's rough treatment, that some people were destined for more protracted confusion. I had been in situations that threatened to become purest phantasm, only to be enlightened after a few seconds or at most a few minutes of bafflement. But here I was, twenty minutes in, and the fog had yet to lift.

The only explanation I could muster was that I was the victim of some spectacular set-up, an outrageous hidden-camera scenario, the inaugural star of some new reality show. I remembered a story a friend of mine had once told, about a play he'd gone to see, a production put on by an interactive theatre group. He did not know when he paid his entrance fee that the audience would become the cast, assisted by actors planted among them, and he had ended the evening having a sword fight with another spectator. I'd heard of ambitious variations on this format, scenarios played out in public, the aim being to see how far people could be pushed, the events gradually escalating till they reacted against the matrix into which they'd been drawn. Was I now participating in one of these real-life fantasies? If so, all I had to do was show that I got it. All I had to do was break the fourth wall, if that's the right term – go back into Coach G and punch the man in the wheelchair, or at least tip him over. The shock of that transgression would bring the whole thing to a halt.

When the sliding door wouldn't open, I assumed it was a standard malfunction. I gripped the side, bracing my feet against the vestibule wall and pulled as hard as I could but I couldn't make it budge, and when I banged on the glass no one inside reacted. I don't how long I kept this up, but everyone kept ignoring me. The Harbinger was doing a Sudoku, the man in tweed playing patience, the little boy marching up and down the aisle blowing into a recorder. Things had already moved on in Coach G. And now that the door was sealed shut, there was only one direction in which to go. At least I had my things.

5

COACH H, YOU'LL recall, I had identified as the extra coach of the new model I believed had just been brought into service. If this was the case, then just beyond here would be the buffet car, now located in Coach I. Perhaps I would find Mark Ramsden there, swirling a brandy in a plastic glass, equally astonished, his own wrist smarting from a confrontation with the man in the wheelchair? I was still unsure whether he was on the train or had alighted at the last moment, via the rear vestibule. But hadn't he taken that call just after the beeps had sounded and the doors were locked? He had definitely boarded, that much was certain, for he had passed me to get to the rear of the quiet carriage, and I convinced myself again that he had somehow managed to get back to his seat afterwards without my noticing. If this was so, given that he had not been there when I got up and went into Coach C, there was no other place for him to be than further downtrain. I didn't recall seeing any toilets engaged on passing through the vestibules, so it stood to reason that he was at large in one of the other carriages.

Had he too been roughed up, ignored, given short shrift by the other passengers? Or had he been cooler, more laid-back about the situation? I could have called him there and then, but I wanted to see if he was in the buffet car first. Plus, it would have felt odd, calling Mark Ramsden, even under these circumstances. I'd never called him before in my life.

I'd texted him hundreds of times, but an actual conversation was unthinkable. We spoke on the office phones regularly, but to do so on our personal handset was too intimate to contemplate. Doubtless the prospect of his calling me was equally unthinkable to Ramsden.

I'd just been physically assaulted in Coach G, but Coach H turned out to present a challenge of a more psychological nature. As the door slid back, the first thing I noticed was the smell, a perfume I remembered earlier from Coach C. It was the foreign woman in the rain mac, the one who'd ignored me before, her blue scented scarf puffing out over the collar of her coat. How had she got past me undetected? The only opportunity to overtake me had been directly after my alter-cation with the Harbinger when I was I lying face-down in the vestibule, but she would've had to have timed it just right.

Improbable though it was that two identical twins had chosen to sit apart, or that two biologically unrelated passen-gers had happened to have put on the same rain macs, done their hair in the same way, chosen the same vintage scarf and scented it with the same perfume, I preferred to entertain either of those options than revive my earlier theory that I was indeed the victim of some avant-garde theatre group. Yet revive it I did as, looking further up the carriage, I saw the lady from Coach G, the one who had been knitting, her purple headscarf now pinned together at the front with a jewelled brooch, and just across the aisle the obese gentleman in the green mohair suit. And there, at the far end, was the student. This time he was facing me. He had a mole in the exact same place, a large oval-shaped blemish on the left corner of his jaw, and his hair was identically styled, brushed back from his face, hooked behind his ears, an unkempt bob, a student haircut, but not one you'd associate with his generation. It was a 90s' style, echoed by his clothing: beige army trousers with pockets on the legs and a baggy hooded top bearing a fractal design. He was as redolent of that period as the woman in the rain mac was of the early eighties. And he had the same annoying habit of allowing a small icicle of snot to gather in his septum before sniffing it back up, a habit which – interestingly – I did not remember in his Coach C counterpart till I observed it in his doppelgänger.

Had Mark Ramsden also noticed these things as he made his way down the train? I hoped so, for I did not want to find myself in the position of defending ostensibly supernatural phenomena as we drank our brandies in the buffet car. If we had both seen something odd, then neither of us would have to defend our sanity. Or maybe we'd both keep quiet about it? Yes, more than likely Ramsden would deny having seen any-thing unusual. In which case I would be forced to deny it too.

The buffet car should have been next. In the older models, it's divided into two halves, the rear half for seating and the front half done out with a counter and a galley kitchen behind a partition; in the newer models it's built into the vestibule bearing onto First Class, a narrow gangway to the left of the counter allowing access to the front of the train. But as the door slid back I saw that the vestibule after Coach H was identical to all the others: beyond this was just another Standard Class carriage.

I continued on through Coach I, again noting one or two familiar faces. There was an elderly gent with a crimson birth-mark on his forehead, smelling of pipe tobacco, and another man with a briefcase who resembled the one who had ignored me in Coach E. The resemblances, I noted, as I moved slowly down the aisle, were not just physical but temporal, not just visual but behavioural. The man in Coach E had had one hand in his briefcase and the other on the keyboard of his laptop, as I'd passed by, and so did the second man in Coach I, though his pastry, I noted, had now been reduced to a morsel. I scared myself with the clarity of this recollection, and decided to make a mental record of some of the other faces here in Coach I that I *didn't* remember seeing before, to see if they recurred later. But when I proceeded to Coach J I found I'd forgotten them and that, instead, I was drawn to certain other details – the buckle on the lapel of someone's jacket, a newspaper open on a certain page, a liver-spotted hand raising a water bottle to a pair of puckered lips – that seemed familiar to me from earlier carriages. Again, it struck me that these details would have been completely lost to my memory, had they not been repeated.

The same thing happened in the next two carriages. And then, in Coach M, I saw him again: the fat man in the green mohair suit, on the left in the middle of the carriage. As on the previous two occasions, he was sat facing me, with his back to the direction of travel, and as I approached he smiled, appearing to catch my eye with the intention of engaging me in conversation. I was about to reciprocate his warmth when I noticed a woman with a trolley behind me, coming up the aisle.

'Tea, coffee, snacks; tea, coffee, snacks, sandwiches . . .'

I couldn't work out how she had got there. There had been no woman with a trolley when I'd boarded, though it's conceivable she could have emerged from the door in the vestibule to the rear of Coach B, where the trolley operators went for their break. I thought I recognised her from the 8:08 service of years ago, a tall mixed-race girl with braids, beautiful lips, bangles on both arms, but it could have been someone else.

I pulled into an empty seat to let her pass. She didn't have to ask what the man in green mohair wanted, pouring hot water from the urn into a paper cup, sealing the plastic lid and serving it in a single smooth movement.

'One Earl Grey.'

'Thank you, my dear. I'm afraid I have only this.'

The trolley woman held the fifty-pound note up to the light. 'I'll let you off the rest,' she said, placing it in her tin, 'give it to me next time.'

I expected the other passengers to laugh, but she took the fifty without giving him change, releasing the brake and continuing on her way:

'Tea, coffee, snacks; tea, coffee, snacks, sandwiches . . .'

Before exiting Coach M, she stopped at another passenger, who only handed over a fiver for his hot drink, and was given change. When she had gone I got to my feet, and as I passed him I recognised him as the student, hunched over his ring binder as before. At that moment, the train swayed violently to one side, and I had to reach out to steady myself, catching hold of his shoulder when I meant to grip the headrest, sending hot tea all over his lap. Most people would have shouted, sworn at me, lashed out, but he remained motionless and silent, apparently unharmed by the scalding liquid. He did not even seem to feel my hand or hear my apology as I regained my balance and quickened into the vestibule.

I continued on, the same passengers reappearing till I fancied there was no one in those subsequent carriages I had not seen before. Most were sat in the same position and performing the same actions: a man hunched over a crossword was in the act of inking in a solution he had proposed five minutes earlier; a baby's dummy had fallen from its lips, caught again by its alert mother; and an elderly couple were eating their apples, slicing off segments with an old-fashioned penknife with a wooden handle. When, in Coach Q, I came across a man asleep in an eye mask who I had just seen in the previous carriage, I decided to return to Coach P to verify the resemblance, but again, there was a malfunction with the sliding door and I was prevented from going back.

As I left Coach Q for Coach R, I knew that I should be right at the front of the train by now, but I had not yet even reached First Class. Here, by my estimations, on the left-hand side of the vestibule, should have been a little cubicle with a frosted glass window: the Guard's office. And beyond this, the bicycle carriage. But there was just another toilet, another sliding door, through which I could see that Standard Class continued.

It was raining hard outside now, and I shut the vestibule window, which began to work its way down again immediately, a problem no one had been able to solve in the entire history of train design. But why was there an openable window on this train? Hadn't they been phased out years ago? There'd been none in the earlier vestibules, none between coaches P and Q, yet there was one here, between Coaches Q and R. And as on trains of old, it would not stay shut. A pool of water had collected in the corner, sluicing across the floor when we tilted into a bend, flowing back again when we went the other way.

It now occurred to me that I really ought to phone Mark Ramsden. If ever there was a situation that called for an armistice, a temporary lifting of our unwritten code, this was surely it. And so, for the first time in my life, I dialled his mobile number.

I was dismayed to feel my heart pound as I waited for him to answer, as though I were not, in fact, phoning a work colleague, but calling a girl to ask her out. The longer it rang the more anxious I got, and the less clear I was about what I ought to say. Ramsden was taking ages to answer, and with each second that passed the more likely it seemed he would be angry when he picked up: 'Why're you calling me?' he might snap, 'I thought we had an understanding?' The longer I waited, the more convinced I was that I would be losing more than I gained by phoning Mark Ramsden. I did not want Ramsden to think that I was trying to 'reach out' to him. We had striven to maintain a neutral relationship, devoid of all the usual politics, the trivial give-and-take that characterised other people's social interactions; why jeopardise this with a single injudicious act?

No, a text would be better. I sent him a simple question: WHICH COACH ARE YOU IN? This was more consistent with the laconic style we had employed for the last decade, requiring as it did a one-letter response.

I thought I should text Dan Coleman too. I punched out the words 'Delayed on the 8:08, reschedule meeting for . . .' But then I stopped. How could I estimate my time of arrival when I had no idea where I was or which direction I was headed? We'd been on the move for forty minutes now, and if the train was heading south, as it usually did, albeit via a different route, then shouldn't we be skirting the edge of the low country by now, maybe somewhere near the fens? But I wasn't aware of any other southbound routes the 8:08 could have followed. We had once been diverted out towards the coast to avoid a storm-damaged section of the track, arcing round and rejoining the usual line further south, but this wasn't that route. I had no idea where we were. I didn't even know if we were north, south, east or west of our original starting point.

It was then that I saw the mountains coming into view. There they were, on our left, veiled in heavy weather, and we seemed to be heading straight for them, the water in the vestibule now rolling back as we inclined towards the foothills. I should probably hold fire on that message to Dan Coleman till I had more information. The more I looked at it, the more meaningless it was. 'Dclayed' was optimistic, and was it really 'the 8:08' that I was on? I was on *a* train, somewhere in the middle of England – I could be no more specific than that. The meeting would go ahead without me anyway. And if I contacted Dan now, he might suggest I join them by conference call. The prospect of offering my thoughts remotely from the vestibule while my colleagues sat there in comfort with a plate of biscuits and a pot of coffee did not appeal, so I put my phone back in my pocket, picked up my overnight bag and entered Coach S.

I know: there *is* no Coach S. Or there shouldn't be, not on the 8:08 service. The coaches stop at R. But I had already negotiated two extra coaches and I was curious, now, as to how many more there were.

Need I add that Coaches S through to Z upheld the same trend inaugurated by Coach G, and maintained in Coaches H through to R, i.e., the replication of passengers familiar to me from Coaches B through to F: the fat man in mohair; the snotty-nosed student; the foreign woman in the rain mac; the lady in the headscarf with the fortune-teller's brooch, and numerous others? Each time something new was added. The fat man was cheerier; the student had a fresh sheet of foolscap; the woman's headscarf morphed into a turban, and she was making headway with her knitting. If I was not mistaken, an Aran sweater was taking shape.

I wasn't mistaken. And it was doing more than take shape – it was nearly finished. And when it was finished, she handed it to me, and I have worn it ever since. Look: I am wearing it now.

II

STANDARD CLASS

1

IT'S NOT A classic Aran by any stretch, but it's 100% wool with the same all-weather versatility. It's also an official garment. That much is clear from the insignia in the middle of the chest, the number '8' embroidered in red, with a small gap at the top of the upper loop. The insignia is reproduced on the visor of my cap – a more recent acquisition. I have reason to believe I am not the first to wear it, nor shall I be the last. The lining is smudged with the perspiration of past incumbents, and I am adding my own even now. Perhaps my successor will inhale my liquors and know something of my era.

But let us return to that first Coach Z. When I closed in on that carriage, I briefly forgot my situation. For there is something pleasing, is there not, about a train which encompasses the whole alphabet? Which commuter, if they are honest with themselves, does not carry around some desire for completion, an exhaustion of all available letters? It's true that there are no Coach A's anywhere on board but this did not diminish my excitement at seeing my first Coach Z.

It's a general rule of Standard Class that folk get friendlier as you advance through any given section of the train, Coach Z being the most convivial and Coach B the least. Each section varies too. In some, the conviviality permeates as far back as Coach L, while in others the good cheer in the later carriages is a little forced. As on my normal commute, every coach has its own distinct signature. I will not detain us with a full taxonomy, but if one is in need of charity, say, or compassion, or empathy, one is advised to wait till at least Coach W, or if in need of mischief and horseplay, to loiter in Coach K - any K will do.

On entering Coach Z, I immediately sensed that its passengers were more approachable than any I'd met so far that morning. Naturally, I was still perplexed at the repetition of passengers from previous carriages, but towards the end of that first section their indifference towards me had softened. By Coach W, people were at least beginning to look up as I went past, and by the time I got to Coach Z attitudes had shifted from borderline hostile to mildly inquisitive. As a rule, during the day not many passengers are up and about, so any wayfarer arouses curiosity. People were not exactly smiling as I completed the end of that first section, but they were doing that thing we all do on trains from time to time: looking up to see who's coming and stopping themselves from smiling at the last moment. It was not much, but it was something.

Only one person spoke to me, however: the woman in the headscarf knitting the jumper. It was the fourth time I'd seen her that morning. There she was, in the last seat on the left, just before the sliding door. As I approached, she looked me directly in the eye and shifted into the window seat, which I took as an invitation to join her. I'm not sure it was, looking back, but she didn't object when I sat down. The only difference, I noted, between herself and the doppelgänger I'd just seen in Coach V was that the sweater was now all but complete. The first time I'd seen her, it had been nothing more than a waistband, and even by Coach V it had progressed no further than the middle of the chest; yet just a few carriages later here she was darting in the insignia I spoke of before, her knitting needles now swapped for an embroidery kit, with only the upper loop of the number '8' to go.

'Looks tricky,' I said, slipping in beside her.

'It *is* tricky.'

I was thrown by her response – not by her words but by the speed with which she found them, already mouthing the word 'it' when I was on the last syllable of the word 'tricky', like she'd known what I was going to say.

She held the sweater up and turned towards me, pulling the sleeves out over her arms, the cuffs drooping down over her hands:

'What do you think?'

I didn't notice how tiny she was till now. She can't have been more than four-feet-nine. Her predecessors seemed bigger when I compared them to the present manifestation. Her skin was darker too – almost Asian, to my eye – and she was bolder by far than the three previous incarnations, who had all seemed so nervous and timid, albeit progressively less so. Looking back now, it's difficult not to see her as a second Harbinger. Where the first Harbinger's job had been to put me on my toes, her function was to redress the balance, return some equanimity to my spirits – of this, I'm convinced.

'Well?'

I studied the sweater approvingly.

'You'll stay awhile,' she commanded casually, laying it down and squeezing my knee.

I'm not normally a tactile man, but the physical gesture bothered me less than the verbal one. It was the second time that she'd read my thoughts, for it happened that I did want to stay. So far, my overriding emotions had been anger and irritation, at the passengers to a certain extent but mostly at myself for boarding the wrong train; but now, having arrived in Coach Z, I was anxious as to what lay ahead of me beyond the end of the alphabet, and I believe she sensed it.

'Yes, you'll stay a while,' she repeated.

That was another verbal trait shared by many passengers in Standard and some in First Class: the utterance of polite orders unaccountably matched to the desires of those to whom they were addressed. She was the first passenger in whom I encountered it, but I observed it in more or less everyone I met thereafter, to lesser and greater degrees.

'I think I will,' I said. 'I think I will stay a while.

She squeezed my knee again: 'Just till I finish.'

'The sweater?'

'Yes. I won't be long now.'

'Then I can go?'

What was I saying? I needed her *permission* to go? What was I playing at? Why wasn't I up on my feet, trying to do something about the situation, looking for the Guard, raising Mark Ramsden on the phone, composing a message to my line manager? I was an hour into a journey that, for all I knew, was taking me in the opposite direction to where I needed to go, yet here I was promising to stay with this stranger till she had finished her knitting.

'But just to make it clear,' she added, as she resumed her embroidery, 'I won't be going forward with you.'

'I'm sorry?' I made it sound like I hadn't heard rather than didn't understand.

'Don't take it personally,' she said, 'but it's a little early for me.'

'A little early for what?'

'Going forward.'

'You mean, a little early . . . in the day?'

'Early in the *week*,' she said, squeezing my knee a third

42

time. 'And I don't want to give up my seat. It's a good seat, isn't it? What do you think? What do you think of my seat?' She was in the one with the extra leg room, that should have had a blue sign above it saying 'Priority Seating'. 'No, I don't think I'll go forward,' she went on. 'Not this week. Maybe not next week either.'

I was nodding furiously throughout this exchange; though the content of her speech was baffling, its tone seemed to demand casual acquiescence. Clearly, 'going forward' was not some coy euphemism, but had some meaning relating to the business of rail travel as she understood it, and I thought it best to let the mystery resolve itself. Why she assumed that I wanted to go forward, or might want to go forward, with her, whatever going forward was – I left aside for the moment, for it was the time-frame that perplexed me here:

'A week, you say?'

'Yes. I can't see me going forward before then.'

'As you say, it's a good seat.'

'It *is* a good seat.'

'A Priority Seat.'

'A what?'

'Never mind.'

'So, you'll stay? Just for a while.'

How long was a while? And why was it necessary to establish these parameters now? But I was so relieved to be spoken to by someone, anyone, however cryptically, I reined in my curiosity. And all that was required was my passive consent. She could have recited the ingredients from the back of a crisp packet and I would have sat there and nodded.

Outside, the scenery had barely changed since we left the station. After passing the football ground and industrial estates, the same collection of concrete huts, wire fencing and defunct electricity substations had appeared in permanent rotation, against the same dreary backdrop of scrub and silver birch, not a single person walking their dog in the drizzle or a single bird in view, no lights on in any of the buildings that rushed past, all of which seemed to be either half-built or derelict. What bothered me, I reflected, as the woman in the headscarf fell silent and continued her embroidery, was not my current predicament per se, but the stealth of the transition, the absence of a clear boundary between things as they had been and things as they were now. The incident with the Harbinger merely ratified a change that had begun much earlier. But when? At the moment of boarding the train or before? On waking that morning? I had been struck, during the first half-hour of my journey, by the strangeness of the landscape, a strangeness that resided not, as I initially thought, in the foreignness of its features, but in their very familiarity. The edgeland usually restricted to the city's outskirts had been sustained well beyond its limits, giving the impression of our passing through a perpetual threshold, and this external liminality mirrored my inability to pinpoint the boundary between things as they had been and things as they are now.

I don't know how long I toyed with these thoughts as the woman in the headscarf completed the sweater. There was twenty minutes' work left at most, but she seemed to string it out. This made the rest of our time together slightly uncomfortable, for she was silent as she applied the finishing touches and I didn't know what to say. Finally, after placing her equipment in a tin from her wicker shopping bag, she folded the sweater neatly, crossing the arms over the back, and presented it to me with a formality that bordered on ceremonial. To refuse the gift was out of the question, and the fact that it was accompanied by no actual words made it harder to do so. I praised the craftsmanship and thanked her, though I was unsure whether to try it on now or later. She had folded it so meticulously, I decided that later was best.

When I looked up again after placing it in my bag, she was bunching her coat into a makeshift pillow, in readiness for a nap, and I took this as my cue to move on.

2

THE VESTIBULE AFTER Coach Z was cold, and the sudden drop in temperature had a sobering effect. The various axes of my predicament – the train's uncertain destination, the behavioural quirks of its passengers, Mark Ramsden's disappearance, my no-show at the meeting – comprised, as it were, a graph on which I had yet to plot a single meaningful co-ordinate. Far from taking decisive action, I had just spent the best part of an hour trading non sequiturs with a stranger rather than trying to reach my colleagues, inform them that I was delayed, that I wouldn't be able to lead the German clients on a tour of the facilities after all, and might even miss the restaurant.

There were still no announcements about our progress, our station stops and so forth. Obtaining this information was paramount, but first I was going to have a cigarette. Usually I'm OK, even on long journeys, but I felt like I needed one. Under the circumstances, I felt like I was *entitled*.

I'd just finished rolling it when the vestibule suddenly darkened. I thought we'd entered a tunnel at first, but when I looked out we were passing along the bottom of a deep gorge, the rock face no more than ten feet away. Our speed was reduced by as much as half, and I could smell the wet moss through the open window, the foliage turning from a tertiary blur to a procession of distinct species adapted to the dark, damp conditions. We continued like this for twenty minutes, on a gradually steepening incline, till the rock became a grassy escarpment, the sky overhead no longer grey but a fierce aquamarine blue.

We emerged from the gorge onto a sort of plateau and there was a purifying sense of having broken through the weather, as when a plane takes off in a storm and settles into its flight path above the clouds. I shoved my head out the window again, looking back as we tilted into a left-hand bend: I could see the carriages curving round, the rear of the train still in the gorge. Again the incline steepened and we entered another gorge, which levelled out after ten minutes onto a second plateau that provided a clearer view of the country through which we had just passed, an undulating landscape of dales and bluffs that could not be seen before, enclosed as we were by the embankment. As we progressed, tilting more acutely through further bends, first one way, then the other, I looked back and was surprised to see that there were more carriages behind me than I had just passed through. And then we entered a third gorge, climbing once more, before emerging onto another plateau, further than ever, it seemed, from human habitation.

The terrain was unlike any I had seen, or was even aware of, in England. It was not quite wilderness nor yet was it shaped by any agricultural purpose I could discern, though its pastures would have made fine grazing. There was no doubting its beauty, but it was the nature of its beauty that bothered me. It was not just picturesque; it was *merely* picturesque: a piece of scenery that existed for no other purpose than to be regarded. Were an animal to have appeared in the viewfinder of the window, the effect would have been like seeing a stuffed exhibit in a diorama. It was indubitably real, vital and verdant, glistening with fresh dew – but there was something moribund about it. At this point I must concede a possible weakness in the veracity of my description. Had I known that I was going to attempt some sort of chronicle, I might have made notes, might have said to myself *This is how it is*, attempting to set it all down with the vividness of the present tense. Instead, I find myself clawing it back with the blunt edge of memory, in all its pluperfect inadequacy, unsure whether what I felt and saw then is clarified or distorted by the words I fumble for now. But who's to say that anything I might've set down at the time would not have been subject to future doubt? *Was that really how it was?* I might later have said to myself, *Was that really how it was?*

I waited a few minutes before looking out again. The train was much longer than I feared, the rearmost carriages not yet visible, an arc of metal terminating at some indeterminate point beyond the entrance to the gorge. I corrected this estimation as more of the train flowed into view, the rear still not in sight, till my neck began to ache and I had to look the other way. The spectacle was repeated on my right. The visible section of the train, then, described a huge crescent, with me at its centre, neither end yet visible, the rear still emerging from the now distant gorge and the front disappearing over the other horizon. I estimated that the length of this section of the train was a mile or more. It should have been a stunning sight, for the sky had cleared and the grass was soaked in sunshine, but I was so disconcerted at the spectacle I reached immediately for my tobacco and rolled another cigarette. As it left the gorge far behind, the train grew in length, a torrent of steel and glass yanked onwards by unfathomable horsepower. The more of it that came into view, the more unlikely it seemed that the end would appear. This had a peculiar effect on my perception: the more of the train that unfolded, the less *whole* it felt. The carriage in which I was standing seemed to belong to the others only in a nominal sense. There must have been two miles between us now, and by the time I finished my second cigarette, it had grown to at least three.

This much I knew: the twenty-five coaches through which I had just passed were a tiny fraction of the total number. It was impossible to judge, from the view of the train I had on that first day, just how much more of it lay to the rear of my original location in Coach B, but I was seized once more by the conviction that, rather than continuing forward, I ought really to try and go back, or at least remain here till I knew which end was closer, the front or the rear. Mark it well, this early fixation with the train's extremities, which was to become the main driving force, the engine of my curiosity.

In fact, I did try to go back, and once again the sliding door wouldn't budge. When the one up ahead opened I assumed it had been triggered by someone coming the other way. But there was no one there, and I suspected it had opened just for me. I'd completed one section of Standard Class and was now being summoned into the next.

3

O N REFLECTION, IT was lucky I joined the train where I did, for I might just as easily have boarded much farther back. Had I done so, I might still be rattling around Standard Class now. As I rolled a third cigarette in the vestibule after that first Coach Z, I was not to know that a mere sixty sections lay between here and First Class, i.e. sixty times twenty-five carriages: fifteen-hundred in all. Half a day would've been enough to complete this distance. You might ask, then, why it took me four.

The long answer to that question forms much of my subsequent account, but the short answer is that I was waylaid by the traction of my own curiosity. Not for an instant did I forget my main goal – to reach the front of the train and locate the Guard – but it didn't take long to see that any occurrence, however mundane, might have some bearing on that objective, and I watched everything closely in those first few days.

The subsequent sections of the train continued to offer up doppelgängers. I was never wholly convinced, when I saw the same person for a fourth, fifth or sixth time, that it was really *them*. Despite the unlikelihood of different people choosing the same outfits, the same paperback novels, the same spectacles; of their having left home that morning with the same kind of briefcase or the same make of scarf soaked in the same brand of perfume; of their arriving at the same solution of the same crossword puzzle at the precise moment I walked past, the possibility that it was all a coincidence remained preferable to the only alternative: the continuous teleportation of individuals from one part of the train to another. The fact that I could only travel forwards meant there was no way of corroborating either hypothesis, for having seen person A in Coach F, I could not go back to compare them with person B in Coach D.

It did not take long to adjust, all things considered. We had yet to make a stop, and though the prospect of our gliding into a station grew more remote with each mile, it did not bother me as much one might think, for our progress was too smooth, too perfect, too finely regulated to brook interruption. On a normal train, the speed undulates, not just when it approaches or leaves a station, but in response to exterior stimuli, something on the track, distractions on the embankment, a signal up ahead; but after we came through those gorges and gained the final plateau, there was not a single moment of deceleration for the remainder of that day. At first I thought our speed was constant, but at some point that afternoon I realised it was increasing by tiny increments. The difference was slight but just perceptible, and it was this continuous increase in our velocity that helped foster a fatalistic attitude to the train's destination, or to the prospect of any destination at all. For it followed that the faster we went, the less likely we were to stop. And the less likely we were to stop, the more pointless it was to worry.

My adjustment to the train's social character was more gradual. Despite the relative good cheer of Coach Z and the enigmatic warmth of the lady who gave me the sweater, the altercation with the Harbinger had primed me for a physical encounter at any moment, and I kept my guard up for now, thinking it better to reciprocate such communication as came my way than try to seek an explanation of the status quo. As long as I made no mention of the journey, of the train and its destination, I found I was taken for an ordinary passenger. And even when I couldn't resist asking after the Guard or the location of the buffet car, and my interlocutor frowned, I found I could easily distract them from my faux pas with some trifling small talk – complimenting the cut of their jacket, say, or commending the colour of their tie. Small talk is out of character for me, but I was just following protocol here, for I observed that few conversations in Standard strayed beyond trivial matters. All had the same serial fault: the lack of progression from first principles of a given theme to its underlying causes and wider consequences, speech less a communicative vehicle than a physiological act akin to breathing or perspiration. Words were jettisoned because it was unhealthy to retain them, the utterance sounding more like an involuntary purgative act than a premeditated one.

It was a different matter when I joined in. I should stress that this was due, not to my own verbal prowess, such as it is, but to my status as an outsider. Only on opening my mouth did I reveal myself as different to the others. Any conversation on which I eavesdropped soon returned, after a few minutes, to the same banalities with which it had begun, but if I joined in it took a more interesting turn. And if I initiated a conversation from scratch, though it might begin in the same unpromising fashion, it would soon develop along more organic lines. I got the impression that, just as the train was a linear collection of components operating in concert, every individual was part of a single conversational machine, used to functioning in the same way, with the same predictable results.

A hint of this was evident in the conversation with the lady in Coach Z, but I can see that a more robust example is called for. The following exchange occurred in Coach E of the next section. Two men in suits were sat facing each other in a table seat. Both had laptops, each having turned his part of the table into an ad hoc office space, with an empty sandwich carton forming a central barrier between them. Occasionally, one of them would nudge the sandwich carton forward to claim more space, and the other would quietly nudge it back into the centre. It was not clear that they were colleagues, till one of them cleared his throat, leaned over and addressed the other. Here, to the best of my recollection, was what was said:

'Has the budget been approved?'

'The budget has been approved.'

'Is the budget accounted for?'

'The budget is accounted for.'

'Has the budget been spent?'

'Effectively.'

'You mean, in principle?'

'In principle. Its being spent is implicit in its approval.'

'I see. The spending of the budget is assumed.'

'Correct. The allocation of a budget presupposes its expenditure.'

'So the budget is accounted for?'

'The budget is accounted for.'

'The budget has been approved?'

'The budget has been approved.'

I was so intrigued by this trajectory that I ghosted into the seat behind them to see how it developed. I wanted to find out what the budget was being spent on, who wielded the purse strings, which of these two colleagues was the senior man. I never found out. They were silent for a minute, then one asked the other whether the budget had been approved – the same question his colleague had just asked him. To which he received the same reply, and the same conversation was had all over again, with the roles reversed.

At the time, I had no reason to regard this as anything but a running joke between two longstanding colleagues who preferred to parody their relationship, lest it fall into indifference and mutual contempt. I was about to give them the benefit of the doubt, when one of them leaned over:

'About the budget,' he said, closing the lid on his laptop.

'Yes?'

And the same conversation unfolded.

I didn't linger long enough in those early carriages to verify it, but I have no doubt now that these stock exchanges are had everywhere in Standard Class, usually between the same individuals. What is discussed is less important than how, the theme subordinate to the form, the whole thing trotted out like a catechism. The satisfaction drawn from returning to the same starting point, time and again, is certainly bemusing, but it's also intriguing, for it has the paradoxical effect of making you listen more closely to what they're saying. As a commuter, I had often noticed that a conversation became banal to me at the precise point where it became meaningful to those who were having it. That was usually the moment when I inserted moistened toilet paper into my ears. But here I hung on every word, transfixed by the neutrality, the inevitability of the outcome.

I completed eight sections of the train that first afternoon, two-hundred carriages in all, taking a break when I found one that wasn't too full. The busier carriages contained too much information for me to process, the repetition of individuals from earlier carriages multiplying the further I went. Sometimes I would forget certain people, only for them to crop up three times in consecutive coaches. The student, for example, had completely slipped my mind, and when I saw him bent over his studies in an otherwise empty Coach D, I mistook it as good honest déjà vu, till my seeing him again in a later carriage triggered my recollection of the previous times I had seen him. Then there was the man in the shell suit, the one I had seen in that first Coach F – always alone, slouched over a table, swirling his tin of cider. Whenever I came across a cold coach where the heating had failed, I knew he would be there, waiting for me in the last table seat on the right, with his back to the direction of travel.

As afternoon shaded into evening, I took a breather in a half-full Coach P. I had begun to notice, in the last few minutes, a more purposeful tone in the conversations, which broke rank from the fixed patterns just described, the solipsistic themes replaced with a new urgency. This, I soon learned, was the symptom of a daily social ritual, widespread throughout Standard Class and much of First Class too. Every evening, at precisely 18:30, at least half the passengers get to their feet, collect their things together and advance further downtrain, while others stay put, placing their bags on the seat next to them if they want to be left alone, or stowing them in the overhead racks if they desire fresh company.

When folk began putting on their coats, I naturally assumed they were preparing to get off. But our speed was still increasing, and I'd seen no stations, not a single blur of signage and platform architecture as the train shoved on to its unknown destination. I put on my jacket anyway and gripped the handles of my overnight bag. I wasn't actually sure I wanted to get off – it was dark outside now, the only thing visible through the windows the reflection of the train's interior – but I wanted to be in a position to disembark should the opportunity present itself.

Though I did not see it at the time, this sudden activity

was an example of what the knitting lady had called 'Going Forward'. I must make a small digression here to disambiguate the term. So far as I am aware, *Going Forward*, in its locomotive sense, has no connection with the language of modern business practice. I dare say that whoever came up with it was unaware of its usage in the corporate sector as a euphemism for progress. Here, its meaning is strictly ambulatory. *Going Forward* is comparable to what the Italians call the *passeggiata*. I don't know whether you're familiar with it. Just after the evening Angelus, the citizens of Rome or Venice, or Siena, as it might be, like to go out for a preprandial stroll round the block. Nothing too taxing – a few hundred metres at most, followed by an aperitif. Or so says my colleague, Bob Buchanan. A champion of all things continental, and a specific advocate of Latin culture, Bob once informed me that the *passeggiata* has no Anglo Saxon equivalent. I remember the solemnity with which he imparted the news that nowhere in Northern Europe were there to be found persons who thought it more cultured to take the air *before* dinner than after. I now know him to be mistaken, for we have our own version here. Admittedly, Going Forward is less flamboyant than the *passeggiata*, but not without some measure of style.

The aisle was rammed as I got to my feet, and it was several minutes before I made it through the vestibule and into the next carriage. This was even busier than the preceding carriage, some of the passengers striking up conversation with folk they seemed to remember from before. Indeed, some of these meetings were quite emotional, intimate friendships apparently resumed after long intervals. There was one old chap who broke right down and cried when he saw someone he clearly thought he'd never see again, a man of similar age and build who, on reflection, might well have been his brother.

Both were wearing kilts of blue-green tartan, and looked like they were on their way to the same party, the newcomer carrying a bottle of Champagne and a small gift-wrapped box. When he took his seat, they appeared to take up where they had left off, falling naturally into the rhythm of an earlier conversation. At least, it sounded like that to my ears, for the first thing the newcomer said was a punchline to a joke – a joke he had not had chance to complete. Something like *And the Irishman said . . .* I don't recall what the Irishman said, I couldn't hear him properly, but the two kilted gentlemen laughed loudly at the upshot.

Only now did I see the connection between this activity and my earlier chat with the lady in Coach Z. I soon learned that it wasn't really done to be up and about after the hour of Going Forward. But I stayed on my feet that first evening, not yet ready to subscribe to the protocols of this unscheduled service. I was nearly twelve hours into a two-hour journey, a journey that was taking me into the black vault of an alien land, but I was still confident of locating the Guard and finding out where I needed to change to get a connecting train.

I took my time on that first day, negotiating no more than 500 carriages in total, taking them in 25-coach sections of B through to Z, eventually coming to rest in a designated quiet coach that must have been at least a mile from my original designated quiet coach. It was there, at the rear of the carriage – in seat 77a, as it happens – that I fell asleep.

4

THE FOLLOWING MORNING I opened my eyes just in time to see a woman with a trolley disappear through the sliding door at the front end of the carriage. I should really have given chase - I'd eaten nothing the previous day - but when I stood up my legs crumpled like cardboard. I'd been in the same position all night, and it was ten minutes before the numbness lifted and the pins and needles kicked in. When I checked my phone, I saw that I had slept for nearly ten hours.

I covered less distance on that second day, the carriages and vestibules so monotonous they could be endured only with regular breaks. Now and then the track inclined, affording a view over the embankment, the country opening out into pleasant pasture, but these interludes were a fleeting respite from the concrete shacks, grey steel boxes and gravel access roads that formed the bulk of the visible terrain as we descended once more into the cutting. The more sections I completed, the more rest I seemed to need, and by lunchtime I was flagging. I had now gone more than twenty-four hours without food, and if I didn't find a trolley soon, or a buffet car, I would have no choice but to appeal to the charity of the other passengers.

I'll pass over the rest of that morning. There was nothing to match the previous morning, the vaulting revelation I had experienced on putting my head out the window, the incident with the Harbinger, the curious amiability of the lady in

Coach Z. I was grateful for the extra garment she had given me, for it was a degree or two cooler than yesterday, which I attributed to our increased altitude. I had to keep reminding myself that we had ascended onto a plateau early on that first day, continuing on a more or less level course ever since.

The passengers continued to replicate themselves, but I was getting used to that now. I thought I detected a new openness among the more familiar faces, a cumulative warmth that ripened with each successive simulacrum, but I was still wary of meeting the eye of the man in mohair, the snotty-nosed student or any other members of the cast, paying just enough attention to note the slight alterations in appearance and behaviour that each incarnation offered up. One of the men in mohair smiled at me as I passed, and another actually said hello when I met him again half an hour later. The third was even more effusive, evidently expecting me to stop and chat. I smiled politely but continued on my way.

The afternoon was more eventful. At three-thirty on that second day, naive as it now sounds, I really thought it was all going to be over. About an hour before, I had begun to notice a substantial decrease in our speed. This had probably started much earlier but – like our acceleration the previous day – was so gradual as to be imperceptible. By two o'clock it was clear that we had slowed to at least half our optimum speed (reached at some point during the night, I guessed), and by half-past we were doing no more than fifty.

How callow it now seems that I really imagined, just a few miles later, when the train came to a halt in a tunnel, that we were approaching our destination, that we had only to wait for a platform to become available before rolling on towards the buffers. When a sizzle of electricity came from the speakers, I thought the Guard was about to make an announcement to that effect. You could hear him moving about in his little cubicle, rustling papers, getting everything in order, and I waited for him to begin his spiel, but all that came was a sort of background rustle, as though he'd engaged the intercom by accident. It was tantalising. At one point he began humming a tune, but there was still no announcement, no information, no advice to passengers to make sure they had their belongings with them, none of the usual things that precede a journey's end.

Nevertheless, when people started getting up, collecting their things from the overhead racks and putting on their coats, I was certain there was a station just beyond the tunnel. What else could provoke this much activity? It was different to the previous evening, when only half the passengers had risen from their seats. Everyone was up now, and I couldn't help but picture my usual destination, the bustling concourse and its plethora of amenities, the snack booths, the newsagent's, the chemist's, the sashed saleswomen handing out free energy drinks, the promotional sports car up on its rostrum, all of which, so familiar to me two days ago, now seemed like the trappings of a fabled land.

I was the last to rise from my seat, bringing up the rear as the others shuffled through the sliding door. The vestibule was heaving, so some of us continued on into the next vestibule, where we stopped, forming two queues, one either side at each door. Then the train creaked into life and we started to creep forward, picking up more speed until, after another minute, we coasted smoothly into the daylight and came to another abrupt halt. I could not see where we'd stopped from my position by the sliding door, only a patch of sky framed in the windows, and when the man at the head of the queue on the left slid his window down but did not make any attempt to open the door, I sensed there was no platform to step onto, that we would not be getting off here. He thrust his head out of the window, closed his eyes and inhaled deeply, and the woman at the head of the queue for the right-hand door did likewise. There they remained, in an apparently meditative state, for thirty seconds or so, before retreating back into the middle of the vestibule, with a slight bow. Then the others took turns to do the same, each passenger leaning out the window and moving aside with the same deferential nod of the head. No one jostled as they waited in line, moving automatically into position when the window was free.

When it was my turn to look out, I saw that we had stopped on the edge of a large declivity of open heathland, flat at the bottom and bordered by high ridges on all sides, the slopes fringed with gorse and heather. The track ran along the east ridge, the November sun already sinking over the opposite horizon, dramatically silhouetting a huge solitary tree in the middle of the declivity, broken two thirds of the way up its trunk, poleaxed by a lightning strike, by the looks of it. As the sun disappeared, the surrounding vegetation began to glow with the silveriness of a partial eclipse, and the tree became a dark silhouette, suddenly transformed into a man bending over, a giant in the act of tying his shoelace. Perhaps I lingered too long at the window, for there was a tap on my shoulder and when I looked round, there was the man in the green mohair suit.

'Sorry,' I said. 'I thought I was last.'

'Take all the time you need, old bean, all the time you need.'

I bowed graciously and stepped aside, just as I'd seen the others do, returning to my earlier position by the sliding door. The man in mohair looked out, drawing the air through his nostrils, respiring with great fanfare, like a Native American chief. When he had taken in the vista, he bowed and turned towards us, whereupon we all joined hands, everyone closing their eyes. I went along with it too, though I kept one eye half-open to see what happened next. We remained in this position for about a minute, waiting. Then the train went forward thirty metres or so, stopped, and lurched back again. This must have happened ten times, and on each occasion everyone made a circular sign on their chest with their forefinger, or a horse shoe, I couldn't work out which. It was a bit like when Catholics cross themselves – everyone seems to do it differently – but no-one objected to the swirl I made as I did my best to emulate it.

As the train began to pick up speed again, advancing towards a tunnel on the far side of the declivity, everyone dispersed, some taking the first available seat in the next carriage, others continuing on.

5

T HE MEANING OF this ceremony may be guessed
at by keener students of rail transportation and those
with an interest in rolling stock, but it took me longer to see
its true significance, and I will preserve my confusion out of
solidarity for the layman. In any case, my thoughts had already
turned to other matters. For all the train's inordinate length,
I'd yet to come across a buffet car. The adrenalin of the last
thirty-six hours had started to ebb and food was now my
immediate concern. I figured that rather than relying on the
on-board catering team, I should try to ingratiate myself with
another passenger, just for this evening, till I could make other
arrangements. It was only half an hour till Going Forward,
and it seemed sensible to incorporate my begging strategy
into that circadian ritual, which was, after all, that time of
day when the brokering of new friendships was encouraged.
I've already described the friendlier atmosphere of the later
coaches in each section compared with the earlier ones, and
I thought it best to focus my efforts there. Of course, in the
event of finding a willing Samaritan, I'd be expected to engage
them in conversation as we broke bread together. I wasn't
looking forward to this, the tendency of most passengers to
adhere to 'stock' themes having prepared me for some fairly
stupefying table-talk. Thankfully this tendency is compensat-
ed for by the occasional prodigy.

I had the good fortune to run into one just before

six-thirty. The thing that drew me to the woman in Coach V was that I recalled seeing her once before, years ago, on my way home from work. My old commute, infested though it was with corporate drones and shabby salarymen like myself, sometimes threw up more bohemian individuals, and this woman had stuck in my mind. Quite what she had made of me that evening, I don't know, but she tolerated my furtive attention as something other than mere lechery, I think, smiling when our eyes met through the gap between the seats, she being seated transversely across the aisle, with her back to the direction of travel, I in a forward-facing seat. Her head fitted perfectly in the gap, and I suppose she saw mine that way too, comically divested of neck and shoulders. It was one of those rare moments when two strangers laugh simultaneously at the same thing: something they think only they have noticed.

When I saw her again in Coach V, I have to say I found it more miraculous than the appearance of the doppelgängers. Here, I had said to myself, on seeing her that first time, is someone I will never see again. I remember the sadness and regret I felt when she'd got off at an intermediate stop, disappearing through the ticket hall, into the clutches of some forlorn provincial town. Yet here she was, half-way down the carriage on the right, with her back to the direction of travel, precisely where she'd been that evening. She was wearing the same clothes too: a two-tone men's suit that shimmered, changing from silver to purple as she shifted about in her seat by the window, and a T-shirt with a yellow lightning bolt on a black background. She was not alone: on her lap was a white cat with a black patch on its side and another on its head.

'Not at all,' she said, on seeing me approach.

I stopped. Was she talking to me?

'Not at all,' she repeated. 'Please do.'

Like the lady in Coach Z, she'd anticipated what I was about to ask: if the seat next to her was taken.

'I was just admiring your suit,' I said, stashing my bag in the overhead rack and sitting down.

'I know.' She held up the arm of her jacket to demonstrate its iridescence. 'You also like my T-shirt – correct?'

'I do. Where'd you get it?'

'Get it?'

'Yes, where's it from?'

'What an odd question. I've always had it.'

'Always?'

'Always. And my shoes? What of them, sir?'

'You're not wearing any.'

Her shoes were on the floor, airing.

'May I?' I reached down and picked one up. Men's brogues, pale brown leather, hand-stitched. 'They look kind of Spanish.'

'And my feet?' She brought them up, tucking her heels under her arse. The cat's head was pushed into her cleavage, but it couldn't be bothered to move.

'Can I be honest?'

'Please.'

'They're big.'

'Are they?'

'Quite big. For a woman. But that's good. That's a good thing.'

There was a now brief hiatus in this flurry of compliments as she asked me if I would be staying or Going Forward. I said that I'd like to stay if it was alright.

'That's settled then. I'm Heobah.'

'Pleased to meet you, Heobah.'

'Pleased to meet you too, Paul.'

I almost let this go. And actually, I now wish I had. It made no difference in the long run.

'Paul?'

She pointed at my chest. I looked down: there was a name sticker on my breast pocket, the kind you get given at a conference, that I hadn't noticed till now. I am not and have never been 'Paul'. Whoever had retrieved my jacket for me in Coach H the previous day had given me the wrong one. The colour was too light, charcoal grey rather than black, and it was looser across the shoulders.

But I was less bothered about the loss of my jacket than by the loss of something more fundamental. For I realised, as I was about to correct this case of mistaken identity, that I could not remember my name.

'You OK?'

'Sorry. I just have to check something.'

I'd forgotten my address before, when drunk, and my pin number once or twice, but my name? Yet it was so. As I held out my hand, nothing came to me. The instinctive utterance offered up a thousand times at dinner parties, meetings, interviews, was irrecoverable. I took the wallet out from the jacket: 'Paul Carver' said the name on the bank card. Definitely not me. Or was it? If I couldn't remember who I was, how did I know who I wasn't? I found something with a photo, an ID pass for a company called SINTEK Industries. Paul Carver bore a cosmetic resemblance to me, but he'd lost more hair and he was wearing a tie pin. I would never wear a tie pin. Still, I had to check my reflection in the window to Heobah's left.

'What's the matter?'

'I was given the wrong jacket. I put it on by mistake. When they gave it to me. Some other guy's. In the confusion.'

'What confusion?'

66

'You don't want to know. It's too much to get into.'

'I see. And now you have his wallet.'

'I guess I need to hand it in.'

'Hand it in?'

'To Lost Property.'

'If something's lost,' said Heobah, 'it is no longer property. Let me see that.'

She grabbed the wallet, leafing through the cards like a kid with football stickers. As she did so, I studied her closely for the first time. She was fortyish, I guessed, her long black hair pinned up in a fashion that suggested she did not know what to do with it, half-beehive, half-teddy-boy quiff, with long bits hanging down over the ears. Her face had the used quality of a workman's favourite tool, flawed with liver spots and one or two scars, crow's feet that she now incorporated into her make-up, the eyeliner ending in three sharp points on her temples, orientalising her other features: the wide mouth, the long nose, the circumflex brows.

'What do you think Paul Carver does?' she said, laying out his cards on the fold-down table. 'What do you think Paul Carver *is*?'

'I've no idea.'

'Well, he's a member of a snooker club,' she said, ignoring the important documents, 'with an interest in – what's this? – gardening.'

She handed me a dog-eared piece of brown card with 'Café' written on it in white letters, below which were nine white circles in a grid, all stamped with a red star. At the bottom of the card were the words 'Have your 10th coffee on us!'

'Gardening?'

'Yes. You can tell it's not a regular franchise. Or an independent outlet. If it were, it would have a name. But it's just a piece of ordinary card that someone's guillotined up. See: it's not been cut straight. From this I infer that it's the loyalty card of a makeshift coffee place, probably just a coffee *area* of some sort, the coffee area of a city farm or petting zoo or an agricultural museum run by volunteers, but most likely a garden centre.'

'That's a big inference.'

'I'm a big inferrer.'

'I guess we'll never know.'

'He was due a free coffee,' said Heobah. 'He'll have to start from scratch now, build up all that loyalty all over again. Unless . . .'

'Unless what?'

'Unless we find Paul Carver and return his loyalty card.'

This was symptomatic of another trait of Standard Class passengers: the tendency to dwell on the peripheral at the expense of the bigger picture. From Heobah's perspective, the image of Paul Carver sitting in the café of some garden centre/ petting zoo/agricultural museum with his head in his hands due to the loss of his loyalty card, seemed more vital to the man's character than anything evinced by his other documents.

'And what do *you* do?' she asked.

I have to admit, I was slightly disappointed at this. I had assumed that such mundane questions weren't asked in bohemian circles.

'Ah. The dreaded question. Guess.'

'How many guesses do I have?'

'Three.'

'Are you an astronaut?'

'Do I look like an astronaut?'

'No.'

'Then why waste your guesses?'

'Makes it more exciting. Puts pressure on the other guesses. Besides, you could have been a resting astronaut.'

'Do astronauts rest? Surely, astronauts *recover*.'

'True. A butcher then?'

'From astronaut to butcher?'

'*Blacksmith* – I meant blacksmith. Are you a blacksmith?'

I asked her to take a second look, to consider my appearance, my bearing, the softness of my hands. Did these things really speak to her of the forge, the anvil, the leather apron? I took this flippancy as a sign that she didn't really care what I did. It was then that I told her I was in cat litter. She took it well. No, I'm doing her an injustice. She did more than humour me as I explained how things stood at work: how we'd all been happy manufacturing just the one product, how everything had been good till Dan took over and told us we'd all be out of a job unless we diversified, and how the probable truth of that prediction just made his regime harder to bear. I told her about the meeting I'd missed with the prospective German clients. How they had a chain of pet stores throughout Germany and were looking to switch the suppliers of their feline range. Potentially, it was a lucrative contract. They had other people to see, but we were first on their list, and our growing markets in Poland and the Benelux territories meant our distribution networks were well placed to facilitate expansion. Then I said I was sorry.

'What for?'

'I'm boring *myself*. Believe me, it gives me no pleasure to speak of "distribution networks" and "growing markets". But it's what I do.'

'Tell me more.'

'Like I say, I preferred it when we just did cat litter. And we only did sacks in one size. Can you believe that? Maybe you remember them? They were everywhere. If you went into your local corner shop, our product was the one on the bottom shelf, the 30kg sack, almost unliftable, and almost invisible too alongside the brighter packaging of our competitors. Now we do 20kg and 10kg, and the packaging has been redesigned. Dan said it was insane that we'd never seen fit to employ a proper designer, that we'd persisted with the same template knocked up by Fred's wife in the 60s. That we'd survived nearly fifty years in a competitive market with no pictures of cats, no feline trappings at all, was nothing short of amazing. That's what he called it: "insane", "amazing". Sorry.'

'Don't be, I get it. Now you're not just in cat litter.'

It was important to convey to her the honour of manufacturing just one thing, the recognition we'd received for it, the certificates and trophies we'd won.

'Do What You Do Do Well,' I said, remembering the old company motto.

'It seems to me,' said Heobah, 'that only now do you see the value of that.'

She was right. Only after Fred had put his signature on his last consignment of Premium Grey did I appreciate the ascetic integrity of our enterprise.

'Give me an example,' said Heobah.

'Of what?'

'Of how things are different now.'

I began the story about the Powder Room, the one I told earlier, at the start, but Heobah interrupted when I got to the bit where Bob Buchanan gets admonished by Dan Coleman for not listening:

'Tell me about him.'

'Bob?'

'Yes.'

'I thought you wanted to know about diversification? Its impact on my wellbeing?'

'Bob too. Tell me about Bob Buchanan.'

Here it was again, the fixation with the peripheral. What was there to say about Bob? Actually, quite a lot.

'Sure. But before I begin, I don't suppose you have anything to eat?'

She produced a lunchbox from the overhead luggage rack, unlidding it to reveal a beautifully arranged selection of sashimi, sushi and rice, and two sets of chopsticks. We were far from the ocean, but it looked fresh enough.

'In many ways,' I began, as Heobah drew her legs up onto the seat, 'in many ways, Bob Buchanan's case is a tragic one . . .'

6

IF EVER THERE was a man not cut out for the corporate sector, it was Bob Buchanan. It was his misfortune to arrive at our company just when the baton passed from Fred Teesdale, an old-school enforcer not averse to accepting the odd bung or bribing the odd accountant, to Dan Coleman, a by-the-book champion of 'best practice'. It's more eclectic than you'd think, the corporate sector. I don't go so far as to claim that it takes in all-comers, but it's something of a refuge for those parted early from their first-choice careers. Over the course of my working life, I've met people who set out to be engineers, scientists, doctors; others who trained as chefs or showed promise at sport, one or two who'd had trials with professional football clubs; others still who excelled in the arts, only to gravitate towards commerce instead, their ambitions checked by the natural inertia of economic constraints. Our company was no different. Among its staff were people who had aimed high and settled for something less. But Fred was a notable exception.

Fred Teesdale *chose* cat litter. Not because he was passionate about it but because he recognised it as a field which, if handled in the right way, would leave him time to pursue his other interests. He was a cultured man, something of an authority on the painter Atkinson Grimshaw, and a devotee of kitchen sink drama. But a jazz man in the main – hence his employment of Bob Buchanan. Before going into cat litter,

Bob had been saxophonist in a successful quartet, but at some point in his early fifties some indiscretion, almost certainly drink-related, had led to his ostracism from the circuit. There was no doubt that he landed on his feet when he met Fred. Bob had never done anything but blow into a piece of brass flecked and tarnished with his own spittle, but Fred created a special position for him.

For a year all was well. Then Fred went down one morning in Despatch with a heart attack. The change of management was a depressing transition for us all. Imagine that your organisation, hitherto guided by Robin Hood, is now to be run by the Sheriff of Nottingham. But it was Bob who bore the brunt. Seemingly destined for a bohemian life – a life partially sustained under the noble protectorate of Fred Teesdale – he was now at the mercy of a man who simply could not see the value of his contrast. On taking over, Dan Coleman sensed the slack that had been cut for him and set about making repairs in the corporate body politic. But he did not fire Bob Buchanan. Far from it, he turned him into a whipping boy, his prime function being to demonstrate the difference between how things had been and how they would be from now on. Which is how Bob went from being our official saxophonist and close-up magician to a superannuated office-boy. He was 54.

It has to be said that sometimes even Fred despaired at Bob's ineptness, his inability to master simple arithmetic and business logic, but his fondness for jazz, and in particular the saxophone, mitigated his annoyance whenever he fouled up. When the wrong consignment went to this or that customer, Fred just counted to ten. I knew for a fact that Bob's instrument was kept in Fred's office. Sometimes Bob would go there under the guise of practising, but in reality to give a private performance for the boss. They had a bond that transcended work. Bob had a Thursday slot in the company bar, and there was no way Fred would have let him go.

As I told all this to Heobah, I expected regular interjections, questions that would cause me to lose my place and start again, but all she did was mumble *Poor Bob, Poor Bob*, as I worked up my sketch of his plight into a full-blown oil study.

I should mention that Bob Buchanan was also a veteran of the 8:08. Like me, he always sat in the same place. He preferred Coach E, the busiest coach – the one that's always full of families on day trips, folk with board games, tourists, holidaymakers. When I walked through to the buffet car, I would often see him chatting to the other passengers, ingratiating himself with children by pulling faces and performing tricks. Train journeys brought it out of him. Where I *withstood* the daily commute, Bob basked in it, especially post-Teesdale. He was never happier than when travelling to and from work, preferring to be among strangers, people who'd never seen him before and would never see him again. He couldn't make mistakes with them, like he did with his colleagues. They would never learn his faults, remembering him only as the fat jovial guy in Coach E. Bob loved Coach E. It was the only place he could get away with being Bob Buchanan. I remember, one time, watching him perform magic to a table of German backpackers. I was just making my way to the buffet car, and as the sliding door drew back, there he was, pulling coins from their ears and so forth, referring to himself in the third person as 'Herr Buchanan', before offering 'to stand them all a tea'. They thanked him, but declined politely, and as soon as he exited the carriage, they got their rucksacks and sprinted uptrain, as far as they could get from Bob's table. Herein is contained the essence of Buchanan, I told myself, as I stood aside to let them pass.

I also remember him pulling a coin from the ear of Dan Coleman one morning, with less than mirthful results. It was just before the first meeting he held after taking over from Fred. Bob had intended it as an ice-breaker, I think, a demonstration of his talents. He seemed to envisage a continuation of his current role as light entertainer, but Dan's reaction put paid to that fantasy:

'Inappropriate!' he shouted, smiting the coin from Bob's hand. 'Inappropriate behaviour, Bob! Completely inappropriate!'

Yet Dan Coleman had use for him as time went on. It might have seemed odd that our line manager preferred as his front-of-house guy someone who most of us agreed would be first out in times of economic hardship, but to Dan it was smart delegation. Bob excelled at being the guy people instinctively knew was *not* the one they had come to see. His task, as he presented himself in the foyer, was to absorb those first few seconds of human contact before the client was passed on to someone more senior. It was what Dan liked to call 'working the buffers', i.e., making people wait before reaching the person they had actually come to see, so that when they met them they were more grateful, more amenable to suggestion. Bob's outstretched hand was rarely accepted as he minced across the foyer, the delegation from Rotterdam or wherever already looking over his shoulder. When the lift doors opened and I or Ramsden stepped out to greet them, Bob would retreat into the margin, mooning under the pot plants, wringing his hands. He never seemed to know what to do with his hands when they were not holding his instrument, which was all the time now, Dan having banned it from the premises. Everything about him told you that he would have preferred a nocturnal existence: the patent leather spats, the three-piece suit, the menthol cigarettes. The night had hidden him for most of his life, but now here he was, out on the catwalk, an owl flushed from its nest.

This was the short version of Bob's story, I stressed to Heobah, and I tried not to impart it with unseemly relish, but I was just trying to convey the dangers of investing too much faith in one man, as he had with Fred, when that man could so easily be replaced by another.

'Why did Fred have to go?' she asked.

I thought I'd already made this clear, but when I reminded her that he was no longer with us, she didn't seem to get the euphemism.

'And Bob,' she went on, 'why does he stay?'

'It's a job.'

'But not allowed to perform his magic.'

'I know.'

'And not allowed to play his saxophone.'

'I know.'

'Not even allowed to bring it in.'

'I know.'

When she asked me about my own relations with Dan Coleman, I explained how I'd managed to appease him so far, but was not confident of doing so for much longer. There were things she didn't understand – she frowned at my daily commute, bemused at the number of train journeys I claimed to have taken – but she didn't pursue it, and I got the impression that these facts, of crucial significance in shaping my life, were secondary to how I spoke and acted now in the judgement she formed of my character. The purpose of that judgement remained unclear, but was not, I believe, motivated by personal curiosity alone.

By ten-thirty, Heobah's head had begun to droop on my shoulder, and the cat was now warming my lap. It wasn't long before I dropped off too. We were approaching optimum speed again, and everyone was now asleep. The faster we went, the smoother our progress, the velocity having a soporific effect.

7

THE FOLLOWING MORNING I was woken by a vibration on my chest. It took a few seconds to realise it was my phone, and when I reached into my pocket I saw that I'd just missed a call from Mark Ramsden. I tried calling him back, but the signal was weak, flickering between one and no bars, so I sent him another text message instead: 'YOU ON TRAIN: Y OR N?'. I kept pressing send; all I needed was a few seconds of continuous signal, though getting the message through obviously depended on our both having coverage. The train was so long only certain sections seemed to have coverage at any one time, but I kept resending till my phone said it was delivered. All Ramsden had to do now was send me a single-letter response.

Heobah had gone, the carriage now empty apart from me and the cat. I noticed he had a tag on his collar, and I could just make out his name from the faded letters on the metal disc:

Companion

Twisted round the top of the collar, behind his head, was a folded piece of paper, which I opened and flattened out over the table. It was a note from Heobah:

Sorry I had to go, didn't want to wake you. Meet me

Saturday PM for dinner in the First Class Restaurant Car.

Though excited at the prospect of seeing her again, I was also unnerved, for she appeared to take it for granted that I'd be on the train for another two days at least.

Now that Heobah had gone, the cat attached himself to me. I could tell he was hungry – no cat showed this much affection without wanting something back – and my first task, after sprucing up in the toilet cubicle, would be to find a trolley or buffet car.

My first stand-up wash went OK. It wasn't an all-over job, just face and armpits. I thought it prudent to eke out my supplies right from the start. It was important to see if I could get by with the bare minimum, so I used the soap from the dispenser, put less toothpaste on my brush, reduced the swipes of my deodorant from six to three and applied a small dab of moisturiser to counteract the dehydrating effects of the dispenser soap. It was better to get used to the on-board facilities now so they didn't come as a shock if I had to rely on them alone.

As I emerged from the cubicle, Companion was waiting for me in the vestibule, rearing up on his hind legs like a miniature horse and showing me the way through the next sliding door.

I spent much of that morning reflecting on how easy it had been just two days ago to acquire the basic necessities of life. I had never been in a situation where I lacked the means to get what I needed, even for a short time, and it was yet possible that I might have to depend entirely on the charity of strangers. There was no cash in Paul Carver's wallet, but I was buoyed to see that his debit card had a contactless payment symbol. All being well, I wouldn't require his pin number.

It was almost noon when we came across a woman with a trolley. We'd just emerged from Coach G in the 35th Parallel of Standard, as I now termed it.* At first, I thought the trolley was unmonitored when I saw it in the vestibule, for its attendant was scarcely taller than the hot water urn. She was wearing a turquoise tabard that hung down over her enormous calves, glaring at me over the lid, each boss-eye missing my face, and as I produced Paul Carver's debit card, she was already shaking her head:

'Cash only.'

'What's that, then?' I asked, pointing at the chip-and-pin machine.

'Broken.'

'I don't have any cash. I don't suppose—'

'What does that say?' She pointed to a handwritten sign: NO CREDIT GIVEN. *Please do not ask as refusal often offends.*

'I'm not asking for credit. I was hoping you would give me something.'

'I see.' Her grip on the trolley loosened. 'And what do I get in return?'

'I'm afraid I don't have much.'

'Your phone?'

'I can't give you that.'

'Your watch then?'

---

* Once the train's length became apparent, I began to record the number of sections I passed through. Each 'Parallel' is equivalent to a section of twenty-five coaches, the point where I boarded being the Equator, as it were, and the latitudes 'north' and 'south' of that region akin to the Tropics. I thus estimated that I had been through 35 sections since boarding. I dispensed with this nautical system on reaching First Class, where the designation of coaches was more confusing.

I drew back my sleeve to show that I wasn't wearing one.

'You have nothing of value?'

I showed her the contents of my overnight bag – a spare shirt, some toiletries, office materials – but she shook her head. Companion, I noticed, had already slipped into the next carriage. This was just as well, for it was conceivable that I would have been prepared to offer the cat in exchange for food at this early stage of our relationship, my better judgement perverted by hunger.

'You have nothing of value,' she continued, 'nothing to barter or trade?'

'Sorry.'

'Then perhaps you're a *man* of value?'

'A man of value?'

'Yes. Perhaps you can be of value? To me, I mean?'

'Possibly.'

'Yes. Perhaps you have a talent of some kind?'

'Perhaps.'

But even as I said this I knew that I didn't. I had a talent for blagging, bullshitting, winging it, getting through my PDR by the seat of my pants, but that was about all. Bob Buchanan had once tried to teach me the coin trick, but I couldn't get the hang of it.

'Your silence tells me everything,' she said. 'I can see that you have no talent. I can see you're not a man of value.'

She released the brake and began pushing the trolley towards the sliding door.

'No. Come back. I am. I am a man of value.'

'That's what they all say.' She stopped, put the brake back on and took a notepad and pen from her trolley. 'Go on then: do my portrait.'

'Ah.'

'What?'

'I can't draw.'

'Pity.' She bent down and took out a sheaf of drawings from the trolley's lower compartment. 'You could've contributed to my collection.'

So this was how it worked. The trolley woman had acquired a substantial portfolio of works on paper, extorted from passengers in need of sustenance, and even the most mediocre of these were substantially better than anything I could manage. The majority were biro sketches done on napkins, I saw, as she began arranging them over the vestibule carpet, passable likenesses of the trolley woman standing over her wares. But one or two were in charcoal, gouache, pen and ink: studies by trained practitioners who had access to proper art materials and who had put her in more imaginative poses.

'These are all by passengers?'

'They sketch me and I give them something. Coffee, a sandwich. Maybe both – depends how good it is.'

'What's your favourite?'

She unscrolled a large study in brown Conté crayon, which depicted the trolley woman nude and pouting, her cleavage gathered up under folded arms.

'I have to say that's impressive,' I said, seeing an opening. 'You know, some of these might be worth something.'

'You think?'

'Look, I may not be an artist, but I do happen to be something of a critic.'

'An art critic?'

'Yes. I may not be a man *of* value, but I *know* value. I know value when I see it. And I like what I see here.'

'Really?'

'I could give you a valuation, if you like. I could put a price on your collection. For insurance purposes. In exchange for something from the trolley. What do you say?'

'OK. Done.'

I was not too effusive in my praise of the better works nor cutting in my judgement of the weaker ones. I had to make a decent stab at objectivity here, so I didn't pull any punches. Much of her collection was of sentimental rather than monetary value, I said, but some pieces were of high artistic merit, no more so than the aforementioned erotic study.

'So how much then?' she asked, when we came to it.

'For this one? A thousand dollars.'

'Dollars?'

'It's how they do it – in the auction house.'

'Right. Dollars.'

'But I'd hang on to it if I were you.'

'You think?'

'The secondary market's not strong at the moment. Everyone's selling. So?'

'So what?'

'You'll give me something from the trolley?'

'Anything. Anything you want. I'll just need my certificate first.'

'What certificate?'

'It's hardly an official valuation, is it, not without a certificate?'

She had a point. My valuation had not been sanctioned by any external governing body. I could have been anyone. I *was* anyone. I told her that, while a valuation would normally come with a certificate, I had none with me at the current time. But I'd be happy to issue one retrospectively.

'Retrowhat?'

''Spectively.'

Then I remembered the other documents in Paul Carver's wallet: 'Sorry,' I said, pulling out his work ID card. 'I should have introduced myself earlier. Here: my credentials.'

'SINTEK Industries?'

'It's a consultancy. We travel around giving valuations to private collectors. Patrons of the arts. Folk such as yourself. I'm surprised you haven't heard of us. Believe me, you should hang on to that Conté study. I meant what I said about the secondary market.'

'I think I'll get a second opinion,' she said, handing back the card.

'Please. A sandwich is all I ask.'

'Sorry.'

'What about my valuation?'

'Your *unofficial* valuation.'

'As I said, I'd be happy to supply you with certification at a future time, if you write down your details. But unfortunately you've caught me on the hoof.'

We stood there in silence, not knowing how to terminate this encounter. The trolley woman seemed just as dissatisfied at the outcome as I was. As a man of value, I had not quite delivered, but she seemed disposed to strike a compromise.

'Look,' she said, 'maybe there's something else you can do for me.'

'Name it.'

She came round to my side of the trolley and reversed into my personal space. 'Take off my tabard,' she said, lifting her arms.

'What?'

'Take off my tabard.'

But I'd misunderstood. I was not to oblige her in that way. She wanted me to take over. If I wanted to eat, I had to take her place. Put on the tabard, do a stint with the trolley. That was the deal.

'And I can have anything I like?'

'Anything.'

What choice did I have? I needed food and here it was in abundance. So I climbed into the tabard, stretching it over my chest while she did up the sides. There wasn't time to discuss the terms of my employment; as I was adjusting my uniform, she gathered up the drawings and bolted into the next carriage, throwing me the key to the moneybox as the sliding door closed.

8

MY FIRST ACT, as trolley guy, was to impound the best merchandise for my own consumption: the brie and bacon baguettes, the salt and vinegar crisps, the short-bread biscuits and individual Bramley apple pies. There was also Companion to think about. I had no qualms about requisitioning the tuna and sweetcorn sandwiches to the rear section of the lower compartment, and I also set aside a substantial quantity of UHT milk. I hoped this would be sufficient for his needs.

Companion was waiting for me at the end of the next carriage, and I followed him into the vestibule, where we stopped and gorged ourselves. He didn't seem to mind the mayonnaise in the filling of the sandwich, though I had to remove the sweetcorn before he would touch the tuna. The bread he declined, and he preferred to have his milk decanted into the lid of a coffee cup than take it straight from the pot, which was too small for his tongue. After I'd ministered to his needs – angling the lid so he could lap up the dregs – I chain-ate two baguettes and downed a miniature from the Junior Collector Whisky Selection Box that I found in the middle compartment of the trolley. I didn't remember single malt being available on the old 8:08 service, only blended whiskies, and as I knocked back my Glengoyne 15-year-old, I reflected that this may have a bearing on our location. For when I put the whisky back, I noticed that the compartment was labelled

Duty Free, well-stocked with Courvoisier, Smirnoff, several bottles of aftershave, and also a bottle of perfume called 808, whose appley scent I thought I'd smelled on the trolley woman. Duty Free, here? The logical implication of this was that the train's route took us beyond UK borders. But that was impossible without passing under a great body of water: the English Channel to the south, the North Sea to the east, the Irish Sea to the west, or the Atlantic to the north, god help us. But we'd already been far above sea level when we'd gone through the long tunnel on the afternoon of the second day, having ascended onto a plateau on the first day, remaining at that altitude ever since, continuing on a level course.

I could have abandoned the trolley right there, put all I needed in a bin liner, slung it over my shoulder and gone on my way. There was no external pressure to don the tabard and take up my predecessor's mantle. I wasn't beholden to her or anyone else in a contractual sense. But I didn't consider reneging on the agreement, not for a second. This acquiescence was highly uncharacteristic, but the truth of the matter was that I was unable to suppress a degree of pride at having been welcomed into the fold. My compliance was automatic. It was not even compliance, as such. I just accepted the role, for no other reason than that the trolley was unmanned, and an unmanned trolley seemed wrong, unnatural. I have no doubt that any other passenger would've done the same in my situation.

Given the empty coaches through which we had just passed, I might have expected to ease myself slowly into my new role, but the next carriage was packed. It was lunchtime, and everyone reached for their wallets as the door drew back and I came clanking into view.

'Tea and coffee,' I announced confidently. 'Savoury snacks. Sandwiches.'

Everyone wanted a hot beverage in that first coach, and several people complained about the temperature of the water, but I think I handled it well. Initially, I was confused when folk handed over a fifty-pound note and expected no change, but I soon got used to demanding, say, £82.95 for a tea and a muffin, as opposed to £2.50, which was the price of the Muffin Deal on the old 8:08; or £68.40 for a packet of crisps and a mineral water. Where I got these figures from, I can't tell you, but they came to me just like that and I rattled them out without thinking.

It took half an hour to get through that first carriage. Like the chip-and-pin machine, the scanning device was out of commission, so I had to add everything up on the notepad the trolley woman had left, which was filled with the sums of earlier transactions. No one looked at their change or the amount of money they tendered, handing you everything they had like tourists on holiday. I could charge whatever I liked. Money seemed abundant enough for no one to question the price of anything. If I charged one person £50 for a coffee and demanded only £36 from his neighbour, there was no argument.

Initially I took great pleasure from being as inconsistent as possible, charging customers whatever I thought they should pay according to their manners, but the novelty of this wore off quickly, for the financial transactions had the same arbitrariness I had marked earlier in the conversations I'd overheard. What I said about words being 'offloaded' rather than spoken with discursive purpose seemed to apply equally to money, here denuded of stable value and reduced to a decorative role. Like language, capital appeared to have slipped its moorings, becoming less significant in the numerical sense, while retaining its symbolic status as a mechanism of exchange.

The demands of my new employment kept me occupied for the remainder of that third day. I felt better now I'd eaten, and after another miniature from the Junior Collector Whisky Selection Box, I was in pretty good spirits. The only downside to the trolley was that Companion had to get used to stopping when he was more naturally inclined to press on. I could not see him properly when he got too close to the front, and I was wary of running him over, so I lifted him onto the top compartment, making space for him in the metal basket at the front. He was not used to travelling at that height, but soon got used to it, and made a charming little figurehead as we cruised along.

The carriages weren't so busy further downtrain, and we made good progress, completing another five sections by four o'clock, with a short rest every twenty-five coaches before negotiating the next Parallel. The further we advanced, the less crowded the train was, and after another five Parallels some carriages were completely empty. In the sparser coaches, my new role felt like a novelty act, a symbolic post I might relinquish at any moment. But make no mistake, when I entered those busier carriages it was a job of work, and I took the responsibility seriously. It's a peculiar admission, I know, but in a way I was now living out a fantasy. Although, as a some-time commuter of the old 8:08, I rarely availed myself of the trolley, I sympathised with those who had to lug it from one end of the train to the other, and often thought about how I would conduct myself if I had to do it. I had gone so far, in these daydreams, as to construct scenarios that demonstrated all the other talents I possessed, in addition to those displayed in my capacity as trolley guy. I changed nappies for single mums. I dealt with drunks using a mixture of eloquent put-downs and martial arts techniques. I 'bantered' with barristers and university professors, while also conversing with manual labourers and those in receipt of state benefits, and gently rebuffed the advances of more than one attractive woman. Once, when the train had broken down, I amused myself by rescuing the other passengers from a gang of terrorists, picking them off individually with the Kalashnikov I'd seized from the first terrorist, who I'd killed with my bare hands.

All this and more I had achieved in my capacity as the imaginary trolley guy, and now that I was the *actual* trolley guy I was determined to act in the basic humanitarian spirit of these fantasies, not seeing my duties as restricted to the doling out of refreshments, happy to assist passengers any way I could. If anyone asked for hot water for a herbal teabag of their own, I didn't roll my eyes, I dispensed it free of charge, even though I was running out. If anyone ordered a drink and didn't have enough money, I accepted whatever they had. I guess I wanted to set an example, be the trolley guy that *counted*, the one that stayed in the memory.

At this stage I had no idea whether I'd continue in my new role till I'd sold everything, or whether fresh supplies would come from an as-yet unknown source. Perhaps the catering crew leader would restock my trolley and send me on my way again when I reached the buffet car, if I was amenable to that arrangement. This speculation was academic, as it turned out, for there was a logistical consideration I'd overlooked, that didn't become apparent till the evening, one that curtailed my tenure. But before that I must tell you about my first contact with Mark Ramsden.

The message came through just before six, when Companion and I were taking a break in the vestibule. You'll recall that I'd invited Ramsden to keep his response brief

– Was he or was he not on the train? – and the length of his reply surprised me. I was also surprised at its tone. This is what he wrote:

I HAVE SPOKEN WITH DAN. HE IS AWARE OF THE SITUATION, WHICH I AM ENDEAVOURING TO FIX. BUT I MUST ASK YOU TO BEAR WITH ME TILL I HAVE MORE INFORMATION. I WILL CLARIFY MATTERS IN THE NEXT 24 HRS, WHICH MAY BE CRUCIAL IN TERMS OF MY OBTAINING CLARITY ON THIS MATTER. SORRY I CAN'T BE MORE SPECIFIC AT THIS TIME, BUT I HOPE TO ACTION ONE OR TWO THINGS GOING FORWARD.

It was wholly out of keeping with his usual succinctness. And why was he using the megaphonic address of our line manager, everything in upper-case – why was he shouting? He was also presenting some of Dan Coleman's other failings: unanchored generality, tautology, pleonasm, disjuncture, grammatical ineptness, above all the inability to communicate anything but the desire to communicate something. Though it promised 'more information', the message did not hint at the nature of that information. Above all, it didn't tell me if Mark Ramsden was actually on the train. I'VE SPOKEN WITH DAN suggested distance, I thought, a phone call rather than face-to-face conversation, which was promising. As was HE IS AWARE OF THE SITUATION. It was certainly a situation we were in, Ramsden and I, and it was heartening to see him acknowledge this. But were we both in the same situation? That was the question, wasn't it? Ramsden could have been referring to some other situation, the meeting with our prospective German clients, the tour of the facilities. I'd almost forgotten about that. I wondered how things had gone, who had taken them round. Probably Jack Meanwell or Don Drinkwater. Or Meanwell and Drinkwater in tandem.

I read the message over and over, but it was impossible to tell if Ramsden was on board. I thought back to the phone call he'd taken in Coach B that first morning. I was now leaning towards the possibility that he had stepped onto the platform after all and boarded another train. HE IS AWARE OF THE SITUATION – what did it mean? HE IS AWARE OF OUR SITUATION would have been more reassuring – implying as it did a degree of commonality.

On a first reading, the message was unworthy of Ramsden, a torrent of meaningless jargon: 'Going Forward', 'In terms of', 'action' as a verb. On a second and third reading, however, it struck me that my colleague may have been reviving an old office joke here. For Mark Ramsden and I have not always been so stand-offish. There was a time when he first joined the company, two years after me, when one might have observed the trappings of a normal friendship between us. This was just after the Teesdale era, when we still had a licensed bar on the premises, and every other night we would all share a pint before heading to the station. In those days, when Ramsden and I had been slightly closer, any correspondence involving the subject of Dan Coleman and his new mana-gerial regime was regarded as an opportunity for sport. I remember them with great fondness now, the private jokes we had at our line manager's expense. I still have some of the text messages we exchanged. When he arrived it was clear from the outset that Dan was intent on imposing his standard management template, without pausing to consider whether it was appropriate for his new team. And one of his favourite techniques for keeping us all on our toes was to send group text messages that were so devoid of meaning they were clearly intended just to test our response time, nothing more. Whenever these came through, we would all roll our eyes – while replying immediately to get him off our backs. But Mark Ramsden and I would also craft something more personal, something we would send only to each other. Here is an example:

THANKS FOR YOUR MESSAGE DAN, BUT I SPENT SO LONG WORKING OUT HOW MUCH OF A SHIT NOT TO GIVE ABOUT IT I FORGOT TO REPLY.

And here's one from Ramsden:

I THOUGHT ABOUT WHAT YOU SAID, DAN, BUT LIFE'S TOO SHORT.

Ramsden's were more gnomic than mine, more menacing. Not that the menace was genuine. We didn't *hate* Dan Coleman, just the situation that had produced him. Let me be clear, when I wrote something like

I GOT THE FILE YOU LEFT ON MY DESK DAN. I HAVE THROWN IT IN THE CANAL AND MARKED THE SPOT FOR MY COLLEAGUES

I wasn't disrespecting the man, I was disrespecting his authority. And when Mark Ramsden wrote something like

he wasn't mocking Dan Coleman, just reminding him of the
work-life balance.

Was it possible that Ramsden was now reviving this tra-
dition? I preferred to think it was so, that the message, far
from evincing a deterioration of his mental faculties, proved
that he had already habituated himself to life on board.
Perhaps humour was simply Ramsden's coping mechanism.
We were both trapped, on a train of indeterminate length,
headed towards an unknown destination, unable to contact
the Guard with a view to catching a connecting train, yet here
he was pretending to be more concerned about work-related
matters.

I thought I owed it to my colleague to reciprocate his good
spirits, and decided to play it with a straight bat, returning
fire with something equally generic. I had spent much of my
working life doing exactly this, drafting messages and emails
that meant nothing – in response to messages and emails that
were either equally meaningless or unclear about what they
were trying to say. I set great store by my ability to calculate
the precise degree of meaning, or lack of meaning, in any given
communication and respond in kind. The problems started
when you over-calibrated, seeking to clarify the initial enquiry,
when it was better to respond neutrally in the *lingua franca*
of the sender, like a tennis player returning a backhand slice
with another backhand slice. I excelled at the 'placeholder'
response – an ostensibly diligent reply that hinted at (but did
not guarantee) a future communication in which you would
deal with the matter more comprehensively. These emails were
taken as evidence of 'good practice' on my part, but in reality

they were the opposite: textbook examples of the collective bad faith under which we all operated. The trick was to send slightly different versions to different people, cc'ing in extra recipients each time, or promoting recipients from the cc box into the primary recipient box, or demoting them, as it might be. The important thing was to *promote or demote people arbitrarily*, with no hierarchic rationale, so that all chain-of-command logic was lost and no responsibility could be attributed. The net result being that no one could be bothered to trace the paper trail back to the original source, and the ultimate consequence being that the request made in the initial email was transformed from a personal request aimed at oneself into a generic request that anyone might be expected to deal with. It's amazing what can be achieved through the simple alteration of a subject heading.

In the end, I took Ramsden's message in its entirety –

I HAVE SPOKEN WITH DAN. HE IS AWARE OF THE SITUATION, WHICH I AM ENDEAVOURING TO FIX. BUT I MUST ASK YOU TO BEAR WITH ME TILL I HAVE MORE INFORMATION. I WILL CLARIFY MATTERS IN THE NEXT 24 HRS, WHICH MAY BE CRUCIAL IN TERMS OF MY OBTAINING CLARITY ON THIS MATTER. SORRY I CAN'T BE MORE SPECIFIC AT THIS TIME, BUT I HOPE TO ACTION ONE OR TWO THINGS MOVING FORWARD.

– and simply extracted the core data, condensing it into

THANKS. CLARITY ON THIS MATTER

WOULD BE APPRECIATED, AS WOULD
ACTION ON THOSE OTHER THINGS,
MOVING FORWARD .

despite not knowing what the 'matter' was or what the 'other
things' were, still less whether our 'situation' was a mutual one.

'Refreshments,' I announced, as the door slid back and Companion led the way into the next carriage, 'cold drinks, muffins, alcoholic beverages . . .'

Trade slackened off as folk settled in for the night, some in sleeping bags, one or two in pyjamas. So far everyone had been content to sleep in their clothes, but passengers were less inclined to rough it in this part of the train. It had only just gone nine, but many were already asleep, and I was careful to reduce the clank of my merchandise as I crept along the aisle, Companion resuming his place in the basket at the front of the trolley. It was just a few carriages later that he too coiled up and fell asleep. The train had this way of dimming its lights so gradually you didn't notice, augmenting the soporific effect of its steady acceleration, which began around noon and continued till midnight.

On I trundled, till we came to a much brighter coach and I felt the same chill I'd felt in that very first Coach F, a mere twenty minutes into my journey. I knew immediately who would be sat at the end, with his back to the direction of travel, in the last table seat on the right, where he always sat: the man in the blue shell suit. He'd recurred less frequently than the other doppelgängers, no more than five times over the last three days, whereas the man in mohair and the lady in the rain mac were well into double figures. Where the latter usually had some change in their appearance or behaviour – both seemed warmer, more receptive, as I advanced – the man in the blue shell suit maintained his standard presentation, which was somehow both slovenly and alert. There he was, slouched over the table, slurping languidly from a half-crushed can, scowling as I approached.

I'd met folk like him before on my normal commute. You

generally got advance warning when you heard the announcement reminding passengers that it was an offence to smoke or knowingly to permit smoking anywhere on board the train, including the vestibules and toilet areas. A few minutes later, someone in sportswear with a cigarette behind his ear would come loping down the aisle, looking over his shoulder. This time he did not just scowl at me. This time he called me a cunt. There could be no mistake – 'cunt' was definitely what he said, and it was definitely aimed at me, for there was no one else there. I was still ten yards away when the insult came and I pretended not to hear, but as I got closer I couldn't resist slowing down to get a better look. The man in the blue shell suit had aged visibly since I'd last seen him, his red hair turning grey, his face more wrinkled, his home-made tattoos more distorted than I remembered: a swastika on his neck with the arms going the wrong way, an inverted cross between his eyes.

I was not that surprised when he called me a cunt. He was obliged to, I think. If I had learned anything since boarding the train it was that passengers, as a rule (with the exception of Heobah and one or two others), tended to behave less as individuals than as archetypes – and he was the flag-bearer of his particular social classification. I'd been called a cunt before, of course, probably more often than most, but not for a long time had I been called one without any provocation, and the immediate effect, I have to say, was one of nostalgia. Here was a throwback to a former epoch, I said to myself, as the word rang out across the empty carriage, an era of baking hot phone boxes and skinheads gathering on benches, when any old herbert would call you a cunt out of sheer boredom as you walked past just for something to do. But that was not all. While it was true that the insult carried the recreational malice of yesteryear, there was something else, something closer to neutral objectivity in his utterance of this Anglo-Saxon expletive: like a species of bird, I was identified, named, *descried*. Prior to this, I would have admitted to being a potential cunt, a would-be cunt – at a push, an occasional cunt. But maybe I was a *proper* cunt? Perhaps I was a *right* cunt? The man in the shell suit doubtless knew a cunt when he saw one. He was, after all, a cunt himself. He was the Cunt in Coach F.

'Refreshments,' I trilled jovially, 'savoury snacks . . .'

'Cunt,' said the man in the shell suit. 'Keep walkin', cunt.'

I slammed the brake on, nearly waking Companion, still asleep in the basket, for the man in the blue shell suit had just lunged over and helped himself to a can of cider from the middle level of the trolley. I hadn't noticed the cider till now; the tops of the cans were the same colour as the stainless steel surround, blending in with the metal, and because no one had yet asked for it I was still fully stocked. The cans bore the name '808' in blue and red, the same name as the perfume in the Duty Free compartment.

'I think you've had enough, sir,' I said, confiscating the drink.

'Cunt.'

'I'd be happy to give you a soft drink, sir, but I'm afraid I can't let you have an alcoholic beverage.'

'Cunt.'

'Not at this time.'

'*Cunt.*'

He was on the verge of kicking off, but I felt in control of the situation. My legs didn't buckle, as they had so often in the past in violent situations, though I hadn't been in a fight since school. I once had to separate Mick Leadbetter and

Les Cundy at a Christmas do, but that's as close as I'd come.

His first blow, when it came, was surprisingly weak, its power diminished by his having to punch up. When I recollect the incident now, it still confuses me why the Cunt in Coach F chose to start a fight from a seated position. Perhaps I should have sat down too? Perhaps to remain standing had been ungentlemanly?

'Now then, sir,' I said, as a second punch glanced my shoulder, 'we'll have less of that, if you don't mind.'

It wasn't how I remembered fighting to be: the scratching and gouging, the hair-pulling, the conclusive headlock, the natural submission of the weaker man, the parting insults as you tucked your shirts back in and returned to your respective schedules – we never made it that far. The inevitable wrestling match on the floor did not happen. I simply stood my ground, so untroubled by his power and hand-speed that, if anything, I was calmer during the fight than before. Even when he stood up and came at me, by the ninth or tenth blow I realised I wasn't feeling anything. The impact moved me sideways, but my body refused to translate it into anything resembling pain. It was a mere diagram of violence, this salvo, and I could have put a stop to it at any moment, but I was so intrigued by the impotence of his aggression that I actually lowered my hands. For the first time in my life I was coming off best in a fight and I wasn't even trying. I hadn't even taken a swing at him yet.

Technically speaking, this would not *count* as a fight till I did, so I clouted my opponent as hard as I could with an open hand. It was a purely contractual blow – the least I could do was reciprocate his efforts – but he went down instantly, clutching his temple and squealing, stunned that I'd been able to generate so much power with such little backswing. As was I. He gave up at once, sobbing into the table, arms curled round his head. I let him whimper a while before placing a hand on his shoulder:

'Really, sir,' I said, lowering my voice, 'there's no need for this, no call for it at all. There, have your cider back. All over. All over now. Go on, have another, have another on me. One for the road, sir. There we are, sir, courtesy of the 8:08. All over. All over now. All over . . .'

And with this, I calmly released the brake and exited into the vestibule.

It may seem that I dealt with this incident quite well, but the truth is it probably unsettled me as much as it did him. How *easily* I'd slipped into the role – like I was implementing years of training. No, it was the other round: it was like the role had slipped into me. What was it I'd said to him? *Courtesy of the 8:08*. I had casually referred to the current locomotive as if it were the normal scheduled service. Where had these words come from? They seemed unbidden, no more voluntary than a sneeze or a bout of wind, my vocal cords producing something that had had no prior germination in my mind. These interludes, when my own volition was countermanded thus, were to become more frequent, foreshadowed by the automatic compliance I had shown in my capacity as trolley guy. I had the feeling that I ought really to get out of Standard Class now, that if I stayed too long I'd become like the others, unable to think for myself, my words and actions running to a scripted programme.

I began stripping the trolley of provisions, putting everything I could comfortably carry into a bin liner and emptying the cashbox into my overnight bag. I removed the tabard, folding it carefully and leaving it on the trolley for the next incumbent. Companion, having slept throughout all of this, now resumed his position on point, leading me through another Parallel of Standard and into a deserted Coach B. Here, he hopped up onto a seat – seat 77a – and we settled down for the night.

III
FIRST CLASS

1

IT WAS FRIDAY. And not just in the calendrical sense.
It was Friday in the spiritual sense too. From what I could
gather, passengers start drinking at daybreak and continue
till midnight. Their preferred tipple is the 808 cider, and the
trolley women do their best to keep everyone supplied. Which
is not to say they are more visible on Fridays. Far from it,
they're as elusive as ever. It seems they come round during
the small hours, ensuring that every table seat has its six-pack,
every double seat a four-pack. There is wine and beer too, but
it's cider in the main.

I was woken that morning by Companion. The usual feline
tactic is to pound the bladder of the sleeping human like a boxer
working the bag, but Companion was gentler, pawing my leg
insistently till I got the message. I collected my things – the
bin liner, the overnight bag, Paul Carver's jacket – and followed
him up the aisle. I expected him to proceed through to Coach
C as he showed me the way into the vestibule, but he stopped,
turned to his left and began scratching at the toilet door. When
I opened it for him, he leapt up onto the seat, perching pre-
cariously with his head facing the sink, his anus hovering over
the bowl, and did what he had to do. A lesser creature would
have befouled the carpet with impunity, but Companion had
taught himself how to use the facilities. In many ways this was
not surprising. As Fred Teesdale was wont to remark, 'a cat no
more rejoices at the sight of its waste than a human'.

When he emerged from the cubicle he put on a little display, arching his back, purring loudly and weaving around my ankles, and I was given to understand by these affections that he was now ready for his breakfast. I gave him some more tuna and decanted some UHT milk into a coffee lid. I wasn't that hungry, so I just had a Balvenie 12-year-old from the Junior Collector Selection Box. It was only eight o'clock, but it was Friday, and I fell in with the wider delinquency, several cans already open as we passed through the next carriage.

No sooner had we gained the vestibule after Coach C than Companion stopped again and started to clean himself, angling his hind leg back over his shoulder like a musket, lapping away at his shank. It was interesting to watch him revert to bestial type after just having mounted a human latrine. He would not be hurried, progressing from his nether regions to his flank, from his flank to his shoulder, from his shoulder to his head, wetting his front paw and swiping it across his face, then hoisting the other leg over his shoulder and repeating on his left-hand side the ablutions just performed on his right.

I left him to it and rolled a cigarette. Morning has broken, I said to myself, looking out the window with faux-pastoral optimism. Then I saw the sun and thought: No, morning *is* broken. Not only did the sun look smaller, more distant than usual, its complexion had changed, greener than I remembered and not quite as circular, a misshapen disc squatting on the embankment as we rose out of the cutting. It had never seemed so withdrawn, so put-upon, so bloodless, our parent star, like an exhausted single mum at the school gates of the cosmos, hoisted reluctantly skyward for the five-billionth time. Somewhere beneath that pale fire was a town, and in that town a street, and on that street a house, and in that house a flat where I lived; and somewhere else a city, and in that city a building that I went to every day, and in that building an office I shared with several other people, with a desk bearing a phone that I sometimes deigned to answer. It was all so vivid, so recent, so plausible, yet I'd forgotten the identity of its chief protagonist. It was only the sun – the one agency that has jurisdiction over all, that encompasses all, sees all – that reminded me of the trappings of that life. I could remember everything but his name: his address of residence, his job, the films he'd seen, the books he'd read, the randomly garnered knowledge. From this store of bric-a-brac I now retrieved a line from a poem, of all things: *Your life slowly becomes more important than you.* I couldn't remember the rest of it, but this had stayed with me, and I felt its relevance now as I mulled over the events of the last few days. I'd begun to feel like I was dissolving, the figure of my being subsumed into the ground of the locomotive environment. My tenure with the trolley had been brief, but I'd submitted almost unquestioningly, and suspected this sense of duty was merely the outward symptom of a deeper assimilation.

We'd slowed down considerably since dawn, counter to our normal habit of accelerating during the day, and as I lingered at the vestibule window there was a marked alteration in the terrain, now more manicured than at any stage of our journey. The embankment on our left was planted with thousands of saplings, arranged in uniform rows, and alongside the track was a freshly laid access road that led to a new development. The foundations for a small building had been set in: a make-shift table sat at the centre of the cement floor, made from boards thrown across two trestles, six folding chairs scattered around it with hi-vis jackets draped over the back. A tarpaulin was tied to a partially-built wall giving shelter from the elements, and there were tools all over the place: jackhammers, shovels, a cement-mixer. These signs of human endeavour were uplifting, especially since we were doing no more than thirty now and I could see them in great detail. But a bigger surprise awaited me. Further ahead, half a mile off, was a bridge over the track with a continuous stream of traffic moving across it, the light glinting from the windows. My cigarette fell from my mouth. At the very moment of resigning myself to an indeterminate stay on board on the train, escape now seemed a real possibility. If we continued to slow, I could open the door, scramble up the bank, flag down a passing motorist. I gripped the handles of my overnight bag, ready to make my move; we couldn't have been doing more than twenty, and I was willing to risk minor injury. But no, I would not injure myself – we were coming to a stop, a hundred metres from the bridge. As we did so, I lowered the window and felt for the handle. To my surprise the door opened, and I descended onto the first step. The temperature outside, I noted, was no different to the temperature inside. I remember my disappointment at the lack of a stiff breeze to mark the threshold I was about to cross for the first time in four days. I put my other foot on the lower step, about to drop down onto the clinker, when I remembered Companion. He had stopped cleaning himself now, front paws planted firmly on the carpet, staring straight at me, eyes narrowing as the sun shone through the open door. I held out a hand, but he wouldn't come.

When I turned again to the bridge I saw that I was mistaken: the windows belonged to train carriages, not cars. This other train had also stopped, the passengers leaning out. I was about to hail them, ask where they were going, get some information about the lay of the land, when we jolted forward, freewheeling for several metres, before reversing again after an abrupt halt. I closed the door and stepped back into the vestibule just as people began filing through from the carriage behind. Again, two queues formed, one at the right-hand window, the other on the left, and we went through the same ritual we'd gone through on the heath, taking turns to look out, making the circular sign on our chest as we stepped back into the middle of the vestibule. This time I stayed at the window, looking over the shoulder of each passenger. Those on the other train were also conducting this ritual, and I was surprised at their indifference to the scenery. None of them looked down as we went back and forth – they didn't seem to notice us on the track below. I found this odd, for the spectacle was impressive: every time we moved, they moved, the two trains in perfect concert. When we went forward, so did they. When we went back, so did they. Thus, the carriages directly overhead soon rolled out of view, and after a few minutes, as our own carriage approached the bridge, I surmised that this choreography was not just ceremonial but functional. Here, then, was my conclusion: this was not another train, but a distant section of *our* train. The synchrony of our movement was too precise for it to be otherwise. But how many carriages lay between us and them? Were they ahead or behind? Were we pulling them, or were they pulling us?

What was going on here, I speculated further, was the addition of more carriages to the train. For the distance we travelled forward before coming to a stop and going back a metre was the same length as an average coach. It stood to reason, did it not, that the train was growing? Or maybe it was shrinking? Might it be that carriages were being removed? I tried to recall my past experience of being on shunting trains. I'd been on trains that had lost carriages and I'd been on trains that had gained them, and could not tell the difference; but

I remember thinking, as I witnessed this spectacle, that now that I'd become used to the idea of a vehicle of inordinate length, the prospect of *losing* carriages was far less appealing than gaining them. If the train had to be long, let it be really long.

There was no joining of hands this time, the other passengers all filing into the next carriage. But there was one who had yet to take his turn at the window, and I knew, without looking behind me, from the heavy mouth-breathing alone, that it was the man in the green mohair suit.

'Beautiful, isn't it?' he said, drawing up to the window.

We watched the other part of the train together in silence, almost directly underneath it now, and before we went under the bridge a familiar face appeared at one of the windows: ruddy and balloon-like, with tiny twinkling eyes, a huge white carnation blooming from his lapel: *it was the man in the green mohair suit.*

He was waving at us, the only passenger on that section of the train to show any awareness of his surroundings. And I was sure the man standing next to me, the other man in the green mohair suit – I was sure I saw him wave back, discreetly, secretively, a slight lift of the fingers, nothing more.

'I'm Marlowe,' he said, as the vestibule darkened and we passed under the bridge. 'Welcome to First Class.'

2

R EVELATIONS, EPIPHANIES – call them what you
will – tend to occur in isolation if they happen at all
in one's life, but here on the 8:08 they come in clusters. The
realisation that the train was even longer than I'd thought, so
long as to necessitate one part passing over another, the spectacle of Marlowe greeting his own doppelgänger on the bridge,
and the news that we were already in First Class, despite
not yet having left Standard, created a riptide of bemuse-
ment that threatened to drag me onto the high seas. I could
see why some passengers just gave up, accepted the status
quo. Marlowe's subsequent claim that 'one is always, to some
extent, in both classes simultaneously' didn't help. Even he
confessed to not having mastered the distinction in all its
nuances, despite introducing himself as a senior member of
the on-board team as we entered Coach D.

We found a table-seat a little way down on the left,
Companion coiling up in the forward-facing berth by the
window and Marlowe sitting next to him. His face seemed
thinner than the one I'd just seen overhead, still clinically
obese but more oblong, closely shaven, pricked with dry
blood, a freshly peeled countenance that preserved the co-
logne's momentary sting, his yellow bowtie imparting a rhu-
barb-and-custard effect. His green eyes were tiny and deep-
set, LEDs pulsing in the circuitry of his brain, and he had
elected to sport, of all things, a flat-top for a hairstyle, wholly

unsuited to his manner, which was one of bluff aristocratic entitlement. He was five and a half feet at most, but there must have been at least twenty stone of him crammed into the mohair three-piece.

'What's in there?' he asked, as I sat down opposite.

'Something from the trolley, sir?' I said, placing the bin liner on the table. 'Soft drink? Savoury snack?'

Again, these words were involuntary, issued, as it were, by locomotive decree, but there was a hint of insolence too, now, a sarcasm all my own.

'And where *is* your trolley?'

I explained about the logistical problem. I thought he might shed some light on how the others got round it, but he wasn't interested, delving into the bin liner and pulling out a tonic water.

'Courtesy of the 8:08,' I said, when he offered me a fifty-pound note.

The carriage was empty apart from us and two other groups: the eight young women in the table seats just ahead of us were already on their third bottle of rosé; further up, a group of men in morning suits were enjoying a Champagne breakfast. Clearly I had some catching up to do, so I cracked open a cider from my stash, which I chased with a Glen Moray 18-year-old from the Junior Collector Selection Box.

'You'll forgive me for not joining you,' said Marlowe, patting his chest. 'A single dram would finish it forever.'

'Must be hard on a Friday. You feel a bit left out, I imagine?'

'GP's advice, old bean, GP's advice.' Marlowe coughed, tilting his Britvic at the young women. He'd deliberately chosen a forward-facing seat to catch the eye of the one in the little black dress with a white sash that said 'Bride-to-be'. The others were also wearing sashes: 'Bridesmaid', and other things

I couldn't make out. All of them had acknowledged Marlowe as soon as we'd entered the carriage, and I was happy to bathe in his celebrity, such as it was. In the earlier sections of the train, the idea that any of his florid predecessors, all dressed in the same green three-piece, with its watch chain and white carnation, could have been members of the on-board team would have seemed absurd, but I saw from the hen party's reaction that he commanded a great deal of respect, a regular patron of their affections, a kind of *paterfamilias*.

'Well?' he said.

'Well what?'

'What do you think?'

'Of what?'

'*First Class*.'

'What do I think? I think it's the same.'

'The same as what?'

'Standard Class.'

Marlowe sighed, as though I had failed some rudimentary test. 'On the face of it,' he said, 'but look again, old bean. Observe details.'

I scanned the fixtures and fittings, but apart from the antimacassars and the extra 808 insignias, the general livery seemed much as before.

'And the passengers?' prompted Marlowe.

I stood up and looked round, at the gentlemen at the far end, the bevvy of girls closer by, the lone individuals hunched over their cans. I gathered from the women's conversation that they were just embarking on their adventure. Various activities were being discussed: cocktails in the afternoon, flamenco in the evening; tomorrow a trip to a spa and a tour of a local gin distillery. As their chat subsided, the men at the far end could be heard discussing their own excursion. They were bound for a racecourse, their top hats stowed in the overhead rack, a newspaper open on the table, the alpha male trying to explain the form to the others. Then the hen party clucked into life again. The bride had hiccups and was being made to drink a whole glass of rosé upside down.

'Go on, Aitch,' said the chief bridesmaid, 'get it down you.'

'Go on, Aitch,' said the others, chanting as the bride-to-be did as she was told: 'Aich, Aitch, Aitch . . .'

'Well?' said Marlowe, as I sat down again.

The best I could offer was that these passengers were not only more verbally adept than their counterparts in earlier carriages, more liberated, more at home, but more aware of the wider picture.

'The wider picture? Not sure I follow, old bean.'

I elaborated that nearly all the conversations I'd heard so far had focused on the past; these passengers were talking about the future. It was an ad hoc observation, but Marlowe seemed pleased with it.

'It *is* tricky to tell them apart,' he said, lowering his voice.

'First and Standard Class passengers, you mean?'

'Yes. Even I floundered at first.'

'At first?'

He hesitated here. 'It's a long time since I myself was in Standard,' he said. 'And yet, even in the middle of First Class, elements of Standard still persist.'

I put it to Marlowe that one of the traditional functions of First Class was to exclude Standard Class passengers. True, he conceded, but there were many different modes of exclusion. And one of the best was to bring both classes into contact with one another. Many First Class passengers felt it was pointless being in First Class unless there were one or two Standard Class passengers to witness it.

'I suppose it affirms their status,' I said. 'Those men up there – they're off to Ascot, right?'

'Ascot?'

'You know. The racecourse. Whereas the women . . .'

'As I say, we operate an integrated system—'

'We?'

'Though it's possible,' he went on, ignoring my interruption, 'it's conceivable that if one went far enough in either direction, one would come across a *pure* First or Standard Class carriage. But one would have to go a long way . . .'

I waited for him to continue, but he'd revealed more than he intended, I think, in his use of the collective pronoun. I got the impression I was being vetted, drip-fed with information to see which way I blew. I have to say, Marlowe wasn't particularly good at it, not used to imparting things on a need-to-know basis.

'So how *do* you tell them apart?' I asked. 'Here, I mean?'

'Here?' This simple word appeared to confuse him, but he let it pass. 'You have conversed, have you not, with some of those travelling *aft?*' he said, throwing a thumb over his shoulder.

'I have.'

'And you marked their verbal limitations?'

'I did.'

'Well, that is the easiest way. Though not infallible.'

'So there's no absolute First Class, as such? No absolute Standard? They're hypothetical realms?'

Marlowe ignored the question, smiling again at the hen party. The chief bridesmaid was trying to open another bottle of rosé, and he motioned her over, drawing the cork with predictable finesse.

'There's something else,' I said, as she went back to her seat. 'The man on the bridge?'

'What man on the bridge?'

'You know – the other, the other . . .'

Marlowe lurched forward, his huge head filling my table-space: 'Yes?'

'You know, the other . . .'

He gripped my hand. 'The other what? You're babbling, old bean. Slow down, take your time.'

The other you was what I had wanted to say, but the words were throttled before I could get them out. I had wanted to ask whether his doppelgänger was ahead of us or to the rear, whether those carriages that had sailed by overhead consti-tuted our future, so to speak, or our past. The carnations in the respective buttonholes of the two men might yet be telling. The one I was looking at now wilted on Marlowe's lapel whereas the other man's had bloomed, visibly resplendent from fifty feet.

'As I say,' said Marlowe, 'it's a long time since I was in Standard. But tell me what *you* have seen. What *you* have heard.'

This time, when he leaned over the table and gripped my hand, it was like the information was siphoned out of me: the exchange between the two businessmen; the two brothers in kilts; my confusion at the ritual of Going Forward; the man in the shell suit; the Harbinger, Mark Ramsden, Dan Coleman, the prospective German clients, everything. Our acquaintance had begun benignly, but now I felt like I was being forcibly debriefed.

'Good, good,' said Marlowe, relaxing his grip. 'But there is something more, is there not?'

'Is there?'

'Yes. There is something else, I think.'

He squeezed my hand harder and the information was

drawn from me once more: my encounter with the woman in the turban ('What was the colour of her headwear?'); my acquisition of the jumper ('May I see it? Marvellous.'); my meeting with the trolley woman ('Ah, an old friend.'); and also my night with Heobah.

'I'm meeting her tomorrow for dinner,' I said. 'In the Restaurant Car.'

He professed not to know her, but I thought this a lie, for he'd let go of my hand at the mention of her name, startled.

'You were saying,' I went on, after a short silence. 'Earlier you were saying that even you floundered.'

'I?'

'Yes – "at first", I think you said.'

This reminder of his exact words was intended to wrong-foot him, referring as they surely did to the time when he first came on board, which I hoped was as disorienting for him as it had been for me.

'Floundered? Did I say that?'

'You did.'

'Well, I suppose there's no denying it. But that was before.'

'Before what?'

'Before I happened upon my station.' Again, he seemed to regret his choice of words, this reference to "before". 'My chief function,' he said, after draining his can, 'is to *embody* First Class.'

'An ambassadorial role?'

'In a system such as ours, there must be some constants.'

'And how does that work, exactly?'

'Simple: wherever I go, that is where First Class is. Another, if I may?'

The only non-alcoholic drink I had left was a bottle of

tomato juice. I handed it to him and he continued, prising off the lid on the edge of the table:

'I suppose that sounds lofty, doesn't it?'

'A bit.'

'I mean it in a purely constitutional sense: as a policeman or judge embodies the law.'

'Am I to understand that you have an *edifying* effect on the other passengers?'

'Not with you, old bean.'

'I mean, do they try harder when you're around?'

'On the contrary, I seem to impel them to further vulgarities, though it is true that some Standard Class passengers are given to self-improvement.'

'An upgrade?'

'Yes and no. Just as it is possible to be *in* both First Class and Standard Class, it is also possible to be *of* both.'

'So no one is exclusively First or Standard Class, then?'

'Depends when you meet them, old boy. You observe yonder hen party?'

'What of it?'

'If I were to say to you that I have encountered those women many times before, you would not be surprised?'

'No.'

'And if I were to add that when I first met them they were different?'

I couldn't see what he was driving at.

'Here,' he whispered, reaching into his pocket and producing a small hexagonal pillbox, 'go and give them this.'

'What is it?'

'Just give it to them. And as you do, look closely at the face of the betrothed.'

There was a chorus of cat-calls as I presented myself to the hen party: 'The gentleman in the green suit has asked me to give you this,' I said.

The chief bridesmaid snatched the box and opened it: 'What do we have here, girls?' she said, pouring the contents onto the table: eight white pills – one for each woman.

'They're not from me,' I said, 'they're from the gentleman over there.'

Marlowe bowed minutely as they swivelled in his direction. Inside the box was a note, which the chief bridesmaid unfolded and read out:

'*Congratulations. A bit of 808 for Aitch's Merry 8.*'

The women necked the pills immediately with a gulp of rosé, and thanked him in turn:

'Cheers, Marlowe.'

'Cheers, Marlowe.'

'Yeah, thanks, Marlowe.'

'Nice one, Marlowe.'

'Bless 'im. Bless ol' Marlowe.'

'Yeah. Give 'im a glass of wine.'

''E don't drink.'

'Give 'im a bloody kiss then.'

There was a cackle of laughter as their gratitude descended into smut and one of them suggested giving Marlowe a hand-job instead. The largest woman – I think it was the chief bridesmaid's mother – went over and planted a loud smacker on their benefactor, leaving a bullet-hole of lipstick on his forehead. I was about to return to my seat, when I realised I'd met the bride before. I'd met her twice, in fact: once several years ago on my old commute, and again two days ago, on the current service. It was Heobah. I couldn't believe it. Her face was deeply tanned, caked in make-up, her hair bleached blonde, poker-straight, the same as the other girls, who all looked identical apart from the sashes designating a differ-ent relation to the bride, and their little black dresses, which ranged from size 6 to 16.

Heobah – or 'Aitch', as she was now called – did not seem to recognise me. What was she doing with these women? Where was her two-tone suit, her lightning flash T-shirt, her men's brogues? Her greying hair and natural forty-something complexion? Who was this peroxided travesty, this devotee of the solarium and straightening tongs? It was the most dramat-ic change yet that I had beheld in any passenger.

'First Class,' said Marlowe when I sat down again. 'Takes a while to get the hang of it, old bean.'

'But I know her,' I said, sliding in opposite, stunned. 'I know her.'

'*Knew* her,' corrected Marlowe, placing his hand on mine. 'Knew her.'

3

WE SPENT THE next two hours playing chess. Marlowe did not say as much, but he clearly felt my mind needed to be directed elsewhere, and I was actually quite relieved when he withdrew the leatherbound set from his inside pocket and began arranging the magnetic pieces. I believe he took no pleasure at all from his five consecutive victories, each achieved with an efficiency I must call *algorithmic*, so immediate were his moves in response to my own. He had obviously studied the game long and hard, and his only interest in playing me seemed to reside in how few moves it took to win. He broke sweat briefly at the beginning of the fifth game, but only to impart commentary on why it was unwise for aggressive players like myself to play the King's Indian as black. And then, halfway through the sixth, just as he was bearing down on my king, he suddenly offered me a draw.

'I have to go now,' he said, pulling out his watch. 'Here.' He pushed the board across the table. 'Work on your opening.'

'Which one?'

'All of them.' He extracted a scrap of paper from a sleeve in the chess set. 'Here are the standard ones. You're actually not a bad player, but you rely too much on talent and not enough on your memory. You must memorise your mistakes and learn not to repeat them. There's a chap downtrain, of roughly the same ability as yourself. I suggest you play him. You would get on well.'

'Who?'

'Oh you'll know him. You'll know him when you see him.'

'Well, it's not like I don't have the time.'

'Precisely, old bean.' He slapped me on the shoulder as he got up. 'Time enough at last, hey, time enough at last?'

It threw me, this comment, implying as it did that my presence on the train was not so much a deviation as a much-needed sabbatical from my normal routine. I watched him shuffle down the aisle, pausing at the hen party to kiss Aitch's hand, through the sliding door and on into the next coach, the interior of which was just visible due to the straightness of the track. I was surprised to see him take the first available table seat there, striking up conversation with an unseen passenger to his left and putting on his spectacles to examine a piece of paper they had just given him. Comical, his leaving so abruptly, on the pretext of urgent business, only to stop again so soon. But if everyone knew him, as he seemed to imply, he would be used to folk flagging him down. Maybe it was part of his 'function' to reach out to newcomers like me? Help us bed ourselves in? A few minutes later he got up again and wandered further downtrain.

After Marlowe had gone, I cracked open another can of 808. The scenery outside had resumed its impersonation of the scenery from four days ago: dead silver birch trees, woebegone common land, abandoned prefabs. But I was by no means disenchanted by this spectacle. The trackside fixtures, the concrete huts and grey metal boxes that presumably housed electrical components, were not unlike those I had seen on my old commute, though there were no cables, I noticed, no signs warning of fatal voltage, the only inscriptions being the graffiti with which they were covered. I have to say, I was cheered by the many tags I saw sprayed and marker-penned onto every available surface. I have always found graffiti uplifting. I like how it occupies the nether region between the track and the world beyond, and it excited me to imagine its practitioners patrolling this liminal zone by night, just so that I, an ordinary commuter, could draw aesthetic benefit in the morning. The authorities are gravely mistaken in their assumption that salarymen like myself are against it. On the contrary, as we gaze out the window, blowing on our hot beverage and unwrapping our pastry, the sight of a tag actually increases our sense of wellbeing. If I happen to look up from my newspaper at the precise moment the word TOXIC rushes past, or ELAMENT, or TWIST, the cosiness of my routine, far from being threatened by this apparently subversive act, is enhanced. I go so far as to say that once I have noticed a particular tag, I await it each morning with something closer to fondness than the sanctimony usually expected of the British taxpayer. It was reassuring to see that, even here, there were so many exponents of the artform, so many individuals prepared to break the law in order to express themselves, and I raised my can of cider, privately saluting their efforts as we sped past.

The hen party had gone quiet now, and I did not care for the change in atmosphere one bit. There could only be one reason why they had lowered their voices: they were talking about me.

Sure enough, a few minutes later Aitch came over. I tried not to think of her as Heobah as she sat down opposite me in the seat that Marlowe had vacated. She was the same age, but had tried to make herself look younger, concealing those used qualities I'd found so attractive in her earlier counterpart beneath a carapace of foundation. She'd gone for white lipstick, to enhance her tan, and her scent was different too, a perfume I'd smelled on a thousand women. She smelled like she'd just had a shower, Aitch, the generic morning smell of the old 8:08, the smell of the spruced-up herd transported south to their desks. I waited for her to speak but she sat there in silence, motionless, looking directly ahead, not at me but over my shoulder. After a few seconds, she closed her eyes and began sighing, lightly at first, then heavily. I asked what was wrong, but she didn't answer.

It was when she started to moan that the penny dropped. It was an old hen party dare: she'd been tasked with simulating an orgasm in public, one of several hoops she would have to jump through as they worked their way through their itinerary, but the act would have no meaning unless she could find a suitable straight man. I had seen this happen before. The victim on that occasion had been a pensioner on an underground train, and I had watched him tough it out, determined not to move, as a young girl in her early twenties had panted and gyrated in the neighbouring seat, in a peach-coloured dress and plastic tiara, an L-plate pinned to her back.

'Go on, Aitch,' yelled the chief bridesmaid. 'Step it up.'

And they all took up the chant: 'Step it up, Aitch, step it up!'

But Aitch would not be hurried. Several minutes passed before her hips began to move, gradually leaving the seat as she thrust her torso upwards, the chief bridesmaid sharking in to film it on her phone. I wondered whether I ought to do anything – respond, make an effort, get involved, enter into the spirit of it a bit more. What had the old man done? Yes, I remembered now: he'd got out a pen, folded his newspaper over his knee and just started doing the crossword. That was good. They'd liked that. He'd done well, the old man – in many ways, his performance had bested the bride-to-be's, and the incident had ended well, with her sitting on his lap, like a schoolgirl in Santa's grotto. He hadn't flapped, like I would have done, the old man, like I was doing now; he'd taken charge, found a way to handle it, turning humiliation into triumph.

'Step it up, Aitch, step it up!'

I, however, had no newspaper, no props as such, and though it was strange to just sit there doing nothing, I felt the mood would turn if I tried to join in, that the playfulness of the situation might flip if I did anything but sit still and ride it out. My role here was simply to bear neutral witness to the orgasm, like a catalyst in an experiment, a substance which speeds up a reaction while remaining chemically unaltered.

'Step it up, Aitch, step it up!'

And now Aitch stepped it up, her climax gaining traction from the very rigidity of my bearing, as I folded my arms, pressed my shoes into the carpet and stared inscrutably into middle-distance. As the others gathered round to film it on their phones, she began to escalate, hyperventilating and shuddering. Implicit in this performance, I sensed, was the determination to surpass the orgasms her friends had simulated on their hen-dos, and also to lay down a marker for the *un*betrothed, those among her party who had yet to undergo this test.

The climax itself was quite disappointing, not as convincing as the build-up, but nevertheless greeted with a fanfare of approval, hoots, wolf-whistles, the banging of tables. I remained in my seat for several seconds out of respect for the show she had put on, then gathered up my things and made my escape, blithely woman-handled as I ran their gauntlet, Companion just ahead of me, oblivious to the meaning of it all, showing me the way, bless him, showing me the way.

'Not bad for his age!' said the bride-to-be's mother-in-law as I rushed past. 'Not bad for his age. You would if you had to, wouldn't you, you would if you had to . . . ?'

4

THE OTHER DOPPELGÄNGERS had changed so gradually, both in terms of their appearance and their behaviour, as to effectively comprise a single person extruded over a long distance. Marlowe, for example, had become friendlier by degrees, the change spread over a handful of intermediate Marlowes, each more genial than the last, and I'd assumed this change echoed the unidirectional constraint of the train, that it was one-way, irreversible. I now hoped this wasn't the case, for the change in Heobah had been manifestly for the worse, and I prayed that it would be her earlier incarnation waiting for me tomorrow in the Restaurant Car and not the one I had just met.

When I ran into Marlowe again, later that afternoon, and told him what had happened with the hen party, he was quick to deny responsibility.

'What the hell did you give them?'

'Placebos, old bean. Power of suggestion. Strongest drug there is.'

The carriage was busy, a well-oiled Coach K, no tables available, and he shifted into the window seat as I slipped in beside him.

'I can see you doubt me.'

'I don't know what to think.'

He took another pillbox out, smaller than the first, more

ornate, with a single white pearl set into the lid, placing it on the fold-down table in front of me.

'Then try one.'

On the side was a tiny inscription, engraved into the silver, but it was in Latin and I couldn't understand it. 'No thanks.'

'It's the only way you'll know,' he said, easing the lid off, 'the only way you'll know whether to trust me.'

'And why would I want to do that?'

He threw up his hands with a whining, emphysemic laugh that turned quickly into a coughing fit.

'It's a reasonable question.'

'And let me ask *you* a question: Who else has taken an interest in your case?'

'My case? Am I to be put in trial?'

'Your affairs, I mean?'

'A number of people, since you ask. Heobah, for one.'

'Ah, Heobah. He-o-bah – or *Aitch* as she is otherwise known.' He took a pill from the box and placed it on my fold-down table. It was white, stamped with '808', like the cider, antimacassars, hip flasks, doors and crockery that would begin appearing just a little further on. 'Well?'

'OK.' I grabbed the box, took a second pill from it and placed it on his fold-down table. 'I will if you will.'

Marlowe consented to the arrangement immediately and we necked them with a mouthful of 808. To my amazement, he then pulled out his pocket watch, noted the time, and informed me that I could expect to begin feeling the effects at around one-thirty.

'What effects?'

'Why, the mind-altering effects, of course.'

'But you said they were placebos.'

'That is correct.'

'And placebos have no effect.'

'Far from it, as I have already stated, the placebo is a potent drug, based as it is on the subject's own confabulations, his desire for release from the bondage of normalcy.'

'But it only works if you think you've been given a real drug,' I said, 'and you've just told me I've been given a placebo.'

'Did I? That was unfortunate.'

'So you have lied to me?'

'Lied? That would imply a concealment of the truth. I have merely passed on my *ignorance* of the truth – in good faith.'

'So you don't know what it is?'

'We are not interested in what it is, only in what it does.'

Here it was again, his use of the third person, more blatant now.

'And what does it do?'

'Its effects are as various as the characters of any two given men – as might be expected of a substance that has only a man's character to work with. All I can say is that in twenty minutes you will begin to feel more *at home*. At least, that's what most people say.'

'Most people?'

'Most people we have tested.'

'So it's a drug trial then?'

'A what?'

'A drug trial. You know, a number of subjects are given a substance. Some get the real thing, others get placebos . . .'

'Oh, I see.' Marlowe's eyes sparkled. 'How interesting. Yes, I suppose it is a bit like that. You might say we're conducting an impediment.'

'Experiment.'

'I'm sorry?'

'You're conducting an *experiment*. But never mind that. How many subjects are there?'

'You mean, how many people have been given the placebo?'

'Yes. And how many have received the real drug.'

'Old bean, the placebo *is* the real drug.'

'Let me put it this way: How many have received the pill marked "808"?'

'In total? Impossible to say.'

'But you must keep records.'

'Difficult to put a figure on it.'

'But you must have some idea? I have a right to know, do I not?'

'Right? To know? Well, naturally everyone is involved.'

'Everyone?'

'Everyone. Everyone is always involved. Stands to reason.'

'What are you talking about, "stands to reason"?'

'Everyone is always involved in everything. I am involved; *you* are involved; *we* are involved: this is involvement.'

'You mean everyone here on the train?'

'What an odd choice of words. Old bean, that *is* everyone.'

'And what have you discovered so far?' I asked. 'May I inquire after your findings?'

Here Marlowe was more circumspect, defensive. 'The results have been inconclusive. So far.'

'So far?'

'We are almost done, almost at the end of – what was that word again?'

'Experiment.'

'Almost at the end of our experiment. Only two subjects remain.'

'Me being one.'

'Yes. Yourself and the other chap.'

'What other chap?'

'Oh, you wouldn't know him. Actually, that's important. It's important the subjects are not known to each other.'

'And what about you? You're forgetting about yourself.'

'Oh, I dropped mine on the floor when you weren't looking. I fear the cat has eaten it. Sorry for the deception, but I must remain neutral, you understand.'

Various expletives formed in my mind but curiosity outranked anger, and I asked him what he expected to discover, whether he was testing out a specific hypothesis: in short, what the *point* of the experiment was.

'We are hopeful of an outcome,' he said evasively. 'We have been very thorough this time.'

'There have been previous times? Other experiments?'

'There is no end to it, old boy. Yet all being well, we are almost *at* an end. We are confident we have involved everyone, by now, and that we have eliminated all but the most promising candidates.'

'I'll take that as a compliment then?'

'Take it how you like, old bean, take it how you like. And one other thing.'

'What?'

'We have introduced another element.' Marlowe lowered his voice. 'It is a piece of genius. It is amazing no one thought of it before.' He looked around to ensure no one was listening: 'This time, one subject has been given a placebo . . .'

'Yes?'

'. . . and the other – the other has been given a *placebo*.'

He said this with utter conviction, and I've pondered its meaning ever since. At the time I thought he really believed two different substances had been administered; but I now think he was claiming that the different characters of each subject would retroactively confer on a single substance the status of a different drug. It was the only available logic in what he said.

'So I'm to be observed under the influence? Interpretations will be made of my actions, inferences drawn?'

'The data will be collected,' said Marlowe.

'And?'

'The data will be analysed.'

'And then what?'

'The data will be processed.'

'Naturally.'

'Compared, cross-referred, you understand.'

'Yes, but with what?'

'Other data.'

'And then?'

'And then,' said Marlowe, rising to his feet, 'then, the data will be *protected*.'

I stood up to allow him into the aisle.

'It's the final stage. Data Protection. The data must be protected, or it is useless.'

'And what does that mean, exactly?'

'I can tell you what it means approximately.'

'Then that'll have to do.'

'It means that the data will not be used to compromise your current interests, only to enhance your future prospects.'

'My prospects for what?'

'Well, we'll have to see about that, won't we? Depends on the data. For now, it suffices to remind you that the placebo only works if the subject believes in it. I can't stress that enough. And now, if you'll excuse me, I have business downtrain.'

Naturally I had further questions, but Marlowe was

already setting off down the aisle. I watched him all the way to the sliding door; but then he stopped, turned and came back, stepping over Companion, now sitting demurely in the middle of the carpet, all four paws tucked under his body.

'What was that word again?' he said, producing a notebook and pencil.'

'*Experiment?*'

I spelled it for him three times, but he still wrote *Impediment.*

5

IT WAS TWENTY past one. According to Marlowe, I would start feeling more 'at home' any minute now. But how to distinguish between the train's inherent strangeness and any synthetic strangeness induced by the pill? There was also Companion to consider. Had he really eaten the one discarded by Marlowe? His pace was certainly brisker as we penetrated further into First Class, but that could be down to his natural impatience, for he liked to press on in the afternoon.

Before relating the other events of that day, it's important to remark on a few topographical changes – I speak, here, not of the surrounding countryside, but of the train's interior. So far, changes to its overall facture had been minimal. There were the sliding windows, the gradually increasing age of the coaches on the first day, the more recent ubiquity of the 808 insignia, and that was about it. From now on the changes to the train's livery and architecture were more marked, with a concomitant alteration of its social character. I did not notice much initial difference in the rest of that section as we advanced, but around five o'clock I began to see, in addition to the trappings of a more traditional First Class 'experience' – bespoke crockery and napkins, leather seats with ashtrays in the armrests and a reclining mechanism at the side – certain other elements that had been absent, not just from Standard Class but from rail travel in general of the last thirty years.

The most conspicuous of these were the compartments,

done out in 1950s style, with long bench seating and wire luggage racks overhead, sparsely distributed at first, but more prevalent as we progressed. Where, before, we were obliged to come into contact with all the other passengers as we breasted the aisles, by late afternoon we occasionally found ourselves emerging from the vestibules into empty gangways that ran to the right, with everyone now seated to the left, facing each other behind windowed façades. However, these compart-mentalised coaches were infrequent at first, separated by a dozen or so Standard Class. It was as Marlowe had said: First and Standard merged rather than separate, with First Class predominating the further you went. But the transition was slow; not till the next day did we begin to negotiate sections consisting entirely of compartmentalised coaches. But there was one thing that didn't change: the sliding doors opening to let you through but never to allow you back.

The compartments themselves were nicely made – the façades done out in lacquered birch, with brass insets between the glass and the window frames, with a blind that came down over the windows, affording privacy from gangway traffic. The interiors were nicely furnished, the bench seats upholstered in luxurious navy-blue velvet, with a table that came out from the thick central mullion of the outward-facing window, ex-tended by means of nested leaves and folding legs all the way to the door, an ingenious piece of carpentry I did not really appreciate at the time. The carpet was blood red and of high quality, most passengers preferring to discard their shoes to feel the warmth of its pile. And yet, I have to say, I found the compartments oppressive compared to the open-plan layout of Standard.

From this point on, then, there was a small degree of lateral movement to one's navigation of the train. In order to enter a compartment, one naturally had to turn left, and continue in that direction for four or five paces if only the window seat were available. It sounds pedantic to remark on this change, but it felt significant. So accustomed was I to going continuously forward, I found it disorienting to perform this simple sideways manoeuvre, which was like coming off the motorway after a hundred miles in the fast lane.

Not till evening did the compartments begin appearing, the next hour presenting a monotonous continuation of aisle, vestibule and sliding door. A more immediate change – and another throwback to an earlier period of rail travel – was the sudden appearance of smokers. So far, I had been the only one.

It was at some point in the late 90s, I think, that smoking carriages disappeared from British trains. The problem, as I recall, was that each time the door opened, a gust of polluted air was released into the vestibule and the next carriage. And what with the vestiges that clung to the clothing of smokers as they went to and from the buffet car, it was not long before the whole train stank like an ashtray. There was none of this on the 8:08. Smoke remained heavily localised, hanging in thick clumps which, rather than diffusing into the surrounding atmosphere, seemed to remain in situ, magically fading into nothingness, thus minimising the infection of adjacent vestibules and coaches. So there was no advance warning when I came upon my first fellow smoker. As the door slid back, and we entered Coach C, the difference in air quality was instantaneous.

So far, there have been several characters who mark, as it were, the various stages of the 8:08's evolution, the Harbinger and the Knitting Lady to name but two, and the source of this pungent emission was another outlier. We shall call him the

Frenchman. I never formally established his nationality, but only a Frenchman could smoke in this way.

As soon as I saw him, at the far end of the carriage, in the last table seat on the left, with his back to the direction of travel, I got the impression that he alone had perfected a habit invented hundreds of years ago, that all subsequent smokers were simply paving the way for his advent. Let us start with his technique. The offering up of the cigarette was at once sexual and veterinary, not unlike the insertion of a thermometer into a cow's anus, the lips tightly pursed, the inhalations punishingly comprehensive, his respiratory system entirely given over to the toxic demands of his calling. For the exhalations he disdained to use his mouth, expelling the smoke through his nostrils like a dragon, both barrels aimed squarely at the mother and baby seated opposite. The mother didn't seem to mind, and the baby gurgled with gleeful fascination, bunched fists flapping, trying to reach the smouldering ember. I come now to his equipment. Need I say that he favoured an unfiltered brand? There was the carton, open on the table, propped up on its lid like a sun-lounger, stylishly chamfered and housing, not 20, but 30 cigarettes, the sheaths whiter than cartridge paper, the tobacco blacker than gunpowder. Next to it, his lighter, a brass flip-top of vintage provenance. There was no ashtray in attendance – for there was no ash. This is important. Somehow, the smoke contrived to carry all the evidence directly into the air. And when he had finished, what do you think he did with his butt? An Englishman would have dropped it in a beer can, but the Frenchman, after allowing it to go out – to die, as it were, of natural causes – placed it carefully in the turn-up of his flares. Quite what he intended for these relics was unclear, but frankly it is not our place to ask.

I slipped into the adjacent table seat, placing my tobacco

pouch in front of me, and he nodded minutely in my direction. There was solidarity in this gesture, but it was laced with irritation, for he was doubtless used to being the only smoker round these parts. He wore faded double-denim, three-day stubble going all the way down into his shirt, his black hair splayed across his head, a sweat-flattened bouffant that resembled nothing so much as a quartered wellington. He did not speak. The gulf in class, as I set to work with my roll-up, was simply too apparent. He watched me struggle with my paraphernalia for a few seconds, sighing wearily at the spectacle of a man who presumed to draw artisanal pleasure from the construction of his own cigarette, before nudging his carton a sixteenth of an inch towards me.

My hand trembled as I reached across the aisle and took one (so short, so thick, so *European*), while the Frenchman unboxed himself another, flicking the cornermost infumation stylishly into his mouth, the flame of his lighter leaning towards the tip like a cobra, the scorch of his first drag audible from seven feet away. Everything about him seemed amplified, and as I withdrew my orange Zippo, I was transformed into his fumbling apprentice, the Frenchman emitting a low murmur of disapproval at this garish appurtenance. He now turned and looked at me for the first and only time, eyes gleaming blackly through a stray forelock, and gave me to understand that his flip-top might be available for work.

'Merci,' I said, reaching across the aisle again.

The flip-top had weight, mass, integrity, with a wick that smelled of paraffin, but what was this engraved into the brass: 'Ostende 1986'. Could it be that the Frenchman was not French? Could it be that he was Belgian?

6

FROM NOW ON the number of smokers increased, as the society and general atmosphere of the train began to take on a more libertarian aspect. The rules here are contingent at best, and nowhere more so than with the train's bewildering entertainments. It is to these that I will turn shortly. But not before recounting another matter.

As a caveat to the following, it should be remembered that there was now a potentially psychoactive element to my perception of anything that happened. Though I remained dubious of Marlowe's claim that a placebo was not a substitute for a real drug but a drug in its own right, I was intrigued as to whether this idea would take hold on my imagination, and if so how. I also had more pragmatic considerations. I thought we could expect to find a proper meal somewhere that evening, given that we were now in First Class, having subsisted solely on the merchandise from the trolley for the last three days. Our supplies were running low. When I emptied the contents of the bin liner out onto the vestibule floor, this was all we had:

> 1 tuna and sweetcorn sandwich
> 1 bag of pork scratchings
> 2 bottles of tomato juice
> 49 pots of UHT milk
> 20 sachets brown sugar

1 half-bottle of vodka
1 bottle of Clynelish 10-year-old from the Junior
Collector Selection Box
3 cans of 808 cider.

I put the whisky and the sandwich in my overnight bag, the
milk in my jacket pockets – I didn't want it going all over my
things – and left the rest where it was.

While I was doing this, Companion began to clean himself,
and I decided I ought to follow suit. I hadn't washed since
Wednesday.

I'd had one or two ablutions in train toilets before, but
this was my first full stand-up wash, and one that I shall
never forget. After checking that the tap worked, I lined up
my best toiletries on the sink – my 46-quid face treatment
from Kiehl's, my Dr Bonner's Castille Soap, my Dermalex
anti-rosacea cream – and took off my shirt and trousers. On
removing my underpants, I was surprised to see I had an
erection. To all intent and purpose, I was impotent, so an
erection would have caught me off-guard, even on my normal
commute; here, it bordered on the uncanny. I attended to
my face and hands, waiting for it to subside, but if anything
the erection redoubled its efforts and I had to work round it.
But this was not all. At the risk of moving directly from the
profane to the sacred, I now had what can only be called a
spiritual experience. I am not happy with that word, but it's
the only one that remotely conveys the subsequent loosening
of inhibitions I felt on completing my wash. If I had to describe my emotional state, I suppose 'euphoric' is the closest
I can come to, but again it won't really do. For, if anything, it
was an absence of emotion: the returning of my mind to some
default setting. I felt purified, cleansed, and as I opened the

cubicle door, I found my hand moving automatically to my chest and making the circular sign, the same one I'd seen the other passengers make during the ritual of shunting. Except that I was not copying anyone now, I was not performing the gesture in rote deference to some protocol I didn't understand, but instinctively, as the only adequate response to the feeling that had passed through me. Whenever I revisit this incident, it still seems to me that the train's waters, as well as performing a sanitary purpose, had some 'baptismal' effect. There is the question of my boner, of course, which does not sit well with this ecclesiastic analogy. But I can only tell you what happened and how it felt.

As if to underline the solemnity of the occasion, when I opened the cubicle door, there was Companion, an 808 insignia above his head, etched into the window of the vestibule, the 'o' forming a halo that crowned my little chaperone, who was transfigured momentarily into the figure from some religious painting, a fleeting transformation that echoed my own. For when I bent down to pick up my overnight bag, I was normal again. Whatever had passed through me had continued on through the cosmos, in search of some other host.

7

A ND NOW TO the evening's entertainment. The first game I played that night is without doubt the most stultifying recreation I ever entered into. *Why Not Sneeze?* is the official game of the 8:08. It is billed as 'a game of skill and chance for two or more players', but from what I can make out requires no skill, only chance.

The compartment in which we played it contained a full complement of passengers, four on either side, and I backed out on opening the door, thinking there was no room. But Companion jumped up onto the lap of one of the occupants, a young man I recognised from my first hours on board. It was the student, a little older now and wearing different clothes, the combat trousers and hooded top exchanged for a brown suede jacket and designer jeans – still a 90s' outfit, but a late-90s one. He also had a goatee, and his bobbed hair was restyled into a quiff. He was filling out a bit too, though he seemed less slovenly now, less withdrawn, more sociable than before, no longer preoccupied with his studies. He still produced a lot of mucous, pulling out a tissue every now then and dabbing at his nostrils, but he no longer sniffed in that annoying way.

It was he to whom Companion was instinctively drawn. I apologised for the intrusion, but he dug his claws into the student's lap as I reached down to pick him up. The student didn't seem to mind, shifting along towards the centre of the bench seat on the right-hand side of the compartment, making space for me in the corner by the door.

I thanked him and sat down. The student was the only person I could see clearly at first, but as my eyes adjusted to the light, I got the impression that everyone was waiting for me to say something. A tall man opposite in a tight black suit was leaning in, eyebrows raised, while a woman in a long black dress with a high collar, seated in the left-hand corner by the window, was staring down her long nose with equal expectation. She had a stick across her lap, a long silver baton, which she rapped on the long table folded out from the central mullion of the window:

'More light, Mr Monroe, if you would.'

The tall man reached up and adjusted the dimmer switch.

'Too much!' said the woman. 'Too much!'

She seemed genuinely pained by the fleeting exposure of her face, the whiteness of which, in that moment, contrasted with the dark high collar of her dress, a concave screen that rose above her head, onto which were projected, so to speak, the various expressions of her facial repertoire. She was sixtyish, her hair dyed black, with black eyebrows and black lipstick, the only colour coming from two green gemstones dangling from the cups of her dress, where the nipples would be. A pair of pince-nez were clamped to her nose, and she snorted at Monroe as he re-adjusted the dimmer, leaving the compartment only a fraction brighter than before.

Again, everyone leaned forward in their seats, as if I had some urgent news to impart, and such was the air of expectation I thought I'd said something after all, or moved my lips in such a way as to make them think I had. A much younger woman, sat next to the one in the high collar, cocked an ear, and Monroe jotted something down in a notebook, which he kept splayed open across his thigh for the next half-hour.

It was much darker here than any part of the train I'd been in so far, and quieter too, almost silent when you entered a compartment and closed the door behind you. The blind on the outer window was drawn, and it didn't even feel like we were moving, such was the smoothness of the train's nocturnal acceleration. I could hear Companion purring, coiled up on the student's lap. In the right-hand corner, opposite the woman in pince-nez, was a gentleman sleeping, covered in a blanket, his hat pulled down over his face. It was a pretty cosy set-up. The table bore the remains of their evening meal: a cheeseboard, grapes, a rustic loaf of bread, chicken legs, half a salmon surrounded with lemon slices, parsley and croquette potatoes, and a decanter of what I hoped was port.

The matriarch rapped her stick again. It was one of those pointers, I now saw, those things rabbis use for reading scripture, a silver hand on the end, with the forefinger extended.

'Why Not Sneeze?' she announced, in a voice that did not seem as loud as she intended, absorbed as it was by the dense furnishings, the crimson carpet, the navy upholstery, the compartment's brown panelled walls.

'Yes, let's,' said the young woman.

'About time too,' said another woman next to her. They were surely sisters, wearing similar white dresses, ruched at the shoulders and waist, like those worn by Bavarian serving wenches. Two other passengers completed our party: a handsome black man in a red velour jumpsuit, and a fat bald man in a butcher's apron, both sat between the student and the sleeping man.

The matriarch nodded at the butcher, and the butcher withdrew a pocket watch from beneath his white coat.

'One, two, three – go!' he said, pressing the button.

Nothing happened. Nothing happened for a very long time. At some point, the butcher unchained his watch and placed it on the table, but other than that no one moved.

'Excuse me?' I asked.

The matriarch's head turned mechanically towards me like a CCTV camera: 'Yes?'

'I don't mean to be rude, but can someone tell me what's going on?'

Monroe made a note of this, and the matriarch pointed to a plaque on the central mullion of the outside window. This, to the best of my recollection, was what it said:

Why Not Sneeze? A game of skill and chance for two or more players. First person to sneeze wins. No stimulants allowed. No pepper or mustard. No massaging of the nasal cavity. No encouragement. No looking at the sun. No looking at the moon. No looking at any lights at all, artificial or natural. No simulation. No ungentlemanly conduct. No swearing or dissent. Sneeze must exhibit a clear beginning, middle and end. Last person to sneeze loses. Game to continue till all players have sneezed or the specified period has elapsed, or at the discretion of the Adjudicator.

'And what is the specified period?' I asked the butcher.

'It is indefinite,' he said.

'Indefinite?'

'Unspecified!' said the matriarch, drawing my attention to the rules. 'Unspecified is as unspecified does.'

'I see. And the Adjudicator?' I couldn't see any officials as such.

'Actually,' said the older of the two sisters, 'We were rather hoping that you would?'

'Adjudicate?'

'Please do!' said her sibling. 'Please say you will!'

'Seems to me,' said the man in the velour jumpsuit, 'seems to me he's already flexing that muscle. Am I right, boss?'

I guessed him at seventy or more, but trim for his age with a full head of hair, his American accent flattened by time spent in England.

'I'd be delighted to act in an official capacity,' I said. 'But the truth is, Companion and I, that is to say, *my* companion and I, were on our way to dinner.'

'But you can dine here,' said the sisters. 'He can dine with us, can't he?'

The matriarch nodded. 'For goodness' sake, Monroe, give the man a plate!'

Monroe got up and fetched a wooden casket down from the luggage rack. It contained just a single plate, a porcelain salver set into the flocking. This was not *a* plate, it was *the* plate – the one they gave to guests, or Adjudicators, decorated with tiny gold swirls that on closer inspection revealed themselves to be a continuous 808 design running around the rim. Monroe put a bit of everything on it and handed it to me with a napkin, before fetching down a smaller casket containing a silver knife and fork, the handles terminating in large art nouveau 808 motifs that protruded from the back of each fist as I ate.

The game continued but they did not make much headway. At one point the butcher gathered himself for a decisive convulsion, but he could not promote it into a sneeze. The student didn't seem that into it, but the sisters giggled continually, unable to bear the tension, the man in velour flirting with them over the table. Monroe had resumed his station in the corner, observing me as I ate, scribbling in his notebook, and the sleeping man continued to sleep, the butcher adjusting his shawl whenever it slipped down, repositioning his hat over his face. Apart from Monroe, none of them did anything else while they were playing. This was the most absurd aspect. Surely it was just the kind of game you could play while doing something else?

'May I have some port?' I asked, as the action reached the half-hour mark.

'Forgive me,' said Monroe, rising once more and unlatching another casket. A single goblet was removed, and when he drew the stopper from the decanter, the liquid glugged copiously till my glass brimmed with nigh-on half a pint. His waiting skills needed work, but I wasn't complaining.

'And a bit of that cheese, Monroe, if you wouldn't mind. That's it. A bit of everything. And some of those grapes. While you're up.'

Monroe was happy to oblige, piling up a plate with some water biscuits and a fresh napkin, while I finished my main course, which did not take long. I also had Monroe set aside some of the salmon for you-know-who.

'I should like it, Monroe,' I said, pushing my luck now, 'I should like it if you could do him a few separate portions in a Tupperware dish or something? For the road. Could you manage that, Monroe?'

Monroe did better than this, separating the remainder of the salmon into five parcels of tin foil that I placed in my overnight bag. They were well appointed here. It seemed like they had everything.

I got halfway through my first proper meal in days before realising I couldn't taste it. The food felt fine in the mouth, the salmon flaking apart beautifully, but I couldn't distinguish one thing from another in a gustatory sense. When I moved on to my cheese course, the stilton was no different to the brie, and when I quaffed my port there was a vague pluminess, nothing more. Even its temperature was uncertain. I imagined it was room temperature, but it would be more accurate to say that it had no temperature. There was no difference between the liquid in my glass and the saliva in my mouth. I may as well have drunk my own spit.

There was one other thing, something that had been bothering me all day, and which seemed more pertinent now I was surrounded by food. Having eaten nothing for the first two days and relatively little since – less than half my usual intake – I would have expected to feel slightly thinner by now. Whenever I'd dieted in the past, I usually had to tighten my belt after a few days. But my waistline was no different, and I wondered whether the food on board had some special nutritional property, in addition to being tasteless.

I was about to ask Monroe who prepared it, where the ingredients came from, when he lurched forward, producing the loudest sneeze I've ever heard, recoiling back into his seat like a crash-test-dummy.

Though the rules stipulate that the game ends only after all players have sneezed, this is only loosely upheld in most compartments, with play continuing after the first sneeze but not so formally as before. The scoring system is as follows: ten points for the first sneezer, eight for the second, six for the third, five, four, three, two and one for each subsequent sneezer. In most compartments, a ledger is kept behind the plaque bearing the rules to the game. It was the man in velour who got up and reached for this document, where, as the Adjudicator, I duly recorded Monroe's victory, the latest of many, I noted.

'You got to sign it, boss,' he said, when I handed it back.

'What's that?'

'You got to stamp it, bossman, or it don't count shit.'

'Sure.' I still couldn't remember my name, so I signed off Monroe's victory as 'Paul Carver'.

The next person to sneeze was the butcher. The matriarch came third, the man in velour fourth, the student fifth, then the two sisters, who for all their early enthusiasm, put in a poor performance. I was about to declare the game over when heads now turned to the man under the shawl in the corner of the compartment, who was still asleep. A minute passed before I intervened:

'I propose a replay.'

'A what?' This was the matriarch.

'In my capacity as Adjudicator. It's only fair. It seems to me that this gentleman is at a disadvantage.'

'A disadvantage?'

'He doesn't even know he is participating in the game. We should wake him and start again.'

As the victor, Monroe naturally objected, but the man in velour cut him short: 'Bossman got a point.'

'Very well,' said the matriarch.

'Excuse me,' I said to the man in the corner. Monroe turned the light up slightly. 'Excuse me,' I repeated, leaning across the butcher and touching his shoulder. I shook him several times, but there was no response.

One by one they all started to chuckle, trying to stifle their laughter, and finally I saw what was going on. The man under the blanket hadn't moved once since we'd entered the compartment. It was a dummy.

Doubtless, this was a trick they played on everyone. They wanted me to remove his hat, but I wasn't falling for it.

'I am the Adjudicator, am I not?' I said to the matriarch.

'Apparently so,' she said.

'I am the Adjudicator, am I not?' I said to the man in velour.

'Damn right you are.'

'As Adjudicator,' I said, putting my plate on the table and getting to my feet, 'I declare this game null and void.'

'Null and void?' said the matriarch.

'Null *and* void. I strike it from the records, forthwith.'

I put a line through Monroe's name, countersigned the amendment – again as 'Paul Carver' – and handed the ledger to the man in velour.

'And now, Monroe, I think I shall have that cigar.'

I don't know where this came from. I felt sure that Monroe would fetch one down from the overhead rack, but either he didn't have any or found the request inappropriate. So I roused Companion, picked up my overnight bag and exited.

Not till we'd passed along the gangway, through the sliding door and into the next vestibule did it occur to me that I'd just made a mistake, that the man under the shawl was not a dummy but a corpse. He'd felt heavy and dense when I'd put my hand on his shoulder, the deadweight of human flesh unmistakable to the touch.

I turned round. The sliding door was still half-open, closing more slowly than usual due to a technical fault. Deciding to go back and confront the matriarch, I took a few paces towards it and stopped; took another few paces, stopped again, leaning on the vestibule wall for support. I was beginning to feel nauseous. The door was still open – there was an eighteen-inch gap I could still squeeze through – but when I let go of the wall and planted my foot it gave way and I fell. I now resorted to dragging myself along the floor, determined to make it through but feeling more light-headed the closer I got. I was only six feet away now; if I made a lunge for it, put my arm in the gap, I might still be able to force my way through. But I passed out as the door drew shut, flailing pathetically at the glass.

When I came round I was only able to pull myself upright after crawling to the front end of the vestibule. So far, it had been possible to go both forwards and backwards within the confines of a single carriage. I now saw that this limited freedom could be revoked, should circumstances demand it.

8

IF THE FIRST game I played that evening was punishing-ly simple, the second was exquisitely complex. Around ten o'clock I ran into a young woman who had left her compartment to take the air in the gangway. She was wearing a 1920s flapper outfit, halter-neck dress, boyish plimsolls, a spangled skullcap drawn down over one eye. She sat fanning herself, perched on the ledge of the outer window, looking out into the night. We were passing through another gorge, the rock face glistening in the light from her compartment, throwing back a spectacle that she seemed to have just noticed, a miniature borealis filling the space between the glass and the rock as the reflected features of the train's interior mingled with those of the gorge, inside and outside meeting on some indeterminate plane. We seemed to hit our optimum speed around this time, and the faster we went the more impressive the display, the view through the window appearing static, like the effect of a zoetrope, as the train accelerated through the darkness.

The young woman was so preoccupied she didn't see us approach till Companion stopped, front paw raised, frozen mid-step.

'Hello, you,' she said, bending down to shake his paw. Then she stood up and kissed my hand, inverting the gender roles in a way that seemed in keeping with her 'bright young thing' outfit. 'Do you have a light?'

I offered my Zippo up to her café crème cigar.

'Sorry – would you like one?'

'Thank you. As it happens, I would.'

'Not at all. Here. London or Yorkshire?'

'I'm sorry?'

'London, or Yorkshire?'

'What of them?'

'You know: "London or Yorkshire"?' This time she put the words in scare quotes with her fingers.

'I'm not from either of those places.'

'Spoilsport.'

'I really don't follow. London or Yorkshire, as in . . . ?'

'As in "London or Yorkshire". Don't tell me you've never played.'

'Played what?'

'You haven't, have you? You've never played it. *He's never played it,*' she said, raising her voice for the benefit of those in the compartment.

'What?' A female voice within, older, posher, scarier.

'London or Yorkshire?' repeated the flapper, turning to me again.

I shrugged. 'Neither.'

'Neither? What do you mean, *neither?*' She extended a foot across the gangway, her long leg fully exposed as she kicked the compartment door open: 'He says "Neither".'

'Neither? What a queer fellow. Tell him it's not in the rules.'

'Very well: Yorkshire.'

'He says "Yorkshire".'

'See!' said the voice within. 'I told you! I told you!'

The flapper led me into the compartment just as a tiny man in a white suit with slicked-back hair and a pencil moustache was signing a cheque.

'Here,' he said, handing it to the woman in the left-hand

corner of the compartment, who was almost identical to her counterpart in the earlier carriage. She had on a black dress of similar design, fake emeralds hanging from both nipples, but this time with an additional element: around each breast cup was a grey moon with a human face, with the emeralds depicted as tears falling from its eyes. Evidently, she was the matriarch here. I supposed that all the matriarchs sat there, in the same place, in the left-hand corner of the compartment.

A man resembling Monroe, though not quite as tall or well dressed, took the cheque on her behalf, stowing it in a small deposit box under the seat. Here, dinner had long finished, the central table pushed back to the window, where a candelabrum sat blazing, with a few bottles of spirits and liqueurs. I took a seat on the right-hand side, in the corner by the internal window, the others shuffling along to accommodate me. The flapper closed the door and came to sit on my knee, where she remained throughout my visit.

'Anyone?' The small man in white got up and went over to the drinks table, brandishing the crème de menthe, which did not seem appetising in his tiny fist, the long neck transformed into a glass penis, the bulb sagging like gonads.

'A whisky would be nice,' I said.

'Oh, it would, would it, Mr Yorkshire? You realise you just cost me £10,000?'

'Sorry.'

'He was sure you'd say "London",' whispered the flapper.

'Just kidding,' said the man in white. 'There, whisky for you, and one for my little princess.'

The flapper hadn't asked for a whisky, but downed it in one, throwing the glass back to the man in white before he'd had chance to put the top back on the bottle. I did the same with mine. Like the port earlier, it was tasteless.

'Now,' said the man in white, 'where were we?'

He sounded Welsh-Italian, his accent alternating between the Latin tendency to go down at the end and the Welsh tendency to go up, a verbal quirk that made him an odd master of ceremonies.

'Yorkshire,' said another man in white, in a similar accent, his outfit augmented by a bolero jacket. 'It was Yorkshire and we're back with Fräulein Braüner.'

'Yes,' said the matriarch. 'Fräulein Braüner?'

'London,' said the woman next to her, in a German accent. Fräulein Braüner was none other the woman in the rain mac, blue scarf billowing from her neck, slightly older than the one I'd met several times that first morning.

'London,' said Monroe II.

'London,' said the bald man in the corner, the one sitting where the corpse had sat in the earlier compartment.

It was back with me again. 'Yorkshire?' I tried.

The flapper looked at the matriarch, and the matriarch looked at the second man in white, the one dressed like a matador.

'Bear with me,' he said, producing a black book, leafing through the pages. 'Ah. Si, si, si.'

He showed the relevant passage to the matriarch, who had to put on her spectacles. 'Yes, here it is: Yorkshire is admissible after three consecutive Londons,' she said, 'but only if you didn't say Yorkshire last time.'

'That's right,' said the flapper, 'let me see if I can remember.' She closed her eyes and put a finger to her temple. '*A Yorkshire may follow three consecutive Londons in two instances and two instances only: when no Yorkshire was offered by the player in question on his last turn, or when no Yorkshires have been offered by any player in one complete round.*'

'Verbatim!' said the matriarch, snapping the book shut and handing it back to the matador.

'Bravo!' said Monroe II.

'Sorry, Señor,' said the matador to me, 'I'm afraid you must drink this.' He handed me a yellow liquid in a shot glass, which I had to knock back in one. Again, it was tasteless.

'Mildred, it's with you,' said the matriarch.

Mildred was the flapper's name. 'London,' she said, looking at me.

'London?' said I. There was a pat on the knee here as I made my first successful contribution.

'London,' said the matador, who now took a seat to my right.

'London,' said the other man in white, who I guessed was his brother.

Now it was with the bald man in the corner again, the only occupant, other than myself, who I could confidently classify as 'normal', for his suit was the colour of goose shit and a lanyard swung from his neck. At his feet, I noticed a laptop bag, with a bunch of documents shoved in the side pocket. He looked like he was bound for some conference. Perhaps he had boarded the train with that intention. But now here he was playing London or Yorkshire?.

'London,' he offered.

It was now back with the matriarch: 'London,' she said.

This was nine consecutive Londons, if we exclude my inadmissible Yorkshire. Three more Londons followed and then it was back with me. Part of me wanted to say something insane, like Sheffield or Manchester, or Halifax, or Southampton, just to see what happened, but I weighed in with another London.

'Uh-oh,' said the matador.

'I can't believe you said that,' said the man in the lanyard.

'I take it that is an official challenge?' said the matriarch. 'Clarify.'

'I think *he* should clarify,' I interrupted, pointing at the man in the lanyard.

The matriarch turned to him: 'Care to elaborate, Ron?'

But Ron had nothing. He didn't have a clue what he was doing either.

'Sorry to jump in again,' said Mildred, 'but may I?'

'Proceed,' said the matriarch.

'If I understand you correctly,' she said to the matador, 'the reason for your challenge is that our guest here has offered a thirteenth consecutive London.'

The matador nodded.

'I thought so. But you appear to have forgotten that a thirteenth consecutive London is admissible when the player in question has offered no Londons in the game so far. At least, under match-play rules. If we were playing *house* rules it would be fine. But as I understand it, this is match play. Furthermore, when the player offering a thirteenth consecutive London, after having offered no Londons in the game so far, is challenged by a player who himself has offered no Londons in the game so far, his challenge is not only invalidated, he has to go and stand outside in the gangway for the next round.'

'What?' The matador was already leafing through the rule-book, looking for precedent. 'I never heard of that before.'

'It doesn't come up often,' said Mildred, 'but I believe it applies in this case. I think it's on page 437? Section III, Subsection a), Clause iv), Scenario b).'

'Spare us chapter and verse, Mildred,' said the matriarch. 'I infer from the gravamen of your enquiry that you are counter-challenging the challenger?'

There could be no complaint. The matador was given a

shot of the yellow stuff and ejected from the compartment.

'It's with you, Pedro,' said the matriarch to the matador's brother.

'London,' said Pedro.

'Ah,' said Mildred.

'Ah?' said the matriarch, 'Ah? Is that another challenge?'

I pass over Mildred's challenge, which had something to do with London not being admissible as a starter when the previous challenge has been successfully counter-challenged – I don't know, she lost me after the first sentence. Whatever, the appeal of the game, so far as I could gather, lay in the fact that it never ended, that it wasn't possible to win or lose, only to continue. Which is not to say there wasn't any objective, just no culminating moment, no resolution, just a collective embracing of the bureaucracy arising from the utterance of these two simple place names.

At length, the matador was called back in and the game resumed:

'Yorkshire,' said the matriarch.

'London,' said Fräulein Braüner.

'Yorkshire,' said Monroe II.

'London,' said Mildred.

'Yorkshire,' said I.

'London,' said the matador.

'Yorkshire,' said Pedro.

'London,' said Ron.

It was back with the matriarch. 'Yorkshire,' she said.

'London,' said Fräulein Braüner.

'Yorkshire,' said Monroe II.

'London,' said Mildred.

'Yorkshire,' said I.

'London,' said the matador.

'Yorkshire,' said Pedro.

'London,' said Ron.

Back with the matriarch. 'Yorkshire,' she said.

'London,' said Fräulein Braüner.

'Yorkshire,' said Monroe II.

'London,' said Mildred.

'Yorkshire,' said I.

'London,' said the matador.

'Yorkshire,' said Pedro.

'London,' said Ron.

'Yorkshire,' said the matriarch.

'London,' said Fräulein Braüner.

'Yorkshire,' said Monroe II.

'London,' said Mildred.

'Yorkshire,' said I.

'London,' said the matador.

'Yorkshire,' said Pedro.

'London,' said Ron.

We alternated like this without breaking step till the game became a chant, the chant a mantra. The longer it went on, the more detached from their meaning the words became, bearing no relation to the places they designated. And then, suddenly, a change: two consecutive Yorkshires. For the first time there was complete silence in the compartment, everyone frozen in the position they had been in when the second 'Yorkshire' was uttered. Minutes passed and still no one spoke. Even Mildred was catatonic, staring into middle distance. It felt colder in the compartment, and as I rose from my seat I noticed that Mildred's bare arms were now covered in goosebumps. I found a blanket on the overhead rack, draped it round her and left them to it.

I'd forgotten about Companion during all this. There was

something about the compartments he did not care for, and he had stayed outside the whole time. When he saw me emerge, he yawned, shivered, arching himself upright, preparing to show me the way.

9

BEFORE PUSHING ON to the third and final entertainment of the evening, I must pause to mention something that may yet be significant, but which, at the time, I found merely irritating. I'd gone no further than a few carriages when I felt a whirring sensation on my chest. Some of the windows were open in this part of the train and I flinched, thinking a bat or an insect had got inside, but when I looked down there was nothing. I reached into my pocket and fished out a warm tablet, glowing in my hand like a children's toy. It took me a few seconds to recognise it as my phone.

'Slide to unlock', said the words on the screen, in grey letters pulsing with white. I did as they asked. 'Enter Passcode', came the next command. I typed in the year of my birth, the phone unlocked, and there was Dan Coleman's text message:

URGENT: GERMAN CLIENTS EXPECTED LATER 16.30. NEED TO REVISE SCHEDULE. PLEASE CALL ME NOW!!

If I focused purely on the screen, I could've been back on my old commute. But the truth was I resented this imposition from my line manager – I resented it so intensely I had to resist the urge to throw my phone out the window. I looked at the message again: it was not just annoying in itself, with its double exclamation marks and capital letters; it jarred with

my current equanimity, the nocturnal smoothness of our progress and the temperate atmosphere of First Class. It was the
mental product of another world, a thought-turd that needed
flushing into oblivion.

I was about to delete it when I noticed the time of its
despatch: 08:43, Tuesday, almost four days ago. I also noticed
six missed calls from Dan Coleman, made a little earlier that
same morning. The notifications had only just come through,
in a pocket of clear reception, four bars now showing in the
top left-hand corner of the screen. That wasn't all. The symbol
in the right-hand corner told me I still had 52% power. I
remember it saying 56% on Tuesday when I'd left home – my
phone ought to have been dead by now. There were at-seat
sockets throughout Standard Class, but I hadn't thought to
recharge it. The delay between the despatch and delivery of
Dan Coleman's message could be explained by poor reception,
but I couldn't account for the battery's longevity, and I still
can't account for it now.

I mention all this in passing. Like I say, it may or may not
be of long-term significance. But I'm more interested to know
what you made of London or Yorkshire?. In my view it knocks
Why Not Sneeze into a cocked hat, though both come a poor
second to the next game – the game that I invented.

I owe its conception to a group of film buffs I ran into
shortly before midnight. It was the smell of pipe smoke that
attracted me to their compartment. Etched stylishly into the
glass of the door were the following words:

8:08 Independent Film Club
Est. 1976

The compartment was full when I went in, and once again a

matriarch presided in the far left-hand corner by the window. This time her outfit was slightly different. The dress was the same – black, with two moons over the breast cups, emeralds dangling from the nipples – but she was also wearing a cloth bonnet of bright marigold yellow, embroidered with an orange ruff that encircled her whole face. That this was intended to represent the Sun was apparent from the costumes of her cronies, all eight of whom, in addition to their black suits, wore balaclavas representing different planets of the Solar System.

'Yes, I know!' the largest gentleman was saying as we entered. 'I *know* that. I can *see* it's an allegory.'

I took him to be Jupiter, for his balaclava was dyed with horizontal layers of orange, red and white, with an opening for the mouth but not the eyes, so that when he spoke his oral vent became, as it were, the giant red spot of that planet.

The others had no vents in their hoods, for eyes or mouth, and their positions in the compartment echoed the order of the planets relative to the Sun, with Mercury seated next to the matriarch, Venus next to Mercury, then Earth, with Mars in the corner by the door. On the opposite bench, Jupiter was sat by the door, with Saturn next, then Uranus, with Neptune over by the window, opposite the Sun. Though membership of the 8:08 Independent Film Club was obviously restricted due to lack of space, they did not object to our entrance. But nobody made space for us to sit down, and we hovered in the asteroid belt between Mars and Jupiter as they continued their discussion.

'I can *see* it's an allegory,' the latter was saying. 'But to what degree?'

'Degree?' said Saturn, pausing to adjust his ring, which was attached to his headgear by means of a special clip. 'Degree? A thing is either allegory or not allegory.'

'You're splitting hairs again, Jupiter,' said the Sun.

'All I'm saying is that I find Buñuel's treatment of the social order a little arbitrary here.'

'Buñuel is nothing if not arbitrary,' said Uranus.

'I agree,' said Mars.

'He is, after all, a surrealist,' said Venus.

'What's a surrealist?' asked Mercury.

Neptune sighed, shaking his head, the bright blue balaclava moving from side to side. 'A surrealist . . .' he began. But Jupiter interrupted: 'Let us return to the moment when the first person is unable to leave the room,' he said, filling his pipe.

''Ang on a minute!' said Earth. ''Ow do we know they're *unable* to leave? 'Oo's to say they're not s'much unable as unwilling, like?'

I had no idea what they were talking about and hoped my counsel wouldn't be sought on whatever cinematic issue had divided them. I was starting to feel awkward. By the window, to Neptune's right, was a tiny slither of seat. 'Here,' he said, as I made my way over, 'you better put this on.'

He handed me a pair of ladies' tights, which I pulled over my head, figuring, by process of elimination, that I must be Pluto, the controversial dwarf planet. Companion, for his part, was the comet that came and went, for as soon as we entered he was scratching at the door to be let out again.

'Where were we?' said Saturn.

Earth recapped. As he summarised the plot of the film they'd been discussing, it began to sound like something I remembered seeing years ago, late one night on TV. A group of Spanish aristocrats meet for dinner in a mansion, but when it comes to the end of the evening, they find supernatural forces prevent them leaving the room. Various things happen while they are trapped: a man dies from cancer, two lovers commit suicide, and at one point a sheep wanders in, which they kill and cook on the fire, using furniture for fuel. When they finally emerge, days later, they see the staff at the gate – the butler, the cook, the maid – who, just as they had been unable to leave the house, had been equally unable to enter it.

'The way I see it,' Saturn was saying, 'one has to place the action within the context of the prevailing political climate. The dinner guests are the fascist bourgeoisie, whose life of privilege is turned into a punishment.'

'With respect,' said Jupiter, 'that is merely received opinion.'

'Let's not start this again,' said Venus.

'Yes,' said the Sun. 'We have been here before, have we not?'

Jupiter lit his pipe in the silence that followed, the smoke merging with the swirls on his headgear, a living, breathing gas giant.

'What do *you* think?' I looked up; the Sun was talking to me, the corona of her bonnet blazing in the gloom of the compartment. 'You're awfully quiet over there. Thoughts? Opinions?'

'About what?'

'Why, Buñuel of course.'

'Ah, yes, Buñuel.'

'Well?'

The members of the 8:08 Independent Film Club all turned towards me. I had seen the inscription on the door, had I not? If I had no interest in film, why barge in, uninvited? I was about to make my apologies when there followed another of those locomotive interventions, my vocal cords producing, once more, something that had not originated in my mind:

'*The Resuscitating Demon* is a highly accomplished piece of work,' I heard myself saying, one leg crossed over the other, like a critic on a late-night discussion show. 'For me, *Resuscitating Demon* is second only to Alain Resnais's *Providence*, in terms of satirical antinaturalism.'

This puzzled everyone, including myself.

'Surely you mean *The Exterminating Angel*?' said the Sun.

But the man to my left was rocking gently with laughter. 'Very good,' said Neptune. 'Very good. Excellent.'

'What?' said Mercury. 'What's excellent?'

'Don't you see?' said Neptune.

'See what?' said Mars. 'Enlighten us.'

'He's inverted it.'

'Inverted what?'

'The title. The title of Buñuel's film.'

'So he has,' said the Sun. 'How clever.'

I saw what had happened just after Neptune. The train had indeed come to my aid, but this time its logic was scrambled.

'*Resuscitating Demon* is the opposite of *Exterminating Angel*,' clarified Neptune for those who had yet to grasp it. 'Let's try another. Here we are: "A Man Appears".'

'What do you mean?' said Mercury. What do you mean, "a man appears"? What man? Appears where?'

'It's a *clue*,' said Neptune.

'Oh I see,' said Mars, 'a *game*?'

'And the answer is *The Lady Vanishes*,' said I, catching on quickly:

'Hitchcock!' clapped the Sun. 'Another!'

I quickly came up with an easy one, 'Trawlermen of the North Sea', for the purposes of illustration, and the Sun got it instantly:

'*Pirates of the Caribbean!* Hang on, I think I've got one . . . Yes, here it is: "Stasis . . . Away from a . . . Periphery of Sky".'

'I still don't get it,' said Mercury.

It was simple, explained Uranus. You just had to take each word in isolation, think of an opposite, then put them all together.

'Stasis Away from a Periphery of Sky,' repeated the Sun.

'*Journey to the Centre of the Earth*,' said Earth.

'Correct! Your turn.'

But Earth couldn't think of one.

'"Everyone Hates Everything Cold",' offered Jupiter.

'*Some Like it Hot*,' I said, without missing a beat. 'There is such a thing as *too* good a clue, Jupiter, if you don't mind my saying. But try this one: "A Diner, a Victim, Her Husband Minus His Nemesis".'

'What?'

'"A Diner, a Victim, Her Husband Minus His Nemesis".'

'Hang on,' said Mars, 'I've got one: "'Panting Heifer'".'

'Please,' I said, 'one clue at a time, or it gets confusing.'

I wrested the initiative from Neptune here, establishing basic etiquette and becoming, in the eyes of his fellow cineastes, the sole inventor of the game I later chose to call *Antonym*. I should really credit him as co-creator, but it wouldn't have happened without me.

'"A Diner, a Victim, Her Husband, Minus His Nemesis". Anyone . . . ? OK, I'll give it to you: *The Cook, the Thief, His Wife and Her Lover*.'

Neptune wasn't convinced by the substitution of 'nemesis' for 'lover', but I explained that flexibility was permitted in those cases where a direct antonym was either not available, too obvious or inelegant. As a veteran of the game, I confessed that I was drawn more to poetic logic than semantic logic.

'But that's just me. And by the way, Mars, "Panting Heifer" is *Raging Bull*. Very good. I like it.'

I felt sorry for Mercury here, perpetually out of his depth in this highbrow clique. I encouraged him to contribute, and eventually managed to coax "Kong King" out of him.

'Kong King!' said Saturn, who had yet to contribute to the game. 'Kong King! You can't have that, he can't have that, can he? Surely that's not a proper one.'

'You don't see, do you,' I said, cutting across his comrades' laughter: 'that's bloody genius. Well done, Mercury. I go so far as to call "Kong King" one of the best I've heard.'

I wasn't just being patronising here. As I saw it, the game was not intended to put wordsmiths at an advantage over the less verbally adept, but to bring both parties into dialogue: a way of comparing one's own understanding of language with others'. It was also very much in the spirit of London or Yorkshire?, in that its rules had to be clarified and debated with each contribution.

As we continued to offer clues, we strayed into new cultural territory: books, songs, opera. The game was expanding, taking shape, the first rules being laid down, and I sensed that my work here was done.

'I have to go now,' I said, removing the ladies' tights from my head and laying them respectfully on the table, 'but I will leave you with this: "'An Infinite Number of Placid Females".' I repeated it as I clambered over Neptune to get to the door: "'An Infinite Number of Placid Females".'

10

SATURDAY BEGAN WITH a stock-take of sorts. The previous night we'd bedded down in an empty compartment a few carriages along from the 8:08 Independent Film Club, and there we remained for much of the next morning. There were blankets and pillows in most compartments, and whatever previous occupants had left behind: clothes, books, litter, occasionally food, though the one I'd chosen was empty apart from the bedding. Companion woke me around seven-thirty, and after giving him some of the salmon from last night, I reached instinctively for a pen.

I was fearful of forgetting what had happened. My memory had been highly erratic since coming on board: lucid with regard to some matters and negligent with regard to others, not the least of which was my name. I wondered how this more glaring instance of amnesia related to the subtler instances during those first few hours. My inability to recall faces and other details from certain carriages until they recurred in later ones suggested a causal connection between forward progress and the retention of mental phenomena. The reluctance of nearly everyone apart from myself to venture very far down-train was striking. Even under the auspices of Going Forward, few passengers advanced more than two or three carriages, and I formed the early theory that the further one went, the more memory, the more identity, the more character was relinquished. I did not know how else to account for their relative stasis.

I found this conclusion a bleak one, for it suggested a resistance to the new character that might be acquired as they advanced. The further downtrain I went, the more entrenched they'd become, preferring to ossify into self-parody than risk mutating into something else. At least in Standard Class. The little cliques in the First Class compartments were different, demonstrating that if the right people came together a 'group character' might emerge, each person a component of a larger social machine. I could see the benefits of this arrangement, though we shouldn't forget that these cliques, as well as requiring figureheads, also appeared to require 'whipping boys', like poor Mercury. If this theory had any credence, then maybe the aim of most passengers was to advance far enough to discard a certain amount of character, but not so far as to relinquish its essence. The appetite for games in the First Class section of the train was instrumental here: if you'd decided you'd gone as far as you wanted, you would need activities, would you not, distractions, diversions, to compensate for the curiosity you might have satisfied had you continued further.

These considerations demonstrate the extent to which my attitude to the train had shifted. Though I still thought of my old commute from time to time, of my colleagues, of my line manager, of the 11:30 meeting and the prospective German clients, and though the current locomotive remained, in some sense, a 'changeling' vehicle, a substitute for the normal 8:08 service, the idea of regarding it as the 'wrong' train now seemed naïve, an innocent solecism borne of my early confusion. I no longer regarded it in a carceral sense either. Though its inducement of nausea to prevent me going back through that sliding door had seemed excessive last night, it might have been for my own good. If anything, I tended to see the train less like a prison now than a book, each carriage a page, each person a sentence on that page. Some of the pages were blank, it was true, and there were whole sections in which nothing much happened, but taken as a whole it was malleable – more malleable than most were willing to believe. Had the previous night not been instructive in this sense? Did the games not testify to a gradual relaxing of rules, the further one progressed? The first was stultifying, the second pedantic, but the third had arisen organically as a consequence of my arrival: evidence – or so I flattered myself – that my rapport with the train was better than most could hope to establish. I felt I had done the train a service, that the vehicle and myself had come to an understanding.

It was for these reasons that keeping a journal seemed like a good idea, so I opened my bag and took out the folio I'd bought in my lunch hour last Monday. My procuring of this item also warrants a mention. Why I'd purchased it, I couldn't say. I don't keep a professional diary, and as for keeping a personal diary, I prefer to discard than preserve the past. So why did I go into the stationer's on my way back to the office that Monday lunchtime, six weeks ago? 'You go on ahead,' I recall saying to Bob Buchanan, 'there's something I need.' What that something was I did not know, and I'm inclined to think these words came, not from within, but from outside of me, as they have at various points on my journey here through the train. It's possible, as I look back, that there'll be more things like this, more events that predate my time on board and seem relevant only now I'm in a position to review them.

Today, of course, was my date with Heobah. I had in mind a relaxing stroll to the Restaurant Car, but as I prepared to set out, I realised I had no idea how far it was – Heobah hadn't given the precise location in her note. It could have been a few carriages away or a whole day's walk, and this in itself was going to make for an odd journey, as I alternated between a fear of being hours late and hours early. The issue of what to wear was more straightforward. I had two choices: the trousers, white shirt and underwear I'd been wearing since Tuesday, or the trousers I'd been wearing since Tuesday, with a fresh (but identical) shirt and clean (but identical) underwear.

On leaving the compartment I pulled into the first cubicle to render my body fit for female consumption. I'd intended to give myself the full once-over. Needless to say, I was limited by the facilities, but what I did not count on was that the train would throw in an existential element to my preparations. I knew something was wrong as I applied the shaving foam, which did not adhere to my jaw with its usual zeal. The shave itself was the briefest I've ever had, for the simple reason that the blade met no resistance as I drew it across my chin, my face perfectly smooth except for a patch under the left ear that I'd missed on Monday night. It was the kind of shave you see on the adverts, where the model has clearly already shaved beneath his beard of foam, so that a single pass of the razor cuts an impossibly clean path. As for the rest of my body, when I removed my shirt, it didn't seem as dirty as it ought to have been, the collar scarcely marked after four days. My kecks were also unblemished, and when I took a reading from my armpits, I deduced that a wash would be pointless verging on decadent. The attempt to evacuate my bowel was equally futile (no change there since boarding), and when I stood, turned, and aimed at the toilet bowl, I found I could offload no more than a pipette's worth of urine.

This existential trend was extended to my physical environment. The gangways and vestibules were normal enough, but when I finally came across the Restaurant Car at 16:30 I was convinced the pill Marlowe had given me, far from being a placebo, was a powerful if slow-acting hallucinogen. And yet, the alteration of my perception was not entirely inconsistent with the claim he'd appeared to make: that any effect of the drug would simply be a result of my own projection. As is usual for a man in the days leading up to a date, I had sketched out many scenarios since Thursday, complete with the desired outcome and its wider backdrop, and initially I mistook the similarity between the actual Restaurant Car and the one I'd imagined as pure coincidence. It was so faithful to that mental picture as to be a physical representation of it – all the more faithful because incomplete, the accuracy residing as much in what was *not* there as what was. There were tables and chairs missing, menus that were blank except for the dishes I'd ordered in those preliminary daydreams, partially clad waiters rushing about, inconsistencies in the setting of the tables – no knives at some, no forks at others – and certain people who only ever presented themselves in profile, or head-on, because that was how my mind had offered them up. But the most spectacular omission was the entire right-hand wall of the Restaurant Car. I don't mean that it gave directly on to outside, that I could see the embankment flying past as I made my way down the carriage; I mean that it was devoid of materiality, that *this area of space had yet to be filled in*. As you faced downtrain, wainscoting ran along the left-hand side of the carriage below the windows, with lamps spaced equidistantly near the ceiling, but on the right-hand side was an indeterminate façade that neither absorbed nor reflected any light. At first I thought it was a grey curtain as I came through the sliding door, but this was simply an optical defence-mechanism, a barrier erected against a phenomenon which had no precedent in my perceptual experience, had neither colour nor substance, nor yet was transparent. How, then, did I know it was *there*? Darkness is the only thing I can compare it to. Most of us have seen a hole that is so dark as to appear like a solid shape on a surface. Imagine decreasing the tone of that darkness while retaining its opacity. It was something like that. When I reached out to touch it - well, what can I say but that I *could* not touch it? When I put my fingers where I adjudged its surface to be, I felt nothing. Though it presented more as gas than solid, my hand did not disappear as I poked it through what should have been the external shell of the Restaurant Car. It had the presence of matter but did not assume any of its known forms. It was impossible, or should have been. And the only way I can account for it is that the vagueness of this part of the carriage when I'd constructed it in my mind's eye was here repeated in its provisional blankness. In all my attempts to envisage its interior, I had ignored the right-hand side of the Restaurant Car; so had the train.

I had no idea how far this apparent conflation of imaginary and lived experience extended, whether my responsibility as the architect of this environment also covered the events that unfolded there: whether, in short, I would be able to realise my best-case scenario, if you know what I mean. I took a stool at the bar, a hexagonal outcrop not unlike a pulpit, built into the left-hand wall halfway up the carriage, clad with white leatherette at the sides and glazed on top, the upper surface doubling as a shallow vitrine housing a collection of insects - beetles, butterflies, moths, scorpions - with handwritten labels bearing their Latin names, an amalgam of elements I must have thrown together subconsciously from various cultural sources: science fiction, contemporary art, furniture catalogues. As I looked around, I realised that everything else was based on some prior experience. The wainscoting and the uplighters I had borrowed from a vintage steam train I'd been on as a boy, the chrome barstools from the American-style diner I went to during my lunch break.

I had the place to myself for ten minutes till an elderly gentleman with an eyepatch came in, the maître d' escorting him to a table at the front of the Restaurant Car near the sliding door. He had not appeared in any of my scenarios, and I did not care to meet his gaze as he sat studying me, showing him my back and turning towards the rear of the carriage. It was there that I drank two martinis in twenty minutes, made with breakneck precision by a young bartender named Brilling. I knew he was called Brilling because that was his name in the various scenarios I'd conjured up when imagining this moment. He had on the white jacket and cream bow tie I'd supplied him with, a short slick of black hair centrally parted. I'd been unable to decide whether to give him a moustache, and his lip alternated between shaven and unshaven for the first hour, before stabilising into two manicured wisps swept away from his philtrum.

Brilling served a complimentary saucer of olives with my second martini then returned to his duties, polishing the glasses fastidiously, holding each one up to the light before placing it carefully by the stem on the shelf behind him.

'Will you be dining this evening, sir?' he said, with his back to me.

This was good. Brilling was following the script. I was about to request a table for two when the man on the stool to my right answered on my behalf:

'We shall require a table for three.'

I hadn't seen Marlowe come in. He didn't look well, broken capillaries criss-crossing his cheeks, his eyes no longer sparkling in their separate depths but bulging, bloated and bloodshot, like two corpses that had risen to the surface of his face. He'd gained at least two stone and spoke more slowly, wheezing between words in a timbre that seemed to match the carnation in his buttonhole, now reduced to a stalk, a saintly relic with a tiny, wizened bulb. He was nursing something powerful, possibly a Manhattan, doing his best to pace himself and failing. I asked if he'd fallen off the wagon, but he wasn't familiar with the phrase.

'Can't say I blame you,' I went on, 'Brilling makes a fine cocktail.' In one sense this last statement was meaningless, for I could taste nothing, but I liked the way he made them, so it was not entirely untrue.

'Another, sir?'

'A whisky, please, Brilling. Marlowe?'

'Why not.'

He seemed tetchy at first, the scarlet folds of his neck juddering as he spoke, but the whisky returned him to a more equable version of himself, his patter strewn once again with his customary 'old beans' and 'old boys' as he gradually became more communicative, encouraged by the ambience. The Restaurant Car was filling up now, couples arriving arm-in-arm, larger parties of four and five in their eveningwear, greeted unctuously by the maître d', a slender man in black tails and white gloves.

'You did well, old bean,' said Marlowe, phlegm rattling in his throat.

'I did?'

'So I hear.'

'And what – what did you hear?'

He put his finger to his lips.

'It's sufficient that I heard, old boy. *What* I heard is . . .' He stopped here to attend to a cramp in his foot, bracing his toe against the bar till the pain subsided, rocking back slightly on his stool. Then he demanded another whisky. Brilling brought the bottle over with ice and a toby jug of water, a charming little knick-knack with a feline face, not unlike Companion, who occupied the stool to my left, alert and upright, sniffing the new air on offer hereabouts.

Marlowe fed his gout with a swift medicinal measure and poured another for recreational. 'And the usual for you-know-who,' he said to Brilling.

'Whiskey Sour, sir?'

'Make it a strong one.'

'I'll make it how I always make it, sir.'

I was pleased with his measured defiance here – there was a lot of myself in Brilling – but there was something amiss. As he reached for the bourbon I intervened:

'I think she'll have a White Russian, on reflection, Brilling.'

'Very good, sir.'

'And Brilling?'

'Sir?'

'Make it how you always make it. Only more so.'

I watched as Brilling worked, bottleneck braced between the knuckles of one hand, the shaker of ice in the other, catching the penile jet, his movements automatic, habituated to the task. The area beyond the bar did not go overlooked either. He watched the guests nervously as they came in, and I sensed tension between himself and the maître d', who did not seem so alert, not as sensitive to the atmospheric shifts. Brilling's eyes narrowed as a large group of women filed in through the sliding door, already the worse for wear. I too was concerned. As the maître d' conveyed them to the long central table, gliding in to remove the Reserved sign and pull back the chairs, I thought I recognised the members of the hen party. They were all in different dresses this time, and I couldn't see Heobah, though there was someone roughly her size just sitting down with her back to me, at the head of the table.

As I watched them, I saw that the neutral façade that had so bewitched me on entry had now been filled in. At what point this had happened I don't know, but I figured it must have coincided with the entrance of someone else, possibly the man with the eyepatch, who might've imagined a different scenario to the one I'd sketched out, preferring wood-effect veneer to my whitewashed wainscoting; stainless steel window frames to my oak frames; and two-seater tables bolted to the floor, not unlike those in the First Class section of a normal train – whereas my furniture was period stuff made from wood. For it followed, did it not, that the others could also contribute their visions, augmenting our shared reality to their own satisfaction? Part of me was relieved to have all four walls now, but another resented it, for I considered myself the Restaurant Car's chief architect.

'There are things I'd like to discuss,' said Marlowe. 'Before dinner.'

I was only half-listening, waiting for the woman with bleached blonde hair to turn round, show her face.

'One or two things regarding the placebo.'

Now he had my attention.

'Just a few formalities, old bean.'

I told him that, with regard to last night, my perception had not been influenced in any way. But I told him nothing about this morning, of the incident in the cubicle, and kept my vision of the Restaurant Car to myself.

'And your behaviour?'

'What of it?'

'It was consistent with your normal character?'

My hesitation at this question told him all he needed to know. I had felt stable, in the main, but there'd been one or two moments of supreme confidence that seemed wholly *out* of character: when I'd asked Monroe for a cigar, for instance, and chided Saturn for making fun of Mercury. I nevertheless gave Marlowe to understand that I would have acted the same, pill or no pill.

'You're sure?'

'Positive.'

'And how *did* you act?'

I now remembered his earlier remarks about collecting data. The data would be analysed, he'd said, processed. What else? Yes: compared, protected. I assumed Monroe had made notes on my conduct, that I'd been similarly monitored in the other compartments – probably by Mildred in the second and by Neptune in the third – and that the relevant information had been fed back to him.

'Well?'

I told him about everyone I'd met: the matriarchs, Monroe, Monroe II, the men in white, the men in balaclavas, Jupiter, Saturn, Mercury. And the games I'd played: my low opinion of Why Not Sneeze?, my grudging admiration of London or Yorkshire? I was about to describe the game I'd invented when he interrupted:

'And what makes you so certain you were not under the influence?'

'The events themselves were sufficiently diverting,' I said piously, 'that I did not require the aid of a stimulant.'

'How do you know the events themselves were not the product of the stimulant?'

'So you admit it's a stimulant.'

Marlowe didn't reply, but I guessed his silence tactical. He was allowing me to believe I'd scored a point here.

'And there's nothing else?'

I shrank away from him as he said this, fearing he was about to take my hand again, as he had done yesterday, and forcibly extract a full picture of last night's events. But this time he didn't need to.

'Actually, there is,' I said. 'There is something else.'

'What?'

'I can't believe I forgot. How could I forget?'

'Forget what, old boy?'

'That first compartment I mentioned.'

'Yes?'

'There's a body in there.'

'Yes, six or seven people, I think you said—'

'No. A *body*. A corpse. There's a dead man in there.'

'A what man?'

'A dead man.'

'I thought that's what you said.' Marlowe reached for the whisky and poured us another double measure: 'Tell me: in what sense was he *dead?*'

'I'm sorry?'

'*How* was he dead?'

'You mean, how did he die?'

'No, I mean exactly what I say: How was he dead?'

'He was just . . . dead. They'd put a blanket over him. And a hat on his face.'

'What kind of hat?'

'I don't know. A fedora?'

'A dark blue one?'

'Yes.'

'With a grey band?'

'Yes. You knew him?'

'*Know* him. We used to play chess together. My only worthy opponent.'

'You were friends?'

'*Are* friends. His name is Albert.'

'Well, I'm sorry. I'm sorry to have to tell you that Albert's dead.'

'And I,' said Marlowe, 'am sorry to have to tell you that he's not.'

'But he *is* dead.'

'I'm afraid not.'

'What do you mean, you're *afraid* not? You want him to be dead?'

Marlowe's grin slackened. 'Much as we might all aspire to that condition,' he said, 'I never met anyone who attained it. No, this chap you saw, he was not dead. I can assure you of that.'

'Then what was he?'

'Bored.'

'Bored?'

'It's his natural condition, old Albert. Sounds like he's got worse though.'

I was at pains to convince Marlowe that the rigor I'd perceived in Albert's body evinced something more than mere boredom, but he wouldn't have it:

'He certainly does take it up a notch, old Albert, he really is exceedingly bored. The most bored man I ever met. *Dead* bored, to be precise.' Marlowe dropped another a lump of ice in his whisky. 'Look,' he said, swivelling towards me on his stool, 'I think I can iron this out. Am I right in thinking that by "dead" you are referring to the cessation, the drawing to a close, of an animate state?'

'What else can I mean?'

'Ah. I feared as much.' He turned to me and gripped me by the shoulders. 'I am so sorry,' he said, with utter sincerity.

'What is it?'

'I really am very very sorry.'

'What for?'

'Please believe when I say that I didn't intend this. I would never have given it to you if I'd foreseen this outcome.'

'The pill?'

'I admit, I hoped for one or two unprecedented symptoms, but I did not foresee this. I only meant to make you more amenable to your environment. You must believe me when I say that I did not foresee such delusion.'

'But he was dead. *Dead.* Don't you understand?'

'With respect, one cannot say of anything that it is dead and only dead. A thing must be dead in some particular way: dead beautiful, dead keen, dead bored.'

What, for me, was a word designating the cessation of life was for him a mere modifier of adjectives. I could not make him see that 'dead bored' was an idiom, a figure of speech that had its origin in something real, the realest thing of all, that *relied* on that thing for its metaphorical effect. It wasn't that he couldn't grasp the concept of mortality, but he did not accept it as a going concern, an actual status quo, could not see it in anything but mythic and metaphorical terms.

Equally rich was his claim that *I* did not grasp the concept of boredom. As he elaborated, it wasn't clear to me whether the two terms were interchangeable, whether 'boredom' was a euphemism for 'death' or a substitute for that condition.

'It is simply the way of things,' he said: 'Some folk just stop caring. Stop talking. Stop listening. Stop moving . . .'

I waited for him to proceed to the respiratory and cardiac

functions, to adduce the biological stasis of the brain and other vital organs, but he trailed off.

'And then?'

'Well, they just . . . stop.'

'Like Albert.'

'Like Albert.'

11

IT WAS A testament to Brilling's class as a barman that
when the ice in Heobah's White Russian melted he simply
made another and placed it on a fresh doily. And when this
too was spoiled, as the hour reached six-thirty, he did it again,
without complaint – and without my having to ask. That
White Russian had to be there when she arrived – it was
part of the drink, and Brilling understood this. Had I not
imagined it thus in the days before our date?

I did not recall factoring Marlowe into my plans, but I
assumed our threesome would be short-lived, that he would
take a hike downtrain once he got wind of my romantic intent.
It was nearly seven when not one but two women showed
up, neither of them Heobah, one in her late fifties, the other
a decade older. They appeared through the sliding door just
after the maître d' showed us to our table, throwing their arms
out to Marlowe and parking themselves on his lap, the younger
woman on his right knee, the older on his left. I guessed they
were sisters. Both wore close-fitting crimson dresses and plati-
num-blonde wigs, their outfits matched to give the impression
of their being twins, despite the age gap, and they spoke in a
transatlantic accent that suggested a life of continuous social
passage, summer balls, polo matches, ambassadorial soirées,
their voices alternating between a dusky contralto and a high-
pitched scream.

Our table was next to the bar – I'd deliberately chosen

a chair facing the hen party in order to monitor the blonde woman – and I was relieved when these interlopers showed no interest in me, not even seeking an introduction, taking it in turns to whisper things in Marlowe's ear: dirty talk, judging by his reaction. He looked tired, Marlowe, doing his best to humour them, but his bonhomie was increasingly forced and I was dreading the evening that lay ahead. Our table seated four, but the sisters had yet to take their places, and Companion had already abandoned us for a place behind the bar, where Brilling was happy to accommodate him.

I couldn't see myself enduring three courses with these women either. I was on the point of asking Brilling if I could be seated elsewhere, when I was rescued by the maître d':

'Excuse me, madame,' he said to the older sister.

She waved him away – she was in the middle of a story – but the maître d' pointed to a table at the other end of the carriage near the sliding door.

'Please. madame,' he said, 'the Count has requested the pleasure of your company.'

The table next to us fell silent, the man setting down a forkful of food, his wife canting her ear. Even Brilling stopped polishing the glasses.

'The Count?'

The sisters looked round. A man nearly seven feet tall was preparing to sit down, a sallow-cheeked ogre with hands the size of baseball gloves, one of which had just tossed his cane into the air. A waiter sprang forward to catch it, while another caught the cloak from his shoulders. A third was ready with his chair, which creaked under the immense poundage. A fourth appeared with a cigar, a fifth with a cigar cutter, while a sixth waiter moved in with a flaming match.

The Count was, on the surface, the most count-like figure I

ever beheld. He had a dark widow's peak swept back from his brow, a long Roman nose nearly touching his lip, and his eyes were so sunken they looked like they'd been fired into his head with a crossbow. But he lacked the natural composure one associates with aristocracy, wracked by some inner precarity perceivable, I felt, to none but myself.

The others seemed to regard him as the real deal, the two sisters already on their feet, shelving whatever arrangement they had with Marlowe. There was competition from a member of the hen party as they closed in, the woman with the bleached blonde hair, who I was pleased to see wasn't Heobah after all. I got a good look as the sisters elbowed her aside and she returned to her seat.

The Count now looked up, acknowledging the excitement spreading through the Restaurant Car (*The Count . . . It's the Count . . . Look, the Count . . . Do you see him?*), whispering something to a waiter, which the waiter now relayed to the maître d'.

'It would very much please the Count,' announced the maître d', 'if everyone accepted a glass of the 808 Special Reserve.'

There was more murmuring here: *The 808 Special Reserve . . . The 808 Special Reserve . . . The Count . . . The Count, do you see him . . . ?*

The Count beckoned the waiter back over, whispered something else, which the waiter again relayed to the maître d'.

'The Count also wishes it to be known,' said the maître d', 'that none shall eat fish this evening.'

The excitement dipped, and the Count motioned once more to the waiter.

'The Count regrets any inconvenience caused by this ruling,' relayed the maître d', 'but it does not please him that passengers should partake of ocean-dwelling creatures at the current time. That is all.'

Most diners agreed that this seemed to make vague gastronomic sense – fish didn't go with Champagne – though they would have accepted anything the Count said. I gathered from their craven compliance that they did not expect him to justify his pronouncements, grateful for such reasoning as his mood disposed.

Conversation resumed, but the Count cast a long shadow and most were unable to concentrate while Brilling poured the Champagne and the waiters carried the flutes off on silver trays.

'What is he the Count *of*?' I asked. 'And why is he looking at me?'

The Count *was* looking at me. The attitude towards him was one of wholesale genuflection, but he had detected a single speck of defiance, surveying the faces in the Restaurant Car and zooming in on mine.

Marlowe nodded at the window: 'His dominions lay all around.'

'Everywhere?'

'Everything. All you can see.'

'It's night.'

'Very funny, old boy. But I fancy he has jurisdiction over that too.'

'And the train?'

'The train? Don't be ridiculous.'

I did not see why it was ridiculous. The train needed permission, did it not, to go through the Count's lands? But Marlowe said this was like saying the sun needed the consent of the sky. He was even more confused when I asked where the Count had got on.

'Not with you, old bean. Got on what?'

'The train. The 8:08.'

'But he was always on it. Like you and me, and Brilling here.'

'But how does one *get* here?' I asked. 'I mean, I got on at, I got on at . . . Odd, I don't remember.'

'Remember what?'

'Where I got on.'

'What are you talking about, *got on?*'

'I can remember getting on the train. I can can remember walking to the station, but I don't remember the name of the station. The name of the town.'

'Town?'

'Or the street where I live.'

'Street? Live? You're babbling, old boy. You're making no sense whatsoever. Understandable, I suppose.'

He put it down to the placebo, reiterating his apology, and I allowed him to believe that my current ramblings were the symptoms of its effects. It was useful cover, allowing me to be bolder when it came to discussing the time prior to my having boarded the train. A subject hitherto out of bounds was now on the agenda. I had the fool's licence to roam.

I asked Marlowe whether it was the same for the others, whether all passengers forgot where they'd boarded, that is, how they'd got here.

'I really don't see how *here* is something one can be in possession of,' he replied. 'One is either here or not here. One doesn't *get* here. Here is not given to be possessed.'

'No, that's not what I mean, you don't see—'

'Please. Please let us not make a scene. Not in front of the Count.'

'I don't give a shit about the Count.'

It came out at precisely the wrong moment, this, the chatter abating for a second or two, my words carrying further than intended.

'Good,' said Marlowe, 'I don't think he heard.'

The Count was no longer looking at me. He was sat back in his chair, addressing the sisters in a long monologue that seemed to consist mainly of orders, the sisters nodding at regular intervals to show they understood. The older sister was holding a cap the Count had just given her, a black one with a shiny plastic peak, while the younger one was entrusted with a note he had just written and folded, sealing it with wax from the candle on his table, into which he now pressed his sovereign ring. When he clapped his hands and bade them leave, it took a few seconds to realise what was strange about their exit: they did not come back up the carriage, past our table, downtrain; they went backwards, via the same sliding door through which they had entered, *uptrain*, against the direction of travel.

After they left, I assumed the Count would dine alone, but when I looked up a few minutes later another woman had joined him, and I couldn't believe who it was. She had her back to me, but I recognised the silhouette, the two-tone jacket, the mussed black hair.

My first thought was that the Count and I were going to have settle this in the vestibule. I openly stared at him now, numb to the disapproval of the other diners, who appeared to accord him mythic status (*The Count . . . The Count . . . Do you see him . . . ?*). I hadn't seen Heobah come in. What was she playing at? Already late for our engagement, she had paused to break bread with another man. Or maybe she'd blown me out, forgotten about me altogether? I was about to get up and go over there when I felt a hand on my shoulder.

'Sorry I'm late,' said Heobah, sliding into her seat. 'Have you ordered?'

There it was: the lightning bolt T-shirt, the men's brogues, the two-tone suit, a different fabric, I now noted, to the other woman's jacket. She'd come from behind us, presumably from the kitchen, which was set into the side of the carriage, on the left, just beyond the bar, and she was nursing the White Russian.

It turned out she'd been here all afternoon: 'I had to help out,' she explained, 'they're a man down back there.'

'That was good of you,' said Marlowe.

'Well, we'll see about that, won't we?'

'Meaning?'

'All I'll say is don't have the Beef Wellington.'

'I wasn't going to.'

'Or the rissoles.'

'Ah.'

'Or the sweetbreads.'

'Or the fish,' I interrupted.

'No,' said Heobah, 'the fish is fine.'

Marlowe nodded at the Count. 'I'm afraid fish is off this evening. By order of you-know-who.'

Heobah rolled her eyes. 'In the name of Guard! Last time it was the lamb. Well, *I'm* having it. I've been looking forward to it all day.'

She'd even earmarked her own portion. It was there on the side, in the kitchen, dusted with flour, ready for the pan.

'What kind is it?' I asked, scanning the menu. It came with celeriac and beetroot salad but there was no other information. 'I mean, where was it caught?'

They both laughed, as though I'd intended this in jest.

'Seriously. What kind of fish is it and were did it come from? Originally?'

I only added this word for rhetorical effect, but Heobah looked at at me like a schoolgirl caught smoking. I have since come to believe that some words are like skeleton keys: utter them, and there is a change, a propitious realignment of the train's agency and a consequent shifting of fortunes. Whatever, she now looked at Marlowe, and Marlowe nodded, pulling the pillbox from his inside pocket.

'I thought so,' said Heobah. 'When?'

'Yesterday.'

'Blue or white?'

'White.' Marlowe repocketed the pillbox and got to his feet.

'Thank you,' said Heobah, also standing, as the two of them embraced, 'you've done well.'

'I have done what was . . . necessary,' he said.

And off he shuffled, ambling downtrain, nodding politely at Brilling as he passed. As the sliding door opened, he turned to face me:

'No hard feelings, eh, old bean?'

He looked completely different, his alcoholic distemper gone, the eyes twinkling once more. The carnation in his buttonhole had been replaced with a flower from a vase on the bar. It looked very much like the one I'd seen on his counterpart yesterday, the one waving from the carriages overhead.

'No hard feelings,' I said, as he slipped into the vestibule.

IV

HEOBAH

1

THAT MARLOWE AND Heobah were in league did not surprise me. They possessed an autonomy lacking in other passengers, an asset that drew them naturally together, though it was clear from the scene in the Restaurant Car that Heobah outranked Marlowe in their secret opposition. The full extent of their cause was to remain a mystery, but they shared an intuition that I was an effective instrument for their immediate objectives; and if either of them foresaw what has happened since, and what – if my structural theories of the train are correct – will happen in due course, they disguised it well. Perhaps I've been used? It's equally conceivable that I have used them. But surely more likely that we are all beholden to a higher power.

What did I make of my fellow insurgents? I assumed that, like everyone else, both Marlowe and Heobah had been numbed into submission, denuded of their memory, either partially or wholly, but had managed to claw something of themselves back, reaching an understanding with the train, as I was beginning to do, as we all must. It is difficult, if not impossible, to resist this natural amnesia, but it appears that some are more resistant than others, finding ways of respecting the 8:08's rubric without fully internalising it. I'd excelled myself with the trolley, partaken of the entertainments, might have settled for a place in First Class, but I distrusted the hierarchies of those compartments, the positions held there by individuals merely a distraction from the more fundamental question of their locomotive berth, that is to say, their *passage*. On they sped, content not to ask where or why, so long as they maintained their little cliques.

Even as I adapted to it, I felt a growing independence from the train, a contradiction I am still unable to resolve. In the short term I wondered whether, if I continued to nurture this impulse, I might recover the things I'd forgotten: my name, my home town, the street where I lived. Curiously, I had not forgotten about my job, my place of work, my colleagues. But the things that were particular to *me* continued to be eroded. My appearance, for example, was beginning to surprise me whenever I bothered to look in the mirror. I was not unduly concerned. It was even possible that the amnesia was productive, enabling one to assume whatever role should come one's way. Marlowe's turn in the Restaurant Car had been instructive here. On leaving us, he had seemed disarmingly sober, having feigned his stupor all along to appear in character for the Count, thereby disguising his sedition. I could see from the behaviour of my new colleagues that a certain theatricality was desirable in a would-be insurgent, and I guessed this was how it started: with a creeping indifference to one's identity.

After Marlowe had gone, I might've expected Heobah to begin fleshing out the train's political constitution, but when she sat there in silence, her hand edging across the table towards mine, it seemed that the onus was on me to ask such questions as I dared, at the risk of ruining what we'd clearly both been looking forward to. The fatigue of the interrogation I would now be expected to mount was already palpable, hanging over us both as the waiter took our orders, and I was relieved when, just as I was about to raise the subject of the so-called placebo, she took my hand, looked me in the eye and proposed that we 'leave all that till morning'. The waiter frowned as we both ordered the fish, but Heobah pointed out that the Count had gone now. He hadn't come past us on the way out, so I figured he'd followed the two sisters uptrain, the doors opening for them alone as they headed against the direction of travel.

Just when I needed to monopolise Heobah's affections, who should appear back on the scene but her old friend Companion, emerging from his place behind the bar and jumping onto her lap. She was delighted to see him, and there now followed a comic debriefing, as she asked my little chaperone for a report on my conduct of the last few days, interpreting his various bodily responses as evidence of my good character.

'Is he eating?' she asked, as he began his ritual distempering of her trousers.

'I think Brilling gave him something earlier.'

'And before?'

I told her of the encounter with the trolley woman, of my stint in the tabard, how we'd survived on UHT milk and sandwiches till we hit First Class.

'I knew you'd be alright. I knew you'd get on.'

'I have to say it's been a pleasure. Surprisingly.'

'Why surprisingly? You never thought of yourself as a cat person?'

'Not really.'

'But your job?'

'I know. I'm still not sure I'd call myself a "cat person" though. And actually I'm not convinced you have to be to get along with Companion here. I go so far as to say that that is his charm.'

'You mean, that he's drawn to non-cat people?'

'It's possible. He's the only animal on board, right?'

'So far as I know.' Heobah went to pet him again, but this time Companion grabbed her hand. His claws were not bared, but his ears were back, his head sleeker, more kitten-like. 'He's the only animal I've come across,' continued Heobah, 'since, since . . .' But she glazed over, unable to complete the sentence.

'Since when?'

'I don't remember.'

'Since coming aboard?'

'Aboard?'

'Since boarding the 8:08. You were on the point of comparing our friend here to those animals you'd seen before, were you not?'

'Before?'

'Before boarding the 8:08.'

'I don't follow.'

I reproached myself for not leaving it till morning. I'd assumed, possibly due to the seniority she held over Marlowe, that her memory of life prior to boarding the train was more comprehensive, for she had used the word 'since', an unmistakable reference to the past.

'And you?' I asked, changing the subject as our starters arrived, a sort of tartlet with artichokes and blue cheese. 'Where did you go while I was making my way here?'

'Oh, you know. Downtrain.'

There was no mention of the food's quality from either of us as we conveyed it mechanically to our mouths, like information fed into a computer, no acknowledgement at all of the fine dining 'experience', the good care taken with presentation, the square plates, the small portions, the *jus* in its little jug that the waiter poured without our asking. The meal was only a pretext, after all, a ritual we'd both rather abandon but for reasons of social etiquette had to see through to the end. In this respect, it was wholly fitting that it was utterly devoid of taste.

It was during the main course that Companion intervened. He'd been pounding Heobah's trousers with his front paws throughout dinner, but now he embarked on more ambitious manoeuvres, mounting her forearm and swinging his hind-quarters into position, appropriating the pit of her elbow as his concubine.

'Has he done this before?' I asked, as he began thrusting gamely.

'No. But I kind of like it.'

'He's having sex with your arm.'

'Technically, no.'

She explained that he'd been neutered, and we needn't fear the prospect of his exciting himself to issue. I was curious how he'd retained a phantom libido, after being broken on the wheel of castration, but this mystery was academic. For there was something about the way he kept looking over, to see if I was watching, that indicated a higher purpose here. Even the most neutral of bystanders could not deny there was a spirit of demonstration in his pageantry. I've spoken often enough of his tendency to show me the way through the sliding doors. It now seemed that he was showing me the way in an altogether different sense, that he was showing *us* the way.

I motioned for the bill. When it came, there was a hand-written note on the tray: *Have this one on me.* I looked round at Brilling, who nodded deferentially, like a character from a matinée. More than likely I'd plucked him from a film I'd seen one Saturday afternoon. He had that air about him: a minor actor of the silver screen.

'Look,' said Heobah, as we got to our feet.

Under the note was a key.

2

AS PREVIOUSLY STATED, I'd been impotent for some time, but my erection the previous day had given me cause for optimism. In maritime fiction, the ship is sometimes shown a sign that bodes well: a porpoise off the starboard or an albatross alighting on the poop. So it was with my boner, a welcome portent after a period in the doldrums.

The conditions couldn't have been more sympathetic, for it was clear, from the many couples we passed in the gangway after the Restaurant Car, that the subsequent section of the train was the 8:08's equivalent of a sex hotel. Compartment 165, just a few carriages down, was the one we needed according to the number on the key. When we found it, I locked the door behind us, and Companion hopped up onto the bench seat on the right-hand side, where he began cleaning himself rigorously, hind leg extended over his shoulder.

The compartments here were different to those I had been in last night. There were blankets and pillows on the overhead rack, as before, but a lot more junk, more evidence of previous users, and a small fridge in the corner under the seat. On the floor by the window was a trunk of clothes and fancy-dress costumes: a pilot's uniform, a Roman centurion's armour, a bus inspector's outfit, an orange codpiece. I put the codpiece on over my trousers, donned the bus inspector's cap and minced about a bit, while Heobah put on the doctor's outfit, which came with a stethoscope that she held to my chest, dancing to the music she imagined coming from my insides. She was an excellent clown. I didn't see what a valuable skill that was till now: how much I loved women who could clown.

'Look,' said Heobah, rummaging inside the fridge, 'Champagne.'

There were no glasses but that was a good thing, our fingers touching as we passed the bottle. We ought by now to have been drunk. I'd had three cocktails, two double whiskies and a brandy, but I was completely sober. The previous day everyone in Standard Class had been drunk by mid-morning, but I don't recall anyone losing control in First Class. Yet alcohol retained its status as a social lubricant, consumed in great quantities by all.

We drew the curtains and laid out the blankets on the left-hand seat, Companion still cleaning himself on the other side, still on the same hind leg as before, which was thrust out horizontally now, like the snout of an Irish bagpipes.

'What do you make of this?' said Heobah.

It was a cream dress with mint green piping, the kind of thing a cheerleader or a drum majorette might wear.

'Nice. Put it on.'

Heobah held it up against herself, then shook her head: 'Nah: you.'

'Me?'

She offered it up to my chest. 'It's your size. See: 18.'

'How'd you know I'm an 18?'

'I can tell.'

'You really want me to put it on?'

'Why not?'

'Seriously?'

'One of us ought to, don't you think? It's such a *nice* dress. Besides.'

She slumped onto the seat, and for a moment I thought she had zoned out again, just as she had done in the Restaurant Car, her mind frozen by some thought that could not be verbalised.

'Besides what? You seem anxious.'

'It's just that . . . well, I think I *need* you to put on.'

'I don't follow.'

'What I mean is, I don't think I can do this – unless . . .'

'Unless what?'

'Unless you're in women's clothing.'

'Right . . . Do what, exactly?'

She got up and came towards me, grabbing me by the lapels. It was the briefest but intensest of kisses, a squall of tongues and teeth, a tender assault borne equally of desire and trepidation, and when we parted it was mutually understood that I had to put on the dress.

I told myself it was just another outfit, like the doctor's white coat or the centurion's armour. She turned round while I changed, not to spare my blushes but because she didn't want to see me naked before seeing me in character. The dress, it turned out, was more like a skirt, the hem not much lower than my arse. It was tight round the waist but fine apart from that – she was right, I was an 18.

She insisted I keep my bus inspector's cap on: a combination of men's and women's clothing was more exciting for her, she explained, than a purely female ensemble. I told her I understood, that it worked for me the other way round too.

'You like women in men's clothing?'

'Er, *hello?*' I emphasised her men's suit, her men's brogues. 'But there has to be a vestige of femininity.'

'A vestige? You mean, like this?'

Whenever I recall this scene now, it's the sound I

remember: the heavy clunk of the belt buckle on the carpet as her trousers fell to the floor.

'That's more than a vestige,' was all I could think of to say.

She kept her jacket on at my request. Nudity from the waist down, I informed her, though unbecoming in men, is desirable in women. As to the rest, the physical side of things can be easily imagined, so I shall limit my commentary to what was said rather than what was done. For much was said. A little too much.

Firstly, it was not enough for her that I was wearing women's clothing – I had to acknowledge it verbally throughout.

'And I mean throughout,' she said, getting down on all fours. 'Don't stop.'

'What do I say?'

'You'll think of something.'

And I did. I thought of lots of things. 'I'm a 45-year-old man,' I began, as we assumed our respective positions, 'I'm a 45-year-old man and I am wearing a cheerleader's outfit.'

'Nice opening,' said Heobah. 'But call it a dress. *Outfit's* too theatrical. Like you're going to take it off any moment. Act like it's for keeps.'

'I'm a 45-year-old man,' I said, 'and I am wearing a cheer-leader's *dress*.'

'Better. Now, what colour is your dress?'

'It's a beautiful cream dress with mint green piping.'

'I can feel it. I can feel it brushing against my ass, the piping round the hem.'

In point of fact, there was no piping round the hem, only on the shoulders and arms, but I allowed her to believe it was so.

'I'm a 45-year-old heterosexual man,' I resumed, 'and I

am wearing a beautiful cheerleader's dress – with mint green piping and ruched shoulders.'

'Good. But please refer to the dress as *your* dress, not *a* dress. At all times.'

'I'm a 45-year-old heterosexual man,' I said, 'and I am wearing my beautiful cheerleader's dress with mint green piping and ruched shoulders.'

'Good, good . . .'

'And the label is chafing my skin.'

'Let's home in on that label. Size 18?'

'As we established.'

'So. You're a size 18, heterosexual, dress-wearing man?'

'That's correct.'

'Say it.'

'I'm a size 18, heterosexual, dressing-wearing man.'

'What else do you see?'

'On the label? I'll have to look.'

'No! Make it up. That's the whole point.'

'100% cotton?'

'Let's go for a blend.'

'OK. I'm a 45-year-old heterosexual man, and I am wearing my beautiful cheerleader's dress, 60% cotton, 40% synthet–'

'Make it 80-20. Let's go for an 80% *synthetic*, 20% cotton garment.'

'I see. I see where you're going. What about washing instructions? Machine wash at 40?'

'80.'

'80? It'll shrink.'

'Exactly. On second thoughts, let's just stick it on a boil-wash. With a bunch of handkerchiefs and shit. And maybe throw in a jockstrap?'

'A jockstrap?'

'And maybe a, I don't know, a vicar's collar or something. Let's fuck this garment up. Let's do it. Do it, do it,' she chanted, banging the seat with the heel of her palm.

'I *am* doing it. Everything I say I'm doing. Everything I say is true.'

'Good. Now put it all together.'

'Everything?'

'From the beginning: I am wearing . . . mint green piping . . . the 80–20 split . . . the vicar's collar . . . the boil-wash . . . Don't leave anything out. And throw in some other elements.'

'Like what?'

'I don't know. Like why you've chosen this dress over all the others.'

'The others?'

'In this scenario you have many other dresses. But you've deliberately chosen this one. What I want to know is why.'

'I can't think why.'

'I wonder, could it be, perchance, because you're a *dirty cross-dressing heterosexual male whore?*'

She turned her head as she delivered this line, straining to look at me over her left shoulder, her angular features foreshortened, chin braced awkwardly against her collarbone, trying to take in the spectacle behind her, mouth open, sweat running, hair hanging down in matted clumps like the ivy of an old, dilapidated building: a woman ten years past her prime. The perfection of her youth was still available behind the façade of her middle years, but its concealment was more seductive, I'll wager, than the sight of that youth in its original glory. I've been unable, so far, to find the right words to describe the beauty of Heobah's face, but I thought I had them now, they came to me in that moment. I wanted to tell her that she had a face like a, a face like a, a face like a ruined priory. The kind Turner might've painted. But it was too cultured, too sophisticated for the scenario we'd developed.

3

THE FOLLOWING MORNING, Companion was up
even earlier than usual, sinking his claws into the fabric
of the opposite benchseat, making a fair old racket. It was a
mark of the creature's diplomacy that he did not come over
and invade the conjugal bed but tried to rouse us from afar. It
was not yet light, and when I got up to give him some salmon,
I caught sight of myself in the window, still in my outfit from
the night before.

'You're a 45-year-old man,' I whispered at my reflection,
'and you are comfortable in women's clothing.'

Then I got back into bed and watched the sun come up
over the ridge that now bisected the train's window. We had
entered another basin, an area of heathland similar to that
which we'd skirted on the second day. Or so I thought. As
we came to a halt and I saw, once again, the solitary tree I
had seen on Wednesday afternoon, I realised it was the same
heathland. The tree was in the same position as before, in the
centre of the basin, and broken in exactly the same place, two
thirds of the way up its trunk, the only difference being that
where, on Wednesday, the broken part had lain to the right
of the trunk, it now lay to the left.

From this I deduced that we were on the other side of the
heath, coming back in the opposite direction, on the home-
ward leg of an enormous loop. My disappointment at this was
telling. Only then did I see that, far from hoping to arrive at

my original intended destination, I'd harboured the subconscious expectation of continuing indefinitely into unknown regions. Now I had to adjust to the possibility of negotiating the same circuit every seven days. So far, the claustrophobia of the train had been offset by the wider agoraphobia of the unknown, the indeterminate nature of our journey, the uncertainty as to its length and destination, one counteracting the other. But now the balance was threatened. It was as if the train had stopped merely to demonstrate this.

After sunrise we got up and sat at the table by the window, and it was there, facing each other across the compartment, the train still stationary, that I tried to edge up to the subject of Heobah's life before she came on board. A verbal slip in the Restaurant Car had convinced me that her memory of that time might be recovered. If I was to arrest my own amnesia, I had to believe others were capable of doing likewise. My memory seemed to be holding up, but I couldn't rule out a decline so gradual you didn't realise it was happening. In the event that it did, I wanted to know the process was reversible. Heobah would be my test case.

I tried to tip-toe up to the claim that I had seen her once before, that evening years ago on my way home from work, when we'd made eye contact and she'd smiled at me, before suddenly getting off at an intermediate station. I was surprised to find, as I revisited this encounter again, that I was able to recollect it more vividly than before. In my experience, once a memory has taken hold in one's mind, it recurs in exactly the same way thereafter, but there was another detail here, as the evening in question resurfaced, that had hitherto lain buried: I remembered now that she ran. That she left the train as if in panic, tearful.

It's not always clear whether the brain is remembering something forgotten or thinking it for the first time, and I couldn't tell if this was a recovered memory or a freshly minted thought. Neither could I rule out the possibility of another locomotive interjection, one that on this occasion I had managed to prevent myself from blurting out. The thought seemed at once familiar and strange. I had no doubt that this memory, if it can be called one, was real, yet it also seemed that it was *not mine*, for it had no basis in what I had seen that evening. I had observed neither panic nor suddenness in her demeanour, and certainly no tears. I couldn't have – I had ducked down, too shy to follow her as she'd left her seat, not looking up again until she gained the platform. And then she was gone, through the barriers, into the ticket hall, off into the night.

All this should have urged me to greater caution, but subtlety was getting me nowhere. It was also difficult to say, as I prodded and probed, whether Heobah sensed I was making a bid for a more profound connection, trying to deepen the meaning of our relationship by dwelling on the one thing she was scared to confront, or whether she thought it a game, that the past I was referring to here was entirely made up, no more credible than the scenario she'd elaborated from the contents of Paul Carver's wallet on Wednesday evening, or the story I'd told about my own past, about Bob Buchanan and my place of work. It was possible she had taken the latter as a facile entertainment, blind to its status as evidence of a wider reality, one that preceded and enclosed that of the train.

In retrospect the plan that came to me was rash, but I implemented it without due regard for the consequences. I figured if I could take that earlier story about Bob, splice it with another series of events that ended with the journey home on the night when I'd met her, I could connect her imagined world with the real world that superintended it, re-uniting her present and past, connecting the purely conceptual domain in which she now appeared to live with the physical one that had engendered her. If I could achieve this, who knew what else might resurface.

So preoccupied was I with this new mission, I saw that I'd forgotten to change out of my cheerleader's dress.

'Would you excuse me a moment,' I said.

There was something I'd always wanted to do as a man. I bent down, grabbing the hem of my dress with one arm crossed over the other, and lifted it over my head in one smooth movement.

'Remember that story I told you,' I said, tossing it back in the trunk, 'the one about Bob Buchanan?'

'The magician?'

'The magician-cum-jazz-saxophonist. There was something I missed out when I told it the first time. I want to tell it again.'

'In your underpants?'

'Give me a minute.'

Rather than put my own trousers and Paul Carver's jacket back on, I selected another outfit from the trunk. I was fol-lowing intuition here. I wanted her to believe my story was imaginary at first, before working my way round to historical fact, and I thought dressing up would be a good rhetorical move. I needed something more formal, so I put my sweater back on - the one I'd got from the lady in Coach Z - and found a pair of navy-blue breeches, which I paired with a jacket roughly the same colour, with brass buttons that did up to the neck, that must have belonged, I think, to an old cavalry uniform. Then I put the black cap on, the one I'd worn last night.

'Like I say,' I began, resuming my place at the window, 'there was something I missed out the first time. Actually, I want to tell a different version.'

This was a test. If she objected, that might indicate she regarded the earlier version as the truth, which might in turn suggest belief in the authenticity of its backdrop, in the world beyond the 8:08 and its environs. But there was no objection. I was free to deviate.

'Earlier we saw things from my perspective,' I said, 'but this time we shall adopt another perspective.'

'Bob's?'

'No.'

'Dan's?'

'Nope.'

'Les Cundy then?'

'Not him either. But let's put aside the identity of this person for now. Let us skip, also, Bob's plight.'

'His what?'

'His plight. His ostracism. How he suffered under Dan's regime.'

'Poor Bob.'

'Poor Bob indeed. But let me take you back to that moment in Coach E. You'll recall that when we left Bob Buchanan, he had infiltrated a group of female backpackers from Germany.'

'Yes, I remember. Bob left them to go to the buffet car, didn't he?'

'That's correct.'

'They didn't want anything, did they?'

'No.'

'They'd already eaten, hadn't they?'

'Yes. I suppose they had. But let me get on with my story.'

I didn't know what the hell I was going to say next. I had to get Bob out of the picture, work my way round to me and her in that carriage on that evening. I now regretted beginning with Bob – it was ever thus with Buchanan – but it was the only way I could think of staging it on a train.

'So. Bob's gone to the buffet car, it's getting late . . .'

'I thought it was morning?'

'This is a different version. Remember?'

'Sorry.'

'Anyway, let's leave Bob there and turn our attention to—'

'But I thought this was supposed to be *about* Bob?'

'Indirectly. Bob's there in heart if not in person. We turn now to Coach F.'

'I thought we were in Coach E?'

'We are. But we follow Bob into the vestibule.'

'To the buffet car?'

'No. Only as far as Coach F. Something distracts us. Or rather, someone.'

'Who?'

'Who indeed? That's the question. Did I mention that this was an interactive story?'

'A what story?'

'Interactive. You get to participate.'

Heobah sighed. She'd already got comfortable, drawing her heels up under her haunches, settling in for a passive reception of events, and the news that she was going to have to help shape them annoyed her.

'You mean *join in?*'

'More than that. You get to decide certain things.'

'Like what?'

'Well, this person in Coach F, for one. I've no idea what she looks like.'

'It's a woman?'

'That's all I know. I'm drawing a blank with the rest. I don't even know what colour hair she has, how old she is. I know where she's *sat* – in a double seat, on her own, with her back to the direction of travel, on the right, halfway up Coach F, sort of slouched, with one foot out in the aisle – but as to her appearance, I'm getting nothing. Help me out here, Heobah. What's she look like?'

'I don't know.'

'Then I don't see how we can continue our story. Unless . . .'

'What?'

'It's the only thing I can think of.' I leaned across the table and took her hands. 'Why don't *you* be her?'

'Me?'

'Why not? You can see the difficulty I'm in. Let's just use you instead.'

'But I'm *here*.'

'We'll put you *there* too.'

'In the story? We can do that?'

'Sure. Just close your eyes. Hang on, I've a better idea . . .' I went over to the trunk and found a scarf, tied it round her head. 'Right, now you're there.'

'In Coach F?'

'Till the blindfold comes off. Agreed?'

'I'll give it a go. I'm sat, how?'

'With your back to the direction of travel. Just like you are now.'

'And my leg out in the aisle – like this?'

'Perfect.'

This was going rather well. She was speaking more loudly

215

now, as if from some other place, the darkness conferred by the blindfold narrowing the distance between the here and now of the compartment and the nocturnal setting of my story.

'It is night,' I began, lowering my voice for atmosphere. 'Clear skies overhead. A full moon.'

'It's not full,' said Heobah.

'You can see it?'

'Yeah. It's not full.'

'What is it then?'

'I don't know. I don't know what they call it. It's sort of lemon-shaped?'

'Let's call it a half-moon.'

'But it's more than half.'

'I don't know what the word is for that. Can we just agree on half?'

'You said I could participate.'

'Fine. A moon shaped like a lemon. A moon shaped like a lemon, on a clear winter's night. The sliding door opens, and in comes—'

I stopped. I was going to say me, but I'd only just gotten Heobah settled in the story – to throw myself in now would be ham-fisted. And didn't I need to already be there? Wasn't that how it had been?

'Well? Who comes in?'

'Er, the trolley.'

'Oh.'

'Yeah, it's just the trolley. You want anything from the trolley?'

'Not really, no.'

'So you decline, nodding politely, and the trolley goes on its way.'

'Actually, I think I will.'

'OK, the trolley comes back. Tea, coffee, savoury snack?'

'On second thoughts no. I don't really feel like anything. I don't really feel, I don't really, what I mean is' – there was a change in her demeanour here, her head drooping, her voice weary and distant, cracked, laboured – 'there doesn't seem . . . much point.'

'In what?'

'There doesn't seem much point to anything, these days.'

This was interesting: the melancholia was out of character, and the temporal slip suggested by *these days*, like her use of the word *since* last night, seemed to imply a concealed past.

'It's odd.'

'What's odd?'

'I've never felt like this before.'

'Like what?'

'I don't know. I don't know how to describe it.'

'You mean, how you feel in the story, or how you feel now?'

This was a clumsy interruption, almost severing the connection I'd opened up between the here and now and the there and then. It was beginning to feel like a séance, as she absented herself from our compartment and inhabited that former Coach F. But she was a fragile medium.

'What happens next, Heobah?'

'How should I know,' she said, regaining control, 'you're the one telling the story. I'm just participating.'

'And you're doing well. I don't think we could have got this far without you. To tell you the truth, Heobah, I'm not much of a storyteller.'

But she wouldn't have it. Her trust in the imaginary, her appetite for narration, was such that she'd sooner settle for the world's worst story than have none at all. I could have told her anything. I could have told her the one about The Glass of Water That Gradually Evaporated, or The Empty Room In Which Nothing Ever Occurred, and she would have been content.

'Tell me,' I said, guiding her more directly, 'tell me, is there anyone else in the carriage? Somebody you know?'

'Should there be?'

'I hope so, because that's the title of my story, Heobah.'

'What is?'

'"Somebody I Know".'

'That's what it's called?'

'You don't like it?'

'As in, somebody I know or somebody *you* know?' Her head moved as the woman she was pretending to be in my story started to scan the faces in the carriage. 'I don't see anyone.'

'Look again.'

'Nope. Nobody I know.'

I guided her to where I'd been sat that evening: 'On the other side, Heobah, on the right as you look. Over by the window, facing you.'

'A man?'

'Yeah. You might have to get up.'

She got to her feet, craning her neck in the direction of where I'd been sat that evening, the Standard Class carriage of my story now superimposed onto the present First Class coach. She was visualising its interior without any trouble, her gaze travelling over the other passengers till finally she locked onto something:

'You mean *him*?'

'Who? Who is it that you see?'

She nailed my appearance precisely, insofar as it's possible to be precise about a generic looking man: the charcoal grey suit, the thinning hair, the new shirt I had on that day, the pink one with the white cuffs that I'd bought in an attempt to make myself less generic. I couldn't be certain that the man in her mind's eye was me. Part of me hoped it wasn't, for she seemed underwhelmed.

'Well, what do you think?'

'This is the Somebody I Know?'

'You don't recognise him?'

'He's kind of familiar. But then, so are a lot of people.'

'What's he doing?'

'He keeps looking. But every time I look back he looks away.'

'That's natural, I suppose.'

'Is it?'

'He's curious.'

'Why's he not come over then?'

'Curious but shy.'

'Shy?'

'Listen, I've an idea. Why don't you go over to him?'

'I can do that?'

'It's a story, Heobah, we can do anything.'

'And say what?'

'I don't know. What's that he's reading, or pretending to read?'

'A book.'

'Ask him about that.'

'Ask him *what* about that?'

'You'll think of something.'

'Hang on. What's happening now?'

'What? What's he doing?'

'It's not him, it's me. I don't feel so good again.'

'What's wrong?'

'I don't know.'

'You want me to take the blindfold off?'

'No. It's alright. Oh, hang on, I'm getting up.'

'You're going over there?'

'I'm getting up, I'm getting my bag from the overhead rack, getting my things together—'

'You're going over to sit with him?'

'I'm walking past him. We're slowing, coming to a halt.'

'The train? The train's stopping?'

'I'm going through the sliding door, into the vestibule.'

'No! Go back!'

'The door's opening. I'm stepping out onto the platform.'

'Go back! Get back on the train!'

'I am on the platform. The doors close. The train moves off. I am alone. Alone on the platform.' Her voice was different now. Calmer. Calm but resigned. 'I am moving into the ticket hall. I am walking out into the night . . .'

'I'm taking the blindfold off.'

'No.' She slapped my hands away. 'I need to stay with her. I need to stay with her till the end. Till it's over.'

I was not privy to the rest. How can I put it? She *saw* what happened but did not recount it, acting it out with her body instead. Now and then her head moved as she looked up at the sky, and occasionally her breath shuddered. At one point she turned her collar up, blew on her hands. Finally, she began rocking, gently at first, on the edge of her seat, then violently, before pitching herself forward. I had to act quickly, springing up to catch her before she fell to the floor.

4

TO SAY THAT Heobah was shaken was an understatement, and little was said during the next few hours as we continued through First Class, covering a good thirty sections, hundreds of carriages, all told. At around 18:30 she came out of her shell, aided by the natural sociality of Going Forward. She understood, I think, as we slumped into another compartment further downtrain, that our story, though beginning in whimsical fashion, had culminated in truth, a personal truth but one that must have felt entirely new to her, rooted as it was in a life now forgotten. I hoped she would be willing to share the rest: what had happened after she'd left the platform and gone off into the night.

These sections of First Class were much busier, and we had to share our compartment with another passenger, a bald man with an expression halfway between a sneer and a smile, who seemed familiar to me. I noticed that where Companion would normally have curled up on the seat, or started to clean himself, he stayed by the door on entering the compartment, staring at the stranger till he left. This was another of his little tricks, the ability to make folk feel uncomfortable simply by fixing them with his expressionless expression that somehow contained all possible expressions. Heobah called it 'mind control'.

'One of the Count's men,' she said, after he'd seen the bald man off.

'I've seen him before.'

'Where?'

'I don't know. Somewhere uptrain.'

I thought it might be the man from the Harbinger's carriage, the one who'd handed me my stuff, but I couldn't be certain. It would've made sense. He and the others had all played their part in ejecting me from that coach, and might have been personally tasked by the Count with sending me forwards rather than backwards. It was not inconceivable that the bald man had been further assigned to monitor my progress, and that more of his cohorts awaited me downtrain.

I'd forgotten about all this in the excitement of our narrative experiment. I wondered what bearing it had on Heobah's arrangements with Marlowe. I would only know after she told me the rest: where she had gone in that blindfold.

There was much to tell, and the telling of it was hard, lacking as she did the vocabulary to describe what had happened, but as we settled in for another night, laying down the bedding and picking at what the previous occupants of our compartment had left in the fridge, she started to open up. I tried to say as little as possible, fearing that if I filled in too much of the silence I would pervert the meaning of what she was trying to say by turning it into what I wanted to hear. But it was difficult, for there were things that were surely once familiar to her, things whose names she now appeared to have forgotten. Much of what she recounted was of a general nature, and it fell to me to infer the particularities through gentle probing.

'The oddest place,' she began, groping for words, 'the oddest place.'

'In what way?'

'Buildings.' She stared at me with incomprehension as she said that word. 'Buildings, everywhere. Nothing but buildings.

And road.' She placed a hand on Companion, who was coiled up on her lap, purring like a nuclear reactor. 'So much road. With more road cutting across, leading off all ways right and left.'

'A town.'

'A what?'

'A town. A place where people live.'

'But the train? They live there. Here.'

'Also in buildings, Heobah. There were lights on in the buildings?'

'I avoided the ones with lights, took those roads that seemed darkest.'

'Took them where?'

'Away from the light.'

'Where to?'

'How were we to know? We had left the train. We'd been . . .'

'What?'

She looked at me gravely: '*Thrown off.*'

'But you left of your own accord. Got up, stepped out onto the platform. No one forced you. No one ejected you from the train.'

'We were compelled to leave,' said Heobah. 'Higher powers commanded.'

'Where did you go?'

'We took the dark roads till the buildings disappeared.'

'And then?'

'The buildings disappeared and the road was single. The road was single and the air hurt. Air that pressed the skin and made our hair stand up.'

'Yes, it was winter, wasn't it? I remember now.'

'Winter?'

'Never mind. Where did it lead you?'

'There was darkness on both sides for a long time. And then a different kind of darkness, on the right, just up ahead.'

'I don't follow – it got darker?'

'No.'

'Lighter, then?'

'No. More solid.'

'Solid?'

'There was a door.'

'In the darkness?'

'The thing the darkness turned into.'

'Describe it.'

'It was large. Large and tall. As tall as some things are long. Do you see?'

'I think so, yes. You went inside?'

Heobah nodded.

'What was there?'

'Seats. Long seats, like the ones here in First Class, but longer and made of wood. With a space down the middle, like the aisle here in Standard. And windows either side. Again, like in Standard. But with colours that shone in the light of the moon. We did not know they were windows at all till we saw the moon beyond. It was then that we knew we were inside. Inside a building.'

'What else?'

It was now that she closed her eyes, trying to sharpen the image: 'At one end, a large table, a table made of – well, what looked like a piece of a mountain.'

'Stone.'

'And above it a man.'

'There was someone else there?'

'A man, also of mountain. Up on the wall behind the table, sort of hanging.'

'Ah.'

'And I spoke to him.'

'Really? What did you say?'

'I told him to come down. I don't know why I said that. I don't know how long he'd been up there. Silly really. I mean, why come down now, just for me? Come down, I said, Come down here where I can see you.'

'And he stayed where he was.'

'He seemed to prefer it.'

'This thing he was attached to, Heobah, the thing you said he was hanging from: it was shaped like this?' I made a cross with my fingers.

'Yes. Yes it was.'

'A church, Heobah. It was a church.'

She frowned, her hand stopping, mid-stroke, on Companion's head.

'A place of religious worship. That's where you were. Sorry. Continue.'

'I turned away. Tried to leave.'

'Back to the road?'

'Where else was there to go?'

'But you couldn't. You couldn't, could you?'

'I got as far as the door. But there was another.'

'Another door? Where?'

'Off to the side.'

'By the entrance – the place where you'd come in?'

'Yes.'

'And you took it?'

'There was no choice. Higher powers—'

'Commanded. Yes, I understand. Go on.'

'It was darker through there. And the wall fell away.'

'How do you mean, fell away?'

'It's hard to describe. It was there at the bottom, near the floor, but in the middle there *was* no wall.'

'No wall?'

'Not at first. Then my eyes adjusted and I saw that it was zig-zag-shaped.'

'Steps. A staircase.'

The word perplexed her. Despite the aspect of the surrounding land, the gorges we'd gone through, the climb into the mountains, she appeared to have no concept of vertical travel, having seen steps only in quantities of two, those leading from the train doors onto the track, probably unused by most passengers.

I held her hand as she edged towards the same conclusion for a second time that day, ascending the spiral staircase to the belfry and out onto the parapet, inching along with her back to the spire, the wind blowing in her face. Again, she started to rock as she imparted the final facts, but this time I was ready and I held her back from the brink.

This experiment was a success – if you define success as getting more than you bargained for. My intentions were noble, but I'd underestimated the consequences of messing with another passenger's memory, and resolved not to repeat my act, to view our acquaintance as beginning here on the 8:08 and forget about the past. And I too had been burned by the experience. When our hands touched and I coaxed her back from the edge, I felt the same sensation I'd felt when Marlowe had seized my hand and drawn from me things not intended for disclosure, only this time the current was moving in the other direction, with me as the conduit. It felt vaguely

Promethean, like I was channelling something I ought not to be, and only when contact was broken did Heobah open her eyes.

5

MONDAY MORNING ON the 8:08 was not nearly as gloomy as one might think – no gloomier than any of the previous Monday mornings of my adult life. I used to fear its pulverising advent – the icy reconciliation with one's job, like choosing to marry again the woman you'd divorced 48 hours earlier – but here it just slaps you with an open hand and waits for you to get back up.

When I gave Companion his breakfast – the last of the salmon – it did not even occur to me that there was nothing for us. Heobah and I ought to have been hungry – we'd eaten nothing yesterday – but there'd been a steady decrease in my appetite since my initial hunger of the first two days, and Heobah's indifference to food was more firmly established. She'd picked at her meal in the Restaurant Car, and wasn't bothered this morning when, rummaging through my overnight bag, she found nothing but a few pots of UHT milk and the bottle of Clynelish 14-year-old from the Junior Collector Selection Box.

'What's this?' she said, pulling out the chess set her comrade had given me.

'A gift from Marlowe,' I said. 'Fancy a game?'

'I don't know how to play.'

'I'll teach you.'

There's nothing more exhausting than teaching chess to a novice. Heobah had the usual issues with the knight's move and the *en passant* rule, but it was the king that came in for most criticism. She couldn't believe it was the weakest piece. He ought to be out there, tearing around, not cowering behind a rank of pawns.

'The king should be able to do anything,' she said, lifting him from his place by the queen. 'The king should be able to do this' – she placed it on my head – 'or this' – she took it from my head and dropped it down her T-shirt – 'or this' – she took it from her T-shirt and placed at the side of the board.

'What's the king doing now?' I asked.

'Watching. That's what he does most of the time anyway. He's just being more honest about it. But I like this business of promoting a pawn to a queen.'

'Yes – but only by getting it to the eighth rank.'

'So, let's do it. Let's promote them *all*.'

Such an endgame would be quite something, I conceded, but more difficult by far than achieving checkmate. She lost interest after this, and I won in about fifteen moves. As I was putting the pieces away, there was a sharp intake of breath when she noticed the backgammon markings on the board's inside:

'Is that what I think it is?'

'You want to play?'

'You think we should?'

'Why shouldn't we?'

I repurposed the chess pieces, setting them up on the points. She claimed to have played it only once before, but took to it immediately when I refreshed her on the rules, narrowly losing the first two games but winning the next two.

'Seems this is your natural game,' I said, setting the board up for a decider. 'Yet you never play?'

'No one does.'

'What's that?'

'No one plays.'

'Why?'

'You mean you don't know?'

She drew my attention to the 'X' that someone had gouged into the board's leather interior.

'Yes, I noticed that. A crass piece of vandalism.'

'Oh, it's more than that. You really don't know?'

'What?'

'You don't, do you? It's a warning.'

'A warning – to whom?'

'Us. Everyone. I thought everyone knew.'

'Knew what?'

'Backgammon: it's not permitted.' She hesitated, unsure of letting me into her confidence. 'You were right the first time. It *is* my natural game. The natural game of the 8:08. Or should be. *Would be*, if we had our way.'

'We? As in Marlowe and you?'

'And the others.'

She gave me to understand that the game was blasphemous. She didn't use that word – she did not know what it meant – but I inferred from what she told me, as we played out the decider, that the spectacle of two opponents trying to reach the home board resembled the objectives of the train's more heretical factions.

'Don't you see?' she said, rolling another double six: 'though it appears to both players that they are going forward, in reality one is going *backwards*.'

'From the perspective of the other player, you mean?'

'Yes.'

'Strictly speaking, backwards and forwards are relative terms here. But yes, they are travelling in *opposite* directions.'

I looked at the cross again: 'So for that reason alone, back-gammon's taboo?'

'I'm sorry?'

'Idolatrous. A graven image.'

I tried to explain, recounting the story of the Ten Commandments, the primacy of word over image in Jewish, Islamic, Protestant faiths, and although she only partially understood, she was adamant that what we were doing now was far more serious.

'You do realise,' she said, 'that we could be *thrown off* for this?' She mouthed these last words silently, with a dread that seemed unwarranted.

'On whose authority?'

'By order of the Count.'

'For playing a game? In which counters happen to go in opposite directions? Who cares?'

'But we could be *thrown off*.' Again, she mouthed these words silently, fearing the walls had ears.

I looked again at the cross on the board, reminiscent of those scored into altarpieces by Protestant iconoclasts. 'But the *Count* goes back.'

'Of course he does. He has Dispensation.'

'Dispensation? From whom?'

'Himself.'

'But what about the sisters?'

'What sisters?'

'The two sisters in the Restaurant Car. I'm forgetting, you didn't see them. They left before you arrived.'

'Describe them.'

'They were wearing crimson dresses. Wigs. Stank of perfume. Had rather a lot to say to Marlowe, as I recall.'

'What of them?'

'Well, they went back too.'

'They had *Dispensation?*'

'It looks like it.'

'Then it's started.'

'What's started?'

'The Count. He's making his move. He's started recruiting.'

'Making his move for what?'

'Control of the train.'

'I thought he already had that.'

'I must speak with Marlowe. We must locate the Guard. If possible, we must locate the Guard, reach the Driver (praise be upon him).'

It was the first time anyone had referred to the Driver, and Heobah made a figure-of-eight sign on her chest as she praised him.

'And why – why must we find the Guard?'

'*Locate* the Guard.'

'Why must we locate the Guard, reach the Driver?'

'Praise be upon him,' added Heobah. 'Isn't it obvious? If what you say is true, that the sisters have Dispensation, then the Count is making not for the front of the train, as we assumed, but for the *rear*. Lucky we put a man there.'

'And what, exactly, is at the rear of the train?'

I thought again of the old 8:08, the rear of which I still remembered fondly; of the daily tussle with Ramsden over seat 77a; of the lockable door behind Coach B where the trolley operators took their breaks. How much of the current train lay beyond that door? And was it more of the same, or another class below Standard – 'Sub-standard', as it might be?

'Nobody knows,' said Heobah, when I put these questions to her.

'Not even the Count?'

'Not even him.'

'Can he be stopped? You said you had a man there.'

Heobah got up and started putting on her shoes. 'We sent one there, just in case.'

'Only one?'

'Yes: one in Standard and another here in First Class.'

'Marlowe?'

She shook her head.

'Then who?'

Heobah went out into the gangway to check we were alone. When she came back in, she knelt down before me and took my hands in hers: '*He who has the blue pill, he shall go aft; he who has white shall go fore.*'

'Me?'

She repeated the incantation, making the figure-of-eight on her chest.

'And this chap in Standard, he got the blue pill?'

'Guard willing, he'll worm his way into the Count's confidence, accompany him to the rear.'

'And then?'

'He will do what he must.'

I waited for her to continue, but she looked away, silent, and I pictured my more heroic counterpart wrestling his antagonist on the vestibule floor. Part of me was glad to have been spared that showdown, but I'd be lying if I didn't admit my pride was wounded. I was not considered a man of action. I was not 'blue-pill material'. Instead, I was the emissary, the errand boy insinuating himself into the bourgeoisie of First Class, ghosting down the aisles and gangways while this other chap sacrificed himself 'aft'.

'Come on,' said Heobah, 'put your shoes on. And don't forget this.'

She handed me the bus inspector's cap from the dressing-up trunk. It went well with the cavalry jacket, which I wore open over the sweater from the lady in Coach Z. The breeches were a little tight, but Heobah assured me these clothes were an improvement on my own, and women are usually right about these things.

6

FROM THIS POINT on, the train's architecture began to change more radically, First Class evolving from the regulation carriages of twelve compartments into disparate arrangements of First and Standard Class coaches, and others that seemed to have no official designation, all letters now out of alphabetic sequence. The compartment we'd just been in was located in Coach F, and as we passed into the vestibule, I noticed that the next one was Coach K. This was followed by Coach E, then another Coach E, then Coach P. I thought this a coincidence, but decided to write down the letters in my folio, and five carriages later I had the following:

KEEPGOING

The letters of the next coaches made no additional words, the only other thing of note being a solitary Coach A – the only one I ever came across on the entire train – but I continued to record them anyway in case they should prove significant.

The second thing I noticed was the dramatic fall in population. The part of the train where we'd spent the night had seemed busy, but with each subsequent section the prospect of seeing anyone at all seemed to diminish.

An hour later we came to an abandoned buffet car, not unlike those on the old 8:08, one of several hereabouts whose only purpose appeared to be to connect one part of the train to another. As we took a table seat by the counter, I asked Heobah how many people she thought the Count had recruited.

'Who knows?' she said. 'As many as it takes.'

'And once they've helped him to the rear of the train?'

'You mean, what will become of them?'

She nodded at the scenery rushing past the window.

'He'll throw them off?'

'Once they've served their purpose.'

'But their Dispensation?'

'A temporary privilege.'

'I see. Whereas you—'

'We,' she cut in, 'would bestow it on *everyone*.'

'Dispensation for all.'

'Naturally.' Heobah got up and went behind the counter into the galley kitchen that ran down the left-hand side of the buffet car. 'Fancy a coffee?'

My loss of appetite was now extending to fluids, but I said yes anyway, out of nostalgic fidelity to my old habit of punctuating the day with a stream of hot drinks I never really wanted, and a few minutes later Heobah reappeared with two steaming mugs.

'What does he look like?' I asked, as she sat down again. 'The Guard? How do we recognise him? He'll be wearing a uniform of some sort? Right?'

'I suppose it's possible, yes.'

'You haven't seen him before?'

'No one has.'

I thought again of the Harbinger, the joke he'd had at my expense: *No Guard hereabouts. Not for a while now.*

'So no one has ever made it this far?'

'If they have, no one has ever come back.'

'For obvious reasons.'

Whether the train's unidirectional policy was a mechanism to prevent folk reporting what they had seen in these furthermost coaches was, and still is, a moot point. When I put it to Heobah that few passengers were willing to sacrifice their position to satisfy their curiosity as to what lay downtrain, she said it was more the case that only certain passengers were *destined* to go downtrain.

'You mean, they're chosen?'

'If you like.'

I thought about it. If the train had the ability to prevent us going backwards, maybe it could regulate forward progress. Maybe, one day, you reached a sliding door that refused to open for you and that was it, you were consigned to a particular carriage. In this way, everyone found their place, be it a First Class compartment or a Standard Class coach.

'But the Count? Surely, he exercises his Dispensation.'

'To reach the Guard, you mean?'

'And come back. Or perhaps he's not that bothered.'

'Not bothered about what?'

'Well, you yourself said he's headed for the rear, making his bid for the train there. Might this tell us something?'

'Oh?' Heobah blew on her coffee. 'And what might it tell us?'

'The front of the train – maybe it's not all that?'

'Not all that! Not all that!'

'Maybe it's not as important as you—'

'Take out your chapbook.'

'My what?'

'Your chapbook. It's time we went over some old ground.'

'What do you mean, old ground?'

'Take out your chapbook and turn to page 1.'

'I don't have a chapbook.'

'All passengers are issued with one.'

'Not me.'

Heobah reached across the table and extracted a brown pamphlet from the breast pocket of my cavalry jacket. 'I think we need to remind ourselves exactly what is at stake,' she said, turning to page 1. 'Here, read.'

The text was faded but legible, the capital letters of each paragraph in pseudo-monastic script: '*In the beginning was Guard*,' I began. '*And Guard created the train. And the train was made in Guard's image. And Guard looked down upon the train and saw that it was good. But the train as yet moved not. So Guard created the Driver. And the Driver caused motion in the train. And Guard looked down thereafter on a thing of manifold beauty. Then one day Guard grew sad at the train, which though it pleased Him much, pained Him too, that He must needs look upon it from afar and not partake of His creation. So Guard joined with the Driver, and Driver and Guard were one. And Driver and Guard sealed their bond with a number. And the number is 808.*'

Heobah made the sign of 8 as I finished, then produced another pamphlet. 'Compare it with this,' she said. 'The Count's *Fully Revised & Amended Edition*.'

The first thing I noticed was that it was more professional, the paper stock superior, the ink less faded, the binding more robust. Neither pamphlet had images, just a blank sepia cover bearing the 808 insignia. The insignias were different too. The one from the cavalry jacket had a small gap in the upper loop of the 8, like the 8 on my jumper, while the one on the revised edition was complete.

'The text is identical till the last few pages,' said Heobah. 'See.'

The Count had inserted several extra passages, recasting the scripture in his own Messianic image. I don't have that copy with me now, so I can't quote from it, but I seem to remember that his amendments followed a vaguely Trinitarian line. If the Guard and Driver comprised a holy union, the Count imagined himself a third part of the equation, a sort of go-between. Heobah stared at me, not altogether blankly, when I said it reminded me of the Father, the Son and the Holy Ghost. She appeared to retain some vague Sunday School memory of these things, but I could tell she found the analogy distasteful, and it was quickly countermanded by her own summary of the recent theological shift.

To begin with, she said, the consequences of the Count's scriptural amendments had been minimal, but soon passengers took it upon themselves to collectively enforce a stricter interpretation of canonical law. A significant minority had objected, suspicious of this new zealotry, but these soon dwindled to such a tiny number they kept their resistance secret. Certain recreations were still permitted – Why Not Sneeze?, London or Yorkshire? – while others – backgammon, for example – were frowned on and subsequently banned. The rituals of Going Forward and Shunting, hitherto 'folk' customs undertaken out of affection for the 8:08, became ultra-formalised, especially the latter, passengers now required to show utmost reverence whenever the train came to a halt, where previously they might have stayed in their seats. The Count was particularly obsessed with this. The original chapter and verse has it that regular observance of Shunting is desirable but not mandatory: *he who oftentimes rises*, runs the text in the first version, *he shall receive Guard's grace, but he who rises seldom shall not be forsaken outright, for he who neglects the vestibuling of his personage, he may atone by making good the shortfall in the perpetuity of time, the fullness of which is infinite according to Guard's wisdom* . . . The Count, on the other hand, insisted on mandatory observance of Shunting on pain of – well, I can quote well enough from memory from the revised version I no longer have to hand: *he who omits to rise and vestibule himself, he shall be cast out, he shall be ejected, he shall be Thrown Off.* It wasn't the only infraction that might be penalised thus.

Despite this zero-tolerance with regard to Shunting, in other respects the Count's moral compass swung this way and that. According to his *Fully Revised & Amended Edition*, in certain parts of Standard Class *not* smoking was bad form, and everywhere on the 8:08 alcohol was prohibited on Tuesdays but mandatory on Fridays. And of course, any intimation of backwards motion was *to Guard's love as sulphur to His skin . . . the malefactors hunted down and Thrown Off.* Again, I quote from memory.

Now I saw why Heobah had uttered those words with such dread. On the old 8:08, 'thrown off' suggested, at worst, a run-in with the Transport Police, but here it conveyed something more terminal, like 'beheaded' or 'shot at dawn'. When seen in the context of the passengers' apparent indifference to the surrounding terrain – which I'd noticed as early as the first day and which now seemed more akin to an *unawareness* – it certainly seemed possible that getting thrown off was, for some at least, tantamount to execution. For I suspect that everything exterior to the train is regarded as a sort of void, an *absolute* exterior to the 8:08's absolute interior. If so, one might fear ejection from it as an astronaut fears ejection from a spaceship.

She drew it out longer than necessary, this history of the Count's scriptural perversions, before asking me to refill our coffee cups. When I went behind the counter, I saw Companion disappearing through the door at the far end of the galley kitchen, trying to show me the way.

'Not yet, Companion, not yet. Give us a moment.'

I followed him into the vestibule and beckoned him to come back, but he just sat there blinking, all four paws gathered under his body. I noticed that he was sat, not directly on the carpet, but on a small black rectangle, which I recognised as my folio. It was then that I made my mistake. Before going to retrieve it, I should have propped the door open. But it slammed behind me before I could make it back, and when I tried the handle, it was locked.

On the old 8:08 there's a gangway that runs alongside the kitchen, to the left, back into the buffet area. But here the wall went all the way across: the door was the only way back. I banged and shouted, but I knew Heobah had planned it this way. The fact that my overnight bag was nowhere to be seen, that she had deemed it surplus to my requirements when removing my folio and placing it here, was just as significant as the note I found inside when I opened it:

> See you at the front one day.
> Or the rear.
> Thank you, and good luck.
>
>   H.

V

THE GUARD

1

RELATIONS BETWEEN COMPANION and myself were frosty in those subsequent coaches, but I bore him no long-term grudge for conspiring to separate me from Heobah. I was more preoccupied by the wording of her note, which seemed to contradict the earlier offence she'd taken when I'd suggested the front of the train was not all that. Having defended it robustly, she now appeared to accord it no more importance than the rear.

We had spent little more than two days together, all told, but it had felt like two months, and I was surprised how quickly I readjusted to life as a single man. Like I say, I soon forgave Companion, whose company I now valued more than ever as we advanced through one deserted coach after another. But he was not the only distraction from my isolation. For the train - who knows, possibly in reward for my choosing the solitude of these far-flung coaches over the communality of the earlier ones - now bestowed a new privilege: from this point onwards, the sliding doors no longer closed behind me. It was true that I was still quarantined - that kitchen door would remain forever locked - but it felt like an honour nevertheless.

The other change was in the train's livery. Not only was there no alphabetised system, or any system at all, to the designation of coaches, there was no aesthetic uniformity either, each possessing, as it were, a freestanding vintage. As Companion and I struck out for the Guard on that

Monday afternoon, we seemed to go from the Noughties to the Nineties, from the Eighties to the Seventies, from the Seventies to the Sixties, and back to the current day. Other coaches seemed to hail from the near future, with plasma screens on the backs of the seats, headphone ports in the hand-rests, and other gadgets I couldn't fathom. I recall that one had cat's eyes in the floor that came on as we progressed up the aisle, with a bespoke section at the far end, a walnut coffee table, R&B music piped from hidden speakers, UV lighting under leatherette benches – less like a train carriage than the fuselage of a rapper's private jet. And then the very next coach would be a travesty, an example of the British network at its most abject, half the seats ripped out, racist graffiti scratched into the windows – like the intercity football trains of the past. What else? Yes, there was also the odd 'heritage' coach, buffet cars done out in wood, with gingham tablecloths and glass-fronted food cabinets, that looked like they ought to be yoked to a steam locomotive. And every so often we'd find ourselves in a facsimile of the old Coach B: the designated quiet coach I'd boarded every day of my working life.

This is just a small selection of the full variety. I figured a train of such enormity had to utilise all available rolling stock, and the result was the creation of a sort of no-man's land, a liminal zone between the passenger section and the front. I seemed to pass through every kind of carriage I had ever been in, and the cumulative effect of this was enchanting rather than disorientating. As the sliding door drew back, presenting a fresh spectacle every thirty metres, I now realised that I felt privileged to be alone rather than daunted. I hadn't yet completed a week on board, but the anxiety of that first morning, my panic at being on the wrong train, felt absurdly remote. There was a new bond with my environment. I felt no less at home here than in my own flat or my own office cubicle. I was no longer bothered, moreover, by those unbidden thoughts that still found expression in my mind from time to time, no longer caring to distinguish between these locomotive assists and the products of my own intellect. I was already confident that the loss of memory suffered by my fellow passengers would not be visited on me, at least not to the same extent; and frankly, that which was jettisoned has not been missed. I made no attempt to recover my name. In fact, I toyed with the idea of adopting 'Paul Carver' as my permanent appellation, so indifferent was I to my actual identity, an indifference that was beginning to extend to my physical attributes, which seemed to me no worthier of comment than the wider locomotive facture. On those occasions when I drew into a toilet cubicle and saw my reflection in the mirror, I did not regard it as a representation of a separate organism but as proof of its absorption into the train's fabric.

And though I still thought of it occasionally, I did not hanker after the old life: the trudge to the station, the walk to the office, the blue-sky thinking of Dan Coleman and men of his ilk. As for Mark Ramsden, he had fallen silent; though my phone continued to display 52% battery power and an intermittent signal, it was surely inconceivable that the screen would ever light up with my colleague's name. If Ramsden was still on board, then he'd better fend for himself. My priorities had changed. The old life was gone. Over.

Yet in some ways it returned with the appearance of the Guard. For there was one aspect of the old life, conspicuous by its absence from my account so far, that came hurtling back into the equation when I at last made his acquaintance.

Up until now, there had been no internet coverage at all on the 8:08. I ought to have noticed this earlier, but I never used it on the way to work, and not till the third day did I see that it was one long digital blackspot. Or maybe access is restricted? Whatever, I can understand, now, why the Guard is never seen. From what I can gather, he spends most of his time online. Where the passengers have no internet, for the Guard there is *only* internet. As we shall see, this is far from saying that he had the whole of cyberspace at his disposal, but the portion of it that was available to him kept him sufficiently occupied that he retained only the faintest recollection of his status as railwayman.

I wasn't to know, but I'd already strayed into the area under his remit. Ostensibly, his domain covers all carriages from the Driver's cab to the buffet car where Heobah and I parted, but he rarely ventures down that far. As for the rest of the train, it's of no more importance to him than the decorative tail of a kite. It's possible he's forgotten it exists. It's possible that, of everyone on board, the Guard is the least qualified to *be* Guard. I posit the following theory: that his indifference to the vast majority of the 8:08 which lay behind him is a result of the amnesia caused by his own progress downtrain. Suffice to say, he as about as far from the deity described in Heobah's chapbook as I myself am from that transcendent being. But let us not stand on ceremony. Let us make haste to his quarters.

2

I MAY HAVE given the impression that there were no other passengers between here and the Guard's carriage. This was true in a technical sense. But there was one other *person* who constituted – I was going to say the Guard's 'deputy', but I can't really confer on him the authority of that office. I shall call him the Nincompoop. No other word will do.

There are some who acquire nincompoopery, take pains to learn its craft, and others who are born to it. This fellow was in the second category. Whether his condition was exacerbated by the aforementioned locomotive amnesia is impossible to judge, but I venture to say that he's the happiest shipmate among us. At first I thought he was a figment of my own making. As the time of Going Forward came and went, with none but Companion and myself Going Forward, I thought I kept seeing a figure up ahead, but the lighting in this part of the train was faulty and it could have been my imagination. Was it the Guard? I hoped not. For the person I thought I'd seen was naked from the waist down. As night fell, I stopped seeing this phantom, and when Companion began to flag, throwing glances over his shoulder, I decided we should pull into a table seat and stay there till morning. I'd always deferred to him with regard to when we needed to press on and when we ought to stop, trusting the soundness of his judgement.

At around four o'clock, I was woken by the sound of scampering feet. I was struck by their animal nature, their speed and lightness over the carpet, and I opened my eyes just in time to see a bare arse disappear though the sliding door, well muscled glutes poking out from under the hem of a green jacket, which bore a logo that looked familiar. But I couldn't be sure I hadn't dreamed it, so went back to sleep. Half an hour later, I was woken again, not by his footfall but by a loud, ear-splitting fart. At first, I thought he was blowing on his arm, in time-honoured schoolboy fashion, such was its volume and resonance; but as he paused at the sliding door, he discharged another, which clearly issued from his fundament.

I couldn't let this go. As he disappeared into the vestibule, trailing gas, I was up on my feet, barrelling through the sliding door.

'Stop!'

I pursued him through a dozen vestibules, but he was too quick. I couldn't understand why he wanted to be chased. Even by the standards of the 8:08, his conduct was perplexing. The fact that he kept looking round to check I was following suggested he thought it was a game, and I considered giving up the chase, loath to humour my fleeter-footed quarry and end up making a fool of myself. But I was awake now, and moving surprisingly quickly for a 45-year-old man who'd never done much exercise. It was obvious that he was toying with me. If I stopped, he stopped. If I moved, he moved, maintaining the distance between us, increasing his speed when I gained on him, slowing to let me catch up, chuckling insanely as he peeled off – a contrived, mirthless laughter, like a magpie's.

It was this tactic that did for him. I'd shortened the distance to half a carriage, and as he peeled off, this time he was too quick for his own good and flew straight into the sliding door, before it was fully open.

'You OK?' I said, my irritation turning to concern.

There was no answer. He was prostrate and motionless, apparently out cold. As I bent down to turn him over, I recognised the logo on the back of his jacket: a kangaroo holding a takeaway bag. I'd always felt for those who had to cycle around with big green cubes on their backs, and as I beheld the former Deliveroo employee, the brand was transformed from an emblem of exploitation into something worthier, a symbol of the Nincompoop's athletic prowess.

I stood up and waited for him to come round. Mistake. Just as an impala will play dead when caught by a lion, then bolt off the moment it relaxes its grip, the Nincompoop sprang up and darted into the vestibule as I took my hand away. The speed with which he became upright was astonishing, his dick slapping against his thigh as he bounded past the toilet.

I sat there panting from my pursuit, and a minute later Companion appeared, sauntering down the aisle, haunches shuffling from side to side like the chassis of an old rag'n'bone cart.

Another two hours passed before I established proper contact with the Nincompoop. Dawn had just broken when I tracked him to one of the old-fashioned buffet cars that continued to recur hereabouts. He was bent over the counter at the far end as the sliding door opened, with his back to us, pushing a toy train over the Formica, winding it up and murmuring to himself as he watched it scuttle along. He didn't notice me come in, so I crept towards him by slow degrees till I was only ten feet away. The nostalgic décor of the coach, with its ersatz 50s feel, its gingham wholesomeness, seemed to calm him. In fact, scanning the merchandise, I saw that most of it was actually produced by the KEEP CALM franchise, their slogans

emblazoned everywhere in upper case: KEEP CALM AND
HAVE A CUPPA; KEEP CALM AND HAVE A BISCUIT.
There was even a special edition cider, KEEP CALM AND
GET WASTED.

I maintained my stealthy approach, shuffling forward a
few inches at a time, Companion tucking in behind me, when
suddenly the Nincompoop's train stopped whirring and he
noticed me.

'It's OK,' I said, holding up my hands. 'It's OK.'

'Gad!' he said.

'What's that?'

'Gad! Gad!'

'Sorry, I don't understand. Look, I'm going to come closer.
Is that alright?'

I inched forward some more, careful not to make eye
contact for too long, and offered my hand. The Nincompoop
looked at it quizzically, making a low sound in his chest,
like those teddy bears that go *Baa* when you shake them.
A half-eaten chocolate bar lay on the counter. He pulled a
piece off and held it out towards me, gooey strings of caramel
hanging down over his knuckles. I guessed him at twenty-five.
He had the sleek body of a dancer, strong and flexible, with
handsome high cheekbones, a jutting brow and thick blond
hair, almost white, and an equally pale complexion bordering
on albino.

'Thank you,' I said, accepting his gift. 'Thank you very
much.' I set the piece of caramel down on the Formica. 'I'll
have this later, I think.'

I thought I should offer him something in return, but
he saved me the bother, coming forward and conducting a
physical examination, running his hands over my body like a
nightclub bouncer, frisking the pockets of the cavalry jacket

and removing my phone, door keys and the chapbook. I was careful to protect my folio, which I still had under my arm.

'Is this by any chance what you're looking for?' I said, producing the ticket I'd purchased last Tuesday morning.

The Nincompoop examined it and shook his head.

'Ah yes, I nearly forgot.'

I found the Mandatory Reservation Coupon, without which my ticket was invalid, and he brought the two halves together, inserting them in his mouth and clipping the card with a tooth specially filed for that purpose, leaving a perfect V-shaped hole.

'Gad!' he said, handing me back my travel documents. 'Gad!'

Another hour's march – we must have covered two hundred coaches – brought us to the Guard's quarters just after eight. The door to his cubicle was identical to the one on my old commute, the one on the left, just before the bicycle carriage, and when the Nincompoop knocked I half-expected to see the same man to whom I'd occasionally complained in the past, about the heating or the behaviour of the other passengers in Coach B.

But the door didn't open. The Nincompoop knocked again, and this time there was a voice within:

'Wait.'

An Irish voice. We waited. Again the Nincompoop knocked, and again the voice answered:

'Wait.'

'Gad!' said the Nincompoop, nodding at the door, 'Gad!'

He knocked a third time and we continued to wait, in silence, for what seemed like an age, the Nincompoop having no English, I having no Nincompoop. The reason for the delay became apparent when we were finally admitted. On the left-hand wall was a large digital clock, and as we entered, the fourth spool on the right was just turning from 7 to 8.

It was now 08:08, precisely one week after embarkation.

3

WHEN I LAID eyes on the man in whom Heobah and Marlowe had invested such hope, I am sorry to say I was crestfallen. That he was topless was not in itself cause for concern, but the fact that his nudity complemented the Nincompoop's was more worrying. For the Guard was wearing the trousers the Nincompoop had discarded, each man sporting one half of a single outfit. The material was the same green and black nylon, faded to the same degree. What brought them together, how they ended up as sentinels of an otherwise deserted section of the 8:08, one that remained ignorant of the wider locomotive struggle, is a mystery I am no nearer solving now than when I first met them, but this sartorial quirk suggested some kind of job-share situation.

The Guard's cubicle was tiny, six feet wide and eight feet long – or so I initially assumed. Just as its door had looked identical to the one on the old 8:08, its interior was a virtual facsimile of that little office, a single square yard of grey moulded plastic for a desk, a swivel chair and a small filing cabinet, the only difference being a curtain at the far end, which appeared to conceal some sort of changing area. There was barely enough room for one, let alone three, especially since the Guard himself was massive. He had none of the trappings of a conventional railwayman, but his height and heavy build conferred natural authority, and I could well understand that once he had laid claim to the title of 'Guard' few would be willing or able to challenge him. He was even taller than Monroe, his physique somewhere between a Channel-swimmer's and a circus strongman's. His head was bowed as he emerged from behind the curtain to greet me, and at first I put this down to some spinal defect, but it became apparent, as he maintained this posture throughout our early acquaintance, that he could not extend himself to his full height anywhere on board. This must have caused him immense irritation, and was probably a factor in how he spent his days, which was lying down for the most part.

He did not offer me a seat, for there was just the one chair, and I was relieved when he tucked it under the desk, inferring that our business lay elsewhere, hopefully somewhere less claustrophobic. But neither he nor the Nincompoop seemed in any hurry, their lack of urgency contradicting the ritualistic nature of my entrance, exquisitely timed as it had been. The difference in the stature of the two men added to the comedy of their shared outfit, the Nincompoop's jacket too big, the Guard's trousers too small, barely reaching his ankles, as though they had purloined these garments from a third man of intermediate size. Two more disparate castaways you couldn't hope to meet, the Nincompoop lithe and wiry, the Guard not unlike a buffalo in appearance: the dark curls of his hair closely compacted, running into his beard, which in turn ran into his chest, his head indistinct from his body. He looked more Greek than Irish, his skin cured in hot climates, and when he stood next to his colleague, the Nincompoop looked like a rind that been carved off him, such was the pallor of his complexion. It was impossible to imagine him as a child. He looked like he had always been his current age, which I estimated at fifty-five.

'You've done well,' he said, slapping the Nincompoop's arse.

The Guard reached into a drawer and took out a small plastic train. It was identical to the one the Nincompoop already had, but he took possession of it with the excitement of someone who had never seen such an object, discarding his other train and winding up this new acquisition, watching the wheels turn with intense curiosity.

'And now,' he said, turning to me, 'I think we shall step into my office.'

Like Marlowe's, the Guard's conversational style was whimsically tangential but raised to a much higher power of verbosity, probing non-existent depths and splitting the finest of hairs. By far and away his most annoying habit was his use of misleading figures of speech. His office, for example, was not so much something we 'stepped into' as descried after half an hour's walk. Naturally, I thought we were already in it, but it turned out that the cubicle was not a cubicle at all; as he drew back the curtain, a long corridor was revealed, extending further than the eye could see.

The Guard shoved his feet into two battered moccasins, and threw some things from the drawer into a carrier bag. 'I've been expecting you,' he said. 'At least, I've been expecting *someone*.'

The corridor was the only part of the train not subdivided, the space between the carriages continuous here, and it reminded me, in its bareness, of the old 8:08's bicycle carriage, into which I'd sometimes poked my nose; but there were no racks, nothing to tie anything to, no clues as its function. There was nothing at all between our current location and whatever was over the horizon, and for the first time the gradient of the surrounding land registered on the train's interior, the vanishing point pitching up and down as we moved towards it.

It was brighter here, and better ventilated, skylights open at regular intervals, not unlike the ones you used to get on coaches, the air fresher than when I had poked my head out several days before. The temperature outside had been no different to the train's interior then, but I could feel a definite draught now.

The Nincompoop, already gambolling on ahead, now stopped, pacing up and down in a state of great excitement. The Guard took a rubber ball from his plastic bag, threw it as hard as he could, and the Nincompoop bolted after it, with Companion in tow.

'You'll forgive me,' he said, 'if ask to see your ticket?'

'Your colleague has already inspected it.'

'A formality, you understand?'

I produced my ticket and he verified the indentation of his colleague's tooth, adding his own crinkled variant with a specially adapted incisor.

'Your travel documents appear to be in order. By the way, I must commend your punctuality. I cannot abide lateness.'

'No?'

'There is only one thing worse than lateness.'

'And what is that?'

'Earliness.'

'You expect people to be exactly on time?'

'Is it asking too much?'

'Possibly.'

'Then I shall continue to ask it,' said the Guard, pulling his pipe from his underpants and knocking the bulb on his heel, 'for it is better to ask too much than too little, so it is. And with respect to moving from one place to another, it is an unforgivable negligence to present oneself either before or after the appointed hour. Any man armed with an accurate chronometer has no business committing such an infraction.'

'And if his watch shows a different time to yours?'

The Guard stopped and turned towards me: 'I'm not sure I follow.'

'I mean, how do you decide whose is correct: your watch or his?'

'In such cases,' said the Guard, filling his pipe with tobacco obtained from another section of his underpants, 'an average reading must be taken between his time and yours, and the resulting figure newly designated as the appointed hour.'

I reminded him that we'd been a few minutes early.

'We shall let that pass, so we shall! The important thing is that our *faces* met at the specified time. I can see that yours is a *good* face. At least not the worst I've beheld this side of Purgatory. But what of your hands?' He pulled me towards him by the wrists, turning my palms to the ceiling, stroking each one tenderly. 'As I suspected: writer's hands. You'll do. You'll do all right, so you will.'

The Guard took out a box of matches and lit his pipe, the flame leaping up from the bowl, the smoke clinging to his beard.

'That's a relief to hear,' I said, pulling out my own tobacco, 'but I'd like to get straight to the point, I think.'

The Guard stopped and turned to me again. 'No one said anything about a, about a – what did you call it?'

'A point. I think the sooner we discuss what is to be done the better.'

This was a misjudgement on my part. The Guard's ritualistic greeting, his careful timing of my entry into his cubicle, the diligence with which he'd examined my travel documents – all this had kindled the hope that he might be cognisant of events happening elsewhere uptrain, that news of the drive for

Universal Dispensation had reached him, and that he therefore knew the reason for my house call. But he showed no inclination to urgency, and I felt it would be better to get to know him, ascertain the extent of his knowledge, before engaging him on the subject of reaching the Driver.

'I'm here to help,' I equivocated, 'however you see fit.'

He seemed happy with this. 'And not before time. You had me worried for a minute there. The last man was fecking *eejit*.'

'The last man?'

'These interns they keep sending me. But you're different, I can see that.'

I reiterated that I was here to help. I felt I had to strike the right note to win his confidence. If that meant acknowledging myself as his subordinate, so be it.

'Grand.' He bent down to light my cigarette for me, torching most of it into the ether. 'That's grand.'

The Nincompoop came back with the rubber ball and dropped it at my feet.

'Be my guest,' said the Guard.

I threw it as hard as I could, and off he bounded, followed by Companion, more uncertainly this time. He did not know what to make of this latest human proposition, who, though biologically similar to the other passengers, appeared to possess animal attributes closer to his own, but I was impressed with how he accommodated the Nincompoop, touched by his warmth as he parried the boisterous affections of his new playmate. Only when the Nincompoop pulled him by the tail did I have to step in. Thereafter, I was happy for them to disappear together almost out of sight, two dots cavorting in the distance.

4

I'D ASSUMED THE Guard's office was close when we set out, but we still hadn't reached it after fifteen minutes. Conversation soon dried up. I had resolved to bide my time, and the Guard was content only to respond to whatever I had to say, never initiating anything himself – as was the case everywhere on the 8:08. Yet when I did speak, he was so adept at keeping a theme in play it seemed that he had introduced it, not I. Like Marlowe, he possessed a singular logic, which, though drawing inspiration from something you had said, soon parted company from the common-sense spirit in which you had meant it; but his trajectories were more disarming, and I had to watch every word, for there was no telling where it would lead. Only now that I'd reached the Guard, in whom the train's verbal anomalies were most pronounced, did I see the importance of how one *began* a conversation. It was impossible to go back, start again. There was no possibility of retraction on the 8:08. Once you opened your mouth, you were committed to a single discursive route, just as you were committed to a single physical one.

'So I'm not the first to knock on your door then?' I offered casually, after a long silence.

As soon as I said it I regretted it. I was now trapped in a part of the train with someone who possessed the ability to overpower me, dominate me, detain me against my will, and anything hinting at the fate of my predecessors was surely a theme to be avoided. Others had been here before me – the Guard had said as much – but where were they now and what had become of them? Fortunately, at that moment the Nincompoop returned, and my question was lost in the rustle of the Guard's trousers as he bent down to pick up the ball.

'What was that?' he said, throwing it as far as he could.

'Oh, nothing.'

'Believe me, I know nothing when I hear it, and it was not nothing that I heard.'

'Really, it's not important.'

'There is little that's not important, to my knowledge. And I should warn you that my knowledge of what's not important is considerable.'

'I don't doubt it.'

'It easily exceeds my knowledge of what is. Important, I mean. Now tell me.'

'Honestly, it was nothing.'

'It was not nothing or you would not have bespaked it.'

Those movies where characters invent something that rhymes with what they wished they hadn't said – that's what I should've done but I couldn't think of anything.

'There's something you should know,' I said, stalling.

'I'll be the judge of that.'

'It's kind of embarrassing, actually.'

'You have a severe form of venereal disease?'

'No.'

'You wish to confess to an appalling crime?'

'No.'

'You have literally minutes to live – is that what you're trying to tell me?'

'No. I – I talk to myself.'

It was all I could come up with. And it wasn't untrue.

The Guard stopped, gripped me by the cheeks and pulled me towards him. 'You are in the habit of communing with your own personage? Is that what you're saying?'

'Yes.'

'Aloud?'

'I'm afraid so.'

He laughed, a long and protracted heaving of the shoulders, all air and no giggle, with a witch's cackle at the end: 'That's it?'

'It's only fair you know. I do it rather a lot.'

'Doesn't everyone?'

'In my experience, no.'

'I beg to differ. The overwhelming majority of folk talk *only* to themselves. All those men and women who claim to be addressing external minds are in actuality addressing their own.'

Maybe he was right. How many conversations could I recall in which the other person wasn't simply waiting for me to finish, before saying what they were going to say anyway?

'It's an indispensable skill,' continued the Guard, 'especially to a man like yourself.'

'A man like myself?'

'Being as you are a writer.'

'I should make it clear that I'm not a professional writer.'

The Guard bent down to pick up the ball. 'An amateur?'

'I suppose so.'

He slapped me on the back, almost sending me sprawling. 'Even better! It's the professionals you've to watch out for. It's them you've to keep an eye on. Oh you'll do. You'll do all right.'

I did well to conceal my curiosity about the others who had made it this far. I wasn't sure, now, if I wanted to know what had happened to these – what had he called them? – 'interns'. Had these individuals also been 'chosen'? Given a white pill and sent downtrain? Or were they merely a smattering of naturally feckless folk who'd wandered too far and lost their minds as a consequence of advancing to these latitudes? But I wasn't so curious as to risk colouring my relations with the Guard. Better to feign indifference for now and excel in whatever task he set me to. I was to be a writer, that much I knew, but a writer of what?

Eventually we came to a halt before a steel security door, a barrier that seemed all the more imposing for our having embarked on a steep incline. As the Guard punched the buttons of the brass keypad, it had the appearance of something bearing down on him in defiance of his great bulk, a labyrinth chiding its minotaur.

When the door swung open, I might have expected anything after the eclecticism of the earlier coaches, but I wasn't prepared for the interior that lay beyond, which was much warmer and stuffier than the ventilated space through which we had just passed. It was a converted Standard Class carriage completely unlike any other on the train. On both sides of the aisle, in place of passenger seats and overhead racks, ran a row of plywood booths, a desktop computer and a swivel chair at each. In place of the windows was an unpainted plasterboard wall, with the screws still showing. It was difficult to make out anything else at first – there was only a single flickering strip light – but as my eyes adjusted I could see a chest-high veneer counter at the far end, behind it a stack of electronic junk, old PCs, discarded printers and an enormous photocopier with the lid up. I could have been wrong, but it looked to me very much like an internet café.

The 'café' part of the operation was moot. There was a kettle on the counter, a jar of instant coffee, with some KEEP

CALM AND HAVE A CUPPA mugs on a filthy old tea towel, and that was it. Throughout the carriage, pinned on the plywood booths, were various photocopied notices testifying to a once thriving business: document-binding services, free legal advice, no-fee consultations for immigrants. On the wall behind the counter was a series of witticisms in the 'You don't have to be mad to work here . . .' vein. 'Stick your chewing gum here please', read one notice. Patrons had duly obliged, covering the surface with different coloured blobs.

In front of the counter was an officially designated Recreation Area where Companion was already making himself at home, pounding the fabric of the orange modular seating that ran along both walls. The right-hand wall of the Recreation Area was a gallery of sorts: pictures of dogs playing pool; a string of faded blue Christmas cards; an old World Cup fixture list from Argentina '78; a tourist-board poster advertising the scenic landmarks of Connemara; miscellaneous oddments culled from the sports pages of Irish newspapers, match reports from the All Ireland Hurling Final of 1972 between Cork and Kilkenny, profiles of prominent Gaelic footballers down the ages. But all this material was dominated by the central exhibit: an enormous Crying Boy portrait, which hung at a 30° angle from a single precarious nail. There was also a long coffee table, piled up with *Encyclopaedia Britannicas* and a special leather-bound *Reader's Digest* edition of *The Complete Works of Vaughan Meredith*, an author I hadn't heard of, but whose novels had been well-thumbed.

On the whole, I was not too dismayed at my new place of work, albeit relieved to see a second security door at the other end of the carriage, through the gangway that ran past the counter. The simple knowledge that there was more train beyond this point was enough to raise my spirits.

5

IT IS HERE, then, in this crepuscular stronghold, that the Guard spends nearly all his time, journeying uptrain only to exercise his sidekick or to interview men like myself. The Nincompoop tends to go aft more frequently, but only with prior permission, for provisions from the buffet cars, or to lure potential candidates into his master's midst. But here is the shocking thing: so far as I can gather, neither has set foot beyond that second security door. The Guard, it would seem, for all his seniority, is nothing more than a paragon of the 8:08's stock mindset: to settle for what you already have. A sad state of affairs, but there it is.

I turn now to the clerical duties I performed under his stewardship. I spent a week with him in total, and the time passed more quickly compared to those first seven days, despite the somewhat purgatorial nature of my employment. The Guard wanted me to start immediately. This would not be a problem, I said, as I had nothing else on – a flippant remark that brought a hurricane of laughter from my obliging host. I was quite keen to put my stamp on the carriage early, to leave a legacy of sorts if I could, while not forgetting my main objective of contacting the Driver. But that could be done, I sensed, only by establishing a base camp here. I felt I had to show willing, ingratiate myself, not just to earn my keep but to obtain further information, win certain privileges, though the only one of interest to me was access through that second security door. Such diligence as I showed was entirely focused on achieving that aim, on coming up with a good reason – a good *professional* reason – why he should send me forward.

The first thing I did was find a new starter for the strip light. To my amazement there was a whole box under the counter, unopened, but the Guard was so inured to the flicker he thought it a substantial impairment of the carriage's ambience when I corrected the fault, the interior blazing for no more than a few seconds before he had me put the defective starter back in. He also objected to my plumping up the cushions on the modular seating and my giving the counter a wipe down with a cloth.

'There is such a thing as too much initiative,' he said.

'My apologies. I can see you prefer things as they are.'

'We have soldiered on for an eternity or two, and we are good for another.'

'I just thought, you know, a little more light . . .'

'Look, the gesture is appreciated. But it's not a housekeeper I am in want of at this time. A man can be too conscientious,' he added, slapping my arse. 'A man can be so conscientious as to be positively ladylike.'

I made it immediately clear that he had crossed a boundary – that while the Nincompoop might tolerate this sort of behaviour, where I came from it was regarded as sexual harassment. His response was that he didn't see how our working relationship could function without some physical contact.

'I am an extremely tactile man,' he said, 'and you're contractually obliged to suffer some degree of passing entanglement as I wander about the place.'

Later, while I was sorting through the electrical equipment behind the counter, I asked him whether he would object to some music. The Guard blanched, as if remembering some delicacy he had once tried and hated:

'Music? Music? What sort of music?'

'Pass me one of those radios.'

There were several stacked on the top shelf behind the counter. He selected the oldest, a beige, semi-circular model with fabric speakers and a leather strap.

'Turn it on.'

He didn't know how.

'That button there.'

'This one?'

He pressed it and there was a hiss of static.

'Now turn the dial on top.'

As he did so, it was clear that he derived greater pleasure from flitting between stations than listening to any single one, and he left the tuner halfway between a channel playing solemn classical music and another playing a lurid 1960s Europop tune, the only lyrics to which seemed to be 'Titty bom-bom'. He wouldn't let me retune it, and there now ensued an argument about working conditions, I protesting that a health inspector would have the place closed down, he replying that he knew of no such officials hereabouts.

'Now,' he continued, setting the radio back up on the top shelf, 'you'll be wondering what it is I have lined up for you. Park yourself on that chair.'

'Which one?'

'That one.'

There were twenty on either side of the aisle, one to each booth.

'No,' he said, when I sat down on the nearest, 'not that one; *that* one.'

I moved to the adjacent seat.

'Not that one; *that* one.'

I got up, sat down in the next.

'Not that one; *that* one.'

And so I continued, getting further and further from the Guard, till I reached the chair at the rear end of the carriage and he was shouting at me from the other. When I'd tried every one, he asked me which I preferred.

'They're all the same.'

'A common misconception. A supposition of the gravest irrectitude. The truth of the matter is that they are unique things *disguised* as serial things. Now tell me: which did you prefer? Bearing in mind you've to sit there for an epoch.'

I pointed randomly to one halfway down on the right-hand side.

'This one?' He walked over to it. 'The eighth one along?'

'I guess so.'

'Excellent!' he clapped, booting up the corresponding PC. 'An excellent choice!'

'May I ask why?'

'Because nobody has ever chosen it. Sit down. Sit yourself down. Now, of all the manifold duties I've to carry out, it's me correspondence that concerns me most. Me emails and what-have-you.'

'You've fallen behind?'

'Behind? I am not just behind. I am across and to the side of it. I am beneath and under. I am all around it. I am everywhere other than on top of it.'

The problem, he elaborated, was that each reply he sent engendered another, almost instantly.

'A common complaint,' I said, 'but if I may say, you've come to the right man.'

I gave a brief summary of my experience in this area. I was

especially adept, I said, at wording emails in such a way as to prevent people emailing back.

'Grand. But you must deal with each enquiry on its merits. As my personal Secretary, you must be firm but fair.'

I assured him that I excelled at what he was asking me to do, and he left me to it, retreating to a cot in a partially closed-off area at the rear of the carriage.

My confidence wavered on logging into his account: 'I can't seem to find anything in your inbox,' I said. 'Where are the emails you want me to answer?'

He came back and pointed to the junk mail. As I opened it, I assumed there was something up with his settings, that his proper mail had been diverted here. But no. This was it. It was the spam he wanted answering. This was his 'correspondence'.

'I'm away for a nap,' he said. 'Please don't disturb me for at least fifteen hours.'

And he retreated again to his cot, which was made from bits of seats, blankets and old towels, the headboard fashioned from wooden panels from a First Class compartment. The Nincompoop was sat by the counter in the Recreation Area, with Companion, rocking back and forth over the coffee table. He had taken his train to bits and didn't know how to reassemble it. I turned my attention to the screen, clicking on the first of 7,648 unsolicited emails, the one with the subject heading 'Write a message to our pretty pussies'.

6

I SAY 'UNSOLICITED'; the Guard was convinced every item of spam was intended for him and him alone. Two hours later, the total number of emails had risen to 7,667. I was losing already, not even keeping my head above water, but I reckoned I could stabilise the figure by focusing on the more persistent correspondents. There was no blocking function on the Guard's account, no way of preventing follow-up emails except through the agency of my own prose. Normally the most effective method is to not reply at all, but that wasn't an option here, I had to answer everything. In my previous job, I'd thought nothing of taking an entire morning to compose an email to someone seated in the same office as myself, the sole intention being to prevent them emailing back; but here I was dealing with emails I would normally have deleted in batches of fifty, and it took me a while to work up an appetite for their various vested interests. And of course, as soon as I responded to, say, Fubar, or Bhumika, or Karamba Slots Casino, another would arrive from RussianWomenOnline or The Australian Institute of Business Institute. No sooner had I dealt with an enquiry from Nesta Roberts at LinkedIn, here was Maureen at MatureShaggers asking me to view her profile, or an anonymous 'Student girl waiting for a man to lick her pussie'.

My equipment didn't help, a beige PC from the early dotcom years, with a cruddy keyboard and defective mouse, the cursor either overshooting its target or limping across the screen, the monitor flickering in syncopation with the strip light overhead. The web browser didn't resemble any I recalled, even from the internet's inception, a swatch of turquoise framed with buttons and tabs that did nothing but turn the cursor into a spinning multi-coloured wheel, menus that dropped down to reveal greyed-out functions, none of them responsive to commands. But the thing that most distinguished online life here from online life as I remembered it was the character of the web itself. How can I put this? There was no web. Or there didn't seem to be. Everything I typed into the browser yielded a 404 Page Not Found. And when I checked the search history there were no websites listed, just the following repetitive ream:

Mail – guardo8@8o8.co.uk
Mail – guardo8@8o8.co.uk
Mail – guardo8@8o8.co.uk
Mail – guardo8@8o8.co.uk
Mail – guardo8@8o8.co.uk
Mail – guardo8@8o8.co.uk
Mail – guardo8@8o8.co.uk
Mail – guardo8@8o8.co.uk
Mail – guardo8@8o8.co.uk
Mail – guardo8@8o8.co.uk
Mail – guardo8@8o8.co.uk
Mail – guardo8@8o8.co.uk
Mail – guardo8@8o8.co.uk
Mail – guardo8@8o8.co.uk

Thus, the only incoming data was the Guard's spam. Effectively, that *was* the internet. If you clicked on any of the links in the emails, you just got another 404, and if you tried to open attachments, the cursor turned into a spinning wheel and you had to reboot. And yet, just as one might infer an entire civilisation from an artefact like the Rosetta Stone, so here one could get a sense of cyberspace as a whole from the fragments siphoned into the Guard's spam. How many of my replies got through, I don't know, but none came back as unreturned mail.

In the main, the emails fell into four categories: sexual, medical, financial, corporate. Some seemed 'kosher' – a press release from an art gallery, an invitation to subscribe to a new literary journal – but when I showed them to the Guard, he told me to delete them as they were 'clearly not intended' for him. The ones I most enjoyed dealing with came from back-packers trapped without a cent in places like Lagos or Manila: 'I am greatly apologise for imposing on your free time with this unusual emergency . . .'; 'I humbly requiring your urgent assistance with the following compelling matter . . .' etc. etc. I liked the work that had gone into these, their inventive syntax and cunning use of the thesaurus, their struggle with English as a second language. I also warmed to the inept con-men, with their tortuous backstories:

Attn:,
Compliments of the season to you. I will try to be brief and laconic. My late client who shares the same last name with you, died leaving a large sum of money to the tune of Five Million United States Dollars. I contacted you because you have the same family name as my client. With your help we can claim the above mentioned financial estate or the holding bank will confiscate the fund due to the fact that I cannot get a

hold of anyone related to the deceased. In the interim please kindly get back to me with your name, address and full bank details so I can accord you more details and steps we have to take to actualize this issue. Should my proposal contradict your moral ethics, I apologize. But if interested do reply me via my personal email, abdulrahbino@gmail.com, to discuss further regarding this issue.

Yours Faithfully,
Abdul Bin Rahman

By midnight I realised I was winning. The number of unanswered emails had come down to 7,613, thanks mainly to the generic templates I'd developed to cater for the full range of demands. Most worked. Follow-up emails were fewer now, secondary and tertiary responses decreasing all the time. All I had to do was keep cutting and pasting. Every so often I had to devise a new template to deal with a new kind of enquiry that came through, but I reckoned a few days would be enough to assemble a comprehensive library of responses.

I had yet to consider two things. Firstly, I had to sleep. And I would wake to a figure in excess of that with which I'd ended the previous day. The total could be reduced only over a period of weeks. The second thing was that there were thirty-nine other PCs.

The following day – I spent the night with Companion and the Nincompoop in the Recreation Area – the Guard confirmed that each work station was dedicated to a separate account. The idea was that once guard08 was under control, I'd move on to guard09 or guard07, while continuing to monitor guardo8. And so on, till I was managing all forty accounts at once, like a grandmaster playing simultaneous chess games. I envisaged diminishing returns. Conceivably, I could manage two or three PCs, but any more than that would be a music hall act. Even with thirty-nine assistants working at the others, it would have taken a month or more to get through the Guard's correspondence.

The Guard himself, though keeping an eye on my daily stats, was not too vigilant in overseeing the actual writing process. This was a blessing, for whenever he did get involved, he succeeded only in slowing me down. Every so often he would rustle over, standing by my chair, breathing loudly through his mouth, his pelvic region uncomfortably close to my head, occasionally dictating a response to any emails whose subject headings caught his eye. Sometimes he would sit down and compose one himself. Whenever this happened, I lost an hour's work, so fixated did he become with the enquiry of the correspondent. He spent most of the time idling in his cot with a paperback from *The Collected Works of Vaughan Meredith*, but when the mood took him to sit down at the keyboard there were no half measures. I remember one subject heading he was particularly moved by: 'Student girls are ready to present free sex to a person which will pay their room rent'. 'A young and beautiful blond is looking for a man', ran the main body of the email, 'Ready to serious relationship, want kids. Pro in sex and ready to everything, i like anal sex.' From someone calling herself Virginia.

'Stand aside,' said the Guard, when he saw this, 'I can see this girl needs my personal assistance. Be a poppet and make us a cup of coffee.'

When I returned, he'd accumulated a substantial block of prose.

'There,' he said, 'I think you'll find that'll do the job.'

'Really? It looks quite long.'

'I think you'll find it's germane to the matter at hand. See for yourself.'

It certainly was germane to the matter at hand – as the Guard understood it. 'My Dear Virginia,' it began, 'Can I first say that to receive such an epistle as this is a heart-warming thing in its own right in these cynical times? Frankly, I was moved by it. I will do you the courtesy, once I have emptied my tear ducts into this handkerchief, of bestowing upon it the full armoury of my attention and talent. But to get to the point: I am delighted, *delighted* to learn that you are desirous of having children, but what's all this about 'anal' sex? Now I'm not much of a man-about-town, but I'd be remiss if I neglected to point out that you'll never conceive if you go about it using that particular methodology . . .' It continued like this for another three paragraphs, presenting anecdotal evidence from his native Ireland, weighing up the evils of bearing children out of wedlock against the greater sin of abortion (' . . . It is not worth it, on the eternal scale, but I know a man in Roscommon who'll do it for a drink if your mind is set . . .').

He continued to apply himself in this fashion till I gave him to understand that his interventions were counterproductive, remaining in my seat whenever he appeared at my elbow. Maybe I should have encouraged him more. I was impressed by his ability to slip back into a world he'd presumably not seen for some time, converting into prose what I guessed came directly from his memory banks without the vetting of his conscious mind, typing away without revising his sentences, in a trance-like state similar to Heobah's when she'd recounted her trip to the belfry; but though it was possible this retrieval of his past might help rehabilitate the Guard, I also knew it

276

would prolong my stint as his secretary beyond all tolerable limits, for my stats dipped dramatically whenever he took the helm and I soon put a stop to his meddling.

Thus it was that a second week sped by, a thousand times quicker than the first, the train's motion scarcely perceptible in these unfenestrated confines. Only when we hit an incline or leaned into a bend did I remember I was on a moving object, so distracted was I by my clerical responsibilities. It pained me to admit, but I missed work, missed filling my time with tasks which, though pointless in the wider sense, were therapeutic in the short-term. And once I'd adjusted to my new role, it wasn't so different from being back in the office. I didn't find it soul-destroying when an offer for a health insurance quote kept coming back or someone from FindBride.com didn't get the hint. And my interest in the language side of things grew. The scammers were still out there on their own, from a literary viewpoint, but I could see merit in everything now. I'd never really looked at spam, never really examined it closely before, and I suppose I was grateful for the opportunity. The subject headings from the sex sites were particularly good. In the hands of a professional writer, they might be turned into poetry:

> Write a message to our pretty pussies
> Enter our club and have sex
> I want to cheat my husband
> The most beautiful models are in our club
> Enter our club as a lover
> I will introduce you to nasty housewives
> Want to fuck a cutie on a first date?

Only now did I see what an idiot I'd been to delete it all before, in the belief that it was less relevant, less interesting than my legitimate mail. I'm not in a position to test this theory, but I'd wager that now I've got the taste for unsolicited mail, it would be difficult to go back to the correspondence of my friends and colleagues.

7

A NOTHER DEVELOPMENT AT this time was the burgeoning friendship of Companion and the Nincompoop. It was fitting that they gravitated to one another, for the Nincompoop was a human with a bestial streak, while Companion was a beast with human qualities, their interests naturally overlapping. And I'd not been paying him much attention. I spent all my time at the keyboard now, and it wasn't surprising when he preferred to sleep with his new friend than curl up with me at day's end. He would still come when called, but it took more coaxing, and when he did come, groysing my knuckle with his cheek and arching his back, it was like he was playing the part of a cat, paying lip service to an obsolete ritual. He would sit by my chair for a minute or so, but when I looked up again, there he was in the Recreation Area, chewing the fat with the Nincompoop.

The Nincompoop, for his part, now went about completely naked, perhaps trying to identify with the creature that had recently come into his life. He saw that Companion had a fine coat of fur that he kept nice and clean, and I can only assume that he wanted to show off his own pelt. This I approved of. It was good to see him discard the Deliveroo jacket, a dismal relic of a dark age.

Only at the beginning of the third week did I begin to consider how I was going to progress further downtrain. I needed a pretext for getting through that second door. In the last seven days I had reduced the Guard's correspondence by just a few hundred emails. As I feared, fresh tranches came overnight, and it took most of the following day to redress the balance. I calculated that a single account might be brought under control after two months if I worked flat out. Multiply this by forty, and you can see the size of the task.

I was free to come and go through the security door at the rear of the carriage, which the Guard allowed me to prop open whenever I went out for a fag, but nothing was said about the security door at the front. The Guard rarely appeared behind me now, somewhat offended, I think, by my preference for working alone. I hadn't done myself any favours there, restricting my opportunities to engage him in any chit-chat that might naturally lead to the subject of breaching that second door.

On Tuesday afternoon an idea began to form: I would compose an email purporting to come from the Driver, requesting my presence at the front of the train. I would send it to myself and alter the sender's address from guard08@808.co.uk to driver@808.co.uk.

It was a bold plan, staking everything on the assumption that the Driver's authority outranked the Guard's. My instinct – notwithstanding the 'theology' of the chapbook – was that whoever caused the train to move must be the supreme locomotive figure. But I would have to test the water, bring the Driver up in conversation, see how the Guard reacted. Perhaps he would make the sign across his chest at the mere mention of his name, as an expression of fealty to his superior? As to why the Driver should contact *me* and not the Guard, especially on the Guard's email, when he didn't even know I existed, I thought I could get round that by addressing the email to 'The Secretary'. The Guard himself had used that title when discussing my role, and it was reasonable to assume the Driver was familiar with it. Here, then, was my first draft:

Dear Secretary,

I thought I would write to formally introduce myself. I trust you have settled in to your new role and that my colleague is not being too demanding. Let me say that, despite your heavy schedule, you are privileged to be working under such a man. But to get to the point. I should like – with his blessing – to meet you myself, with a view to fostering greater cohesion between the various parts of our locomotive operation. In short, I should like to see a new collegiate spirit on board, beginning here with our own small team. We must set an example to the others, must we not?

As to the place of our meeting, much as I would like to come to you, you'll appreciate that my responsibilities prevent me from leaving my current station. I therefore invite you to make your way to my cab at your earliest convenience. I look forward to seeing you.

Best regards,
The Driver

I sat on this for a couple of days, wondering if I was forcing things too soon. But how much longer did I want to remain in this chicken coop bashing out copy for the Guard? I sensed he thought more highly of me than the interns he'd mentioned before, but I doubted that this was a good thing. The worst thing to do would be to make myself indispensable.

On Thursday morning I made a few edits. I was happy

with the content, the way it appealed to the Guard's vanity while letting him know who was boss: the fact that the Driver already knew about my appointment as the Guard's secretary was ample demonstration of his oversight. But it wasn't quite hitting the right stylistic note. I needed the Driver to sound less avuncular, more managerial, so I threw in some jargon culled from the many text messages I'd received from Dan Coleman over the years, changing the word 'meeting' to 'team building exercise', and rebranding my trip to the Driver's cab as an 'Awayday'. Then I hit send and made the necessary adjustments to the address when the email came back.

Not till lunchtime, however, did I bring the matter up with the Guard. But before I come to that, this mention of food raises an issue that cannot be put off any longer. I shall try to keep this brief. It may have been noted that, since my unsuccessful trip to the toilet ten days ago on the Saturday of my date with Heobah, subsequent visits have been few and far between. Just as my appetite has diminished daily, so have the functions of bowel and bladder. An air of anachronism already attaches to these organs and to the cubicles in which I was wont to service them. So it is with everyone on board, for I've never seen anyone enter or leave a toilet. Just as the Frenchman's cigarette produced no ash, the many meals had on the 8:08 appear to engender no waste products. Where it all goes, no one knows. But here is the real conundrum: where all other passengers are deaf to nature's call, Companion remains a regular patron of the facilities. What can be deduced from this? How is it that lesser mammals pass under the radar, their biology unchanged? And need I labour the irony of a cat being the only user of the human latrines? I've painted myself as something of a Crusoe figure, at times, with Companion as my Man Friday, but there's surely a case for casting him as the deracinated sailor, for it is I who fall into the habits of the natives while he preserves his Western dignity. Fortunately, there is a toilet at the front end of the carriage to cater for his needs.

This may have accounted for the ceremony of our meal-times in the Guard's carriage, for once food is divested of nutritional purpose, there is *only* a ceremonial aspect. Every day he insisted on our eating together in the Recreation Area, at midday and at six o'clock. The sole purpose of this was social, but because the Nincompoop had no English and the Guard spoke only when spoken to (albeit profusely when prompted), I always had to take the lead. I found this exhausting, but today I was grateful for the chance to pursue my own agenda, dropping the Driver into conversation several times without any quizzical looks.

The Nincompoop had been sent out earlier that morning for new supplies, returning with a sack of provisions from the buffet car where we'd first met. So lunch was a KEEP CALM AND TUCK IN sandwich and a KEEP CALM AND FORAGE drink, something in a carton made from berries 'harvested from the verges and by-ways of England'. The Nincompoop had also found a cache of non-edible merchandise, including a KEEP CALM AND LEARN colouring-in book and a KEEP CALM AND KEEP CALM rosewater spray that was supposed to combat negativity and enhance our wellbeing, but which he was using as perfume, pressing the dispenser and parading through the mist, egged on by the Guard, who seemed to find it highly amusing, smiting the arse cheeks of his Chief Ensign with his free hand, while eating his sandwich with the other. When the Nincompoop had been sent out for supplies on the first day, I had instructed him to procure more pots of UHT for Companion. This I was able to do by pointing at one of the pots I still had, but I was hard-pressed to explain to him the difference between a tuna and sweetcorn sandwich and other kinds of sandwich. Fortunately, he brought one back in that first consignment, and I gave him to understand that this would the cat's preferred meal from now on.

As we ate, I opened with a few comments about my workload, how I was meeting my targets, how important it was to set goals for myself – Colemanesque drivel, for the most part. Then I added that, though happy in my work, I sometimes felt frustrated that I couldn't meet in person with some of the more interesting correspondents.

The Guard was sat opposite, bare feet up on the coffee table: 'The personal touch, you mean?'

'Exactly.'

'Like who? The young girls, I'll warrant?'

'Not them, no.'

'The mature ladies then? The, what do they call themselves?'

'Cougars. No, not them either.'

'The turf accountants? The funeral directors? The insurance people? The Quebec Spiritualist Society? The Seventeenth Day Adventalists?'

'I was thinking of those closer to home.'

'Home?'

'Our colleagues. You know: those here, on the 8:08.'

The Guard leaned across the table, manboobs sagging as he reached for a serviette. 'You've had word from them?'

'There's something I think you should see.'

'Show it to me, and I will tell you whether I think I should see it or not. And if I don't . . .'

'What?'

'I shall unsee it, so I shall.'

There was a moment, after we went over to the computer and the Guard sat down, when I thought I'd lost the email I'd spent so long composing, but there it was in the spam box, under a heavy bombardment from The Australian Institute of Business Institute. The Guard's lips moved slowly as he read, and it was then that I realised I might have used some words he wasn't familiar with, or had forgotten. Like Marlowe's, his vocabulary was excellent, but there were blind spots. He didn't seem to know what I'd meant by 'home' just now, for instance.

'An expert piece of prosemanship,' he said, looking up at me when he'd finished. For a second I thought he'd rumbled me. But his praise was sincere: 'I can see why you were seduced by this gentleman. A nice turn of phrase. This bit here for instance, *Reading from the same hymnsheet*. Kind of spiritual.'

'There's no problem then?'

'Why should there be?'

'So I can go? I can go and meet him at the front? Tomorrow maybe?'

The Guard stood and got out his pipe. 'I don't see why not,' he said, filling it with tobacco.

'Thank you. *Thank you.* I'll be back before you know it.'

'Grand. I'm away for a lie-down.'

Before reaching his cot, he stopped, turned to me again. 'There's just one thing,' he said.

'What?'

'This Driver fella. He seems to know me, but I'm damned if I know him.'

8

A MERE DOOR was all that stood between me and the front of the train. But it was a security door and I didn't have the code. It was a brass mechanism with buttons numbered 0-9, and all I had to do was try every possible combination. This was the Guard's advice, offered in the belief that such an undertaking was not only eminently feasible but might be an interesting way of passing the time.

'You're sure you don't know it?' I asked.

'I think it had an 8 in it. Something 8, something, something, something, something, something. I wrote it down on my arm once, but time and the sweats of my own personage have washed it from view.'

We'd already tried various sequences of 8s and 0s – 80808, 8080808, 08080808 – but I could tell the Guard was just going through the motions.

'This Driver fella,' he said, as he watched me pummelling the mechanism, 'this Driver fella – did you ever consider the possibility he might be *aft*?'

'Aft?'

'To the rear of our current location. Did you ever stop to contemplate that?'

'But he's the *Driver*.'

'So you keep calling him.'

'It's what he calls himself. It's what he *is*.'

We had not made much progress here either. This was how our earlier conversation had ended:

Me: 'But he's the Driver.'

Guard: 'The what?'

Me: 'The person that controls the train.'

Guard: 'Surely you have it arse-about-face? Surely you mean the train that controls the person?'

The Guard suggested – not unreasonably – that if the Driver really was who he said he was, then he might know the combination to the door:

'Just email him. I'm sure he'd be delighted to give it to you.'

So I had to pretend to email him, and of course the Driver didn't have it. The Guard seemed pleased when I told him:

'I assume you'll be cancelling your appointment then?'

'Doesn't look like I have much choice.'

'He'll understand. And look on the bright side.'

'Which is?'

'You still have us.'

'But what about the Driver? It won't do to let him down.'

'I'd forget about him. He's out of the reckoning now.'

'What do you mean, out of the reckoning?'

I waited for him to continue, but he didn't elaborate. There was sadness in in his eyes, a new vulnerability as he trudged back to the rear of the carriage and lay down in his cot. He spent the rest of the afternoon there with a paperback, while I persisted with the lock, trying different combinations of 8s and 0s.

After another hour of trying, I needed a drink, so I downed the Clynelish 14-year-old from the Junior Collector Selection Box that I'd been saving for a special occasion. Then I asked the Guard if he had anything else.

He was still in his cot, lost in his novel, an historical saga set in Napoleonic times, and he scarcely looked at me when he spoke: 'I regret to inform you,' he said, 'that this a dry carriage.'

'Temperance? Here? From an Irishman?'

'A what?'

'Forget it. There's nothing at all?'

'There might be something knocking about aft, but I'd have to ask you to consume it off the premises.'

The Nincompoop was duly despatched, returning with a large bottle of whisky in a brown paper bag. He'd seen me drink the Clynelish 14-year-old, and he took the bottle as a guide.

'Do what you have to do,' said the Guard, as he handed it over, 'but I must ask you to keep the vessel hidden, out of respect for the local by-laws.'

Unsurprisingly, it was a KEEP CALM brand - KEEP CALM AND something or other, I don't remember - and I spent most of that evening in the corridor to our rear, with the bottle at my side, smoking the last of my tobacco and pretending to get drunk. The whisky purported to be distilled in the usual way but had no intoxicating effect, and as I sat there, looking up through the skylight, I gave serious consideration to climbing out, making my way along the roof of the train, traversing the Guard's carriage and dropping down through the next skylight, like a stuntman in a film. It wasn't that I couldn't be bothered. No, there were certain ethical issues here. I realised that my attitude to the external environment had come full circle. It wasn't that I no longer noticed it, as I fancied was the case with the other passengers, but it definitely seemed subordinate to the locomotive environment now. If I jumped, I could easily pull myself up, force my way through that 18-inch gap, but to reach the front of the train by such measures was unthinkable. I had to pass *through* it. I had to experience the interior of every carriage. If I didn't, my entire journey – my journey-within-a-journey – would be invalid. In other words, I had to have the code for that door.

The following morning I put it out of my head and resumed my work at the computer. The Guard was in a strange mood: affable but nervous, like he'd done something wrong, and was laying the groundwork for an apology. I'd noticed a change in his behaviour from as early as the third day of my employment, less inclined to whimsy and merriment and increasingly self-conscious, more careful with his words and watchful of their effect. A new style of management, I told myself – he had cracked the whip too often with my predecessors and was trying something different with me.

When he began altering his appearance, I should really have guessed what was afoot. He had taken to styling his hair differently every day, going through as many permutations as its close curls would allow. Today he had wetted it down and slicked it back, but there was no pomade to hand and it was already beginning spring up from the dome of his head. He also had on a waistcoat, with a Paisley front and a lilac backing, quite a nice garment but too tight on his huge frame. Usually he slept in till eleven, but today he was up at 8:00 and he'd made me a coffee.

'Did you notice anything different this morning?' he said, slamming the mug down in my booth.

'What?'

He nodded at the strip light overhead. 'I put a new starter in.'

'Oh. Yes. Thanks.'

'I thought about what you said. About working conditions.'

'I appreciate it.'

'So.' The Guard edged closer, his pelvis almost touching my earlobe. 'How's it going then?'

'Fine.'

'What's that there you're working on?'

'Another reply to the Australian Institute of Business Institute. I explained in my previous email that we are not in a position to consider overseas study, even under their reduced tuition fees for Distance Learning students, but they're quite persistent.'

'You've given up on your friend then?'

'The Driver? Not entirely.'

'Well, his loss is my gain.'

'Nice of you to say.'

'I mean it.' The Guard placed a hand on my shoulder here. As he brought it away, he brushed my cheek tenderly with his little finger. 'It's the truth, so it is.'

'Look, I should get on. I'm a bit behind here.'

The Guard had felt me flinch, and was now trying to make himself smaller, shuffling from foot to foot and looking at the floor. 'Sorry.'

'Don't be. It's OK.'

'It's just that – there's something I need to tell you.'

I swivelled round and looked up.

'It's better out than in,' he went on.

'What is?'

'I think – I think I'm in love with you.'

I logged off calmly, stood, pushed my chair under the booth.

'I can't help it,' he continued, with a mixture of embarrassment and relief, 'I can't help the way I feel.'

'I see.'

'I've been bottling it up something wicked.'

'And you're sure of it? You're certain of how you feel?'

'I am as sure of it as I am of my own backside. I knew it as soon as the curtain drew back last Tuesday week. *Here is the one*, I said to myself, *Here is the one*. Besides, I've done my re-search.'

'Re-search?'

The Guard produced the paperback from his waistcoat pocket, a Napoleonic saga by Vaughan Meredith, about a countess who falls in love with a soldier.

'He's away to battle,' he said. 'But he hasn't told her how he feels about her yet.'

'Ah. Something tells me he might not come back.'

'Don't think I haven't thought about that. I'm scared to continue, so I am.'

'And you feel the same way as – what's his name?'

'Private Attwood.'

'*Private* Attwood? A Private and a Countess?'

'It's a romance.'

'Evidently. And you feel the same way as this Attwood?'

'I do.'

I gave him the usual guff one gives in instances of unrequited love. I told him I was flattered. I told him I was honoured. But I was trouble. I had all sorts of unresolved mental issues from previous relationships. I used the word 'baggage' quite a lot to demonstrate how unsuitable I was, but he kept interrupting – that was what Private Attwood had felt, he said hopefully, that's what had stopped him proposing to the Countess before going off to engage the French.

'The fact is, I am betrothed to another,' I said.

The Guard emitted a tiny, agonised yelp. 'I feared as much,' he said, pulling out his pipe. 'The Driver.'

'No, *no*. Not him. My business with the Driver is strictly professional.'

'Then who?'

'I'd rather not say.'

I'm not proud of my conduct during this scene. But any sympathy I had for his predicament was outweighed by the suspicion that he was still keeping something back. In confessing his true feelings towards me, he had just revealed a motive for preventing me from leaving, and in the silence that followed I saw an opportunity to exploit the situation.

'Let's imagine I *was* interested,' I said. 'Hypothetically speaking.'

'Hypothetically?'

'In principle.'

'Go on.'

'Well, a relationship is built on honesty, is it not?'

'To tell you the truth I wouldn't know. It's the first time I've thrown me hat into the ring.'

'Trust me, a relationship is built on emotional honesty. The question is, are you honest?'

The Guard was confused.

'What I mean is: Have you *been* honest? With me, I mean?'

He was still nonplussed. He had shown his hand. He had virtually gone down on one knee. What more did I want?

'I'm talking about the door.'

'Oh. That.'

'The code. You know it, don't you?'

'I do and I don't.'

'What's that supposed to mean?'

'It means that I would know it if there was one.'

'There's no code?'

'No. All you've to do is open it.'

'But I've tried.'

'I know. I've been watching. You've pressed the buttons, turned the dial, pushed, banged, punched, kicked, screamed at it. You've done everything it is humanly possible to do to a closed door. Except one thing.'

He led the way past the counter. 'All you've to do,' he said, when we got to the end of the gangway, 'is to depress the handle, like this, as with any conventional door, and pull it towards you. Thus.'

He held it ajar for a second. Beyond the threshold was a continuation of the corridor that lay to our rear, wooden floorboards, skylights, emptiness. I was astonished. I didn't see how it had opened now, but not before.

'Pick a number,' said the Guard, closing it again. 'Any number.'

'874573.'

He punched it in. 'Now try.'

The door wouldn't open.

'Now count to sixty.' We counted together. 'Now try it again.'

I turned the handle. The door opened.

'Pick another number. Any amount of digits.'

'7469383682.'

The door wouldn't open.

'Everyone thinks a code need be entered before engaging the handle,' explained the Guard. 'But the opposite logic applies: entering a number *prevents* the handle from turning. You've to wait a full minute before trying again.'

'That's ingenious.'

'It is ingeniousness crossed with witchcraft,' said the Guard, 'with a side-helping of knavery. You're not angry with me, are you?'

I was furious, but I told him I understood – he had done it out of love, his better judgement clouded by passion.

'That author,' I said, 'what's his name?'

'Meredith.'

'Meredith. He probably says something about love being blind, right?'

'I think he does. I think I recall reading something to that effect.'

9

NOW THAT I could leave the Guard's carriage any time I wanted there was no hurry, and I didn't strike out for the Driver's cab till mid-afternoon. How far it was, the Guard couldn't say, for he swore he had never crossed the threshold of that second security door, not once, and I believed him.

'I suppose a kiss is out of the question,' he said, as I put on my cap and retrieved my folio from behind the counter.

'You may kiss me on the cheek.'

He kissed me full on the lips and patted my arse, but it was not too much of a liberty under the circumstances. I was actually feeling quite good about myself for awakening his desires, and I hoped the next incumbent would be more receptive to his advances. Maybe they would make a home together, here among the plywood booths.

Before saying goodbye, I left a few instructions for my successor. I was quite thorough here. I'd saved all my templates in the draft box of the Guard's email account, specifying which templates should be sent to which recipients. I explained to the Guard that the next person should begin here, at guard08, and build on my legacy, before moving on to guard09, guard10 etc . . . It occurred to me that I could have done more as his secretary, that I had not been as conscientious as I might. Only now did I see that I ought really to have trained the Nincompoop up. He could not be trusted to compose anything so important as an email, but might have been taught to perform basic cut-and-paste operations, using keyboard short-cuts. I added this suggestion to the instructions. *He may prove an errant pupil*, I wrote, on a page torn from my folio, *but the Nincompoop has a good heart. I believe in him.*

As I was about to log off, another email arrived from the Australian Institute of Business Institute, and a certain professional doggedness prevented me from ignoring it. *Dear Sir*, I replied, *It's been a privilege. Warmest regards, the Secretary.*

And now I must negotiate the most painful scene of my account. I had gone a few metres into the empty corridor, and as I turned to look at the Guard and the Nincompoop framed in the doorway, the sight of a third, more diminutive figure caused me to wonder whether I shouldn't go back and throw my lot in with them after all. By all means laugh at the sentiments that attach to a mere quadruped, a piebald moggie of middling looks, but they outrank any feeling I ever had for a member of my own species, with the exception of you-know-who. I'd envisaged us together till the end, but it was not to be. Had Companion *chosen* to stay, or was he subject to the same locomotive constraint as the others? The Guard was physically unable to enter the space that lay to the front of his carriage, and so it must have been for the Nincompoop. We'll never know if Companion would claim likewise, had he the verbal wherewithal, or whether he had found his natural place under the steam of his own animal instinct.

But let us not remember him thus. Let us remember him rearing up on hind legs like a little stallion and pirouetting through the sliding doors, showing me the way, showing me the way, arrowing along the carpet; as a figurehead perched resplendently at the front of the food trolley; as a black and white galaxy of fur coiled up on my lap in the evening . . . Let us remember the pleasure we took in providing for his wants and needs, decanting the milk from the UHT pots, the roughness of his tongue on our finger as we angled the coffee cup lid, the separation of the tuna from the sweetcorn in the tuna and sweetcorn sandwiches; his habits at the latrine; his shenanigans in the Restaurant Car; the many positions he got himself into as he conducted his many ablutions; his shrewdness in judging the characters of the various people we met, who to avoid, who to take into our confidence. Fleeting pictures, as I then thought them, now transformed into permanent mental exhibits.

VI
THE DRIVER

1

I F THERE'S ONE thing I regret, it's that there haven't been more jokes. So here's a joke. Two electrons are circling the nucleus of an atom. 'I don't like it here,' says the first electron, 'I'm off, you coming?' 'I think I'll stay,' says the other, 'I'm in my element.' Courtesy of Fred Teesdale, that. And topical too. For I am in my element. Of all Fred's jokes, it's no coincidence that this one should come to me now. Most jokes work by omitting information: *ex*formation, if you will. Here, the exformation is that the first electron doesn't realise its electron-ness is bound up with the element. In the parlance of the second electron, it's not just *in* its element but *of* its element, indivisible from it. There is no absolute division between things, no point where one thing begins and another ends, no clear boundary. If there were, there could be no causal logic between any two given things.

It's the cardinal error of humans to suppose otherwise, to imagine themselves an entity apart, and I still regarded myself as such as I closed in on the Driver's cab. I had removed my cap out of deference, prior to knocking on his door, to underline my status as a mere passenger. I didn't want him thinking I had pretensions, ideas, delusions. Every boy wants to drive the train, I know, but a grown man? I feared he would think it a little *off*.

Two hours' walk had brought me there. The cab itself lay just beyond the bicycle carriage, exactly the same as the bicycle carriage on the old 8:08, a cold, drab interior with metal bars for securing goods. This gave on to a sort of quarter-vestibule, no more than six feet deep, reached by means of an open archway cut into it, framing the pale blue door that marked the end of my journey. That much was evident from the single word it bore:

DRIVER

Below it was a lever under a glass panel, with a smaller sign: **ACCESS RESTRICTED: BREAK ONLY IN EMERGENCY.** There was also a yellow plastic seal joining the lever to the door, the kind you get on lorries to prove the trailer has not been tampered with during transit. I had always imagined, on my old commute, the Guard having to pay occasional visits to the Driver, perhaps in the event of a breakdown, and I'd assumed there was protocol in place, that the Guard had to utter a password before the Driver would open the door, to prove he was not a terrorist or something. I wondered what the form was here. I thought it unlikely that the only way of gaining entry was to smash the glass. Surely the door opened from inside?

I knocked and waited. There was no answer. I knocked again:

'Hello? Excuse me? Anyone there?'

My voice sounded small and distant, the aural equivalent of looking down the wrong end of a telescope. I knocked again, but either the Driver did not hear me or did not want to be disturbed. Just behind me, to the left of the arch, was a door that led to a toilet. I checked it but it was empty. There was nowhere else for the Driver to be but through that door.

Fifteen minutes passed before I broke the seal. I did not

take this decision lightly, and as I removed the fragments of glass, I felt mildly ashamed at the damage. Yet I also understood that this violation was necessary, that I could not consummate my relations with the train by any other means.

The door opened inwards, closing again behind me, and the first thing I saw was the track up ahead. I stared at it for some considerable time, bewitched by those lengths of converging steel, a spectacle that was both exciting and disturbing, and which seemed to require some readjustment of my perceptual faculties. Such was the suddenness of this frontal perspective after a fortnight of only being able to look sideways out of the train, I found I had to avert my gaze as I slumped into the Driver's seat.

The cab itself was, is, quite unprepossessing. I had expected a fancy nosecone, I suppose, a flashy appendage jutting out onto the track, but there's no nosecone at all. The cab of the 8:08 is no different to the cabs on those ugly, two-carriage trains you may have seen shuttling up and down branch lines from one town to another: flat at the front, with a door in the middle, a sort of hood shaped like a bellows extending eighteen inches or so, enabling it to couple with other coaches. The Driver's seat is just to the left of this. On the other side is a small cot, with a thin mattress and a single grey blanket. There's a cabinet built into the rear wall of the Driver's cab, which I imagine once contained crockery, utensils, books, other functional items, but which is now empty except for the centrefold from a 1970s porno mag, stuck to the back panel with a single piece of Blu Tack. The model is called Tessa. Tessa from Sunderland.

I was not greatly perturbed by the Driver's absence. Nor did I find the train's ability to run by itself that disconcerting in light of its foregoing ingenuities. The instruments on the binnacle occasionally flashed, the speedometer's needle climbing slowly as evening drew in, falling again in the morning. There were buttons I pressed, just for the hell of it, switches I flicked, dials I turned in that first hour, but if my meddling affected our progress it was quickly overridden.

I was not at all anxious about the lack of options that now suddenly confronted me. I could not go forward and I could not go back, but this caused me no distress. I did not even bother trying the door behind me, for I knew it would be locked. I didn't care whether it was locked or not. I had already adjusted to the new situation. Part of me still felt that a man in my situation ought to try to amuse himself, distract himself, take his mind off recent events, at least till he was in a position to influence those events, but the vestiges of that old commuter were draining away fast.

At some point I remembered the chess set Marlowe had given me, and it came as no great surprise that I was able to have a reasonably competitive game with myself, which ended in perpetual check. I dozed off around midnight, just as we reached optimum speed. Just before retiring to the cot, I thought I caught sight of something on the track, in the far distance up ahead, but I was too tired to keep my eyes open.

2

IN THE MORNING I woke late, at ten o'clock, and when I rose from the cot I found that we were stationary. Climbing back into the Driver's seat (there was nowhere else to sit), I saw that the thing on the track was still there: a smudge on the horizon where the two rails met. Even in daylight, it was difficult to tell if it was an optical effect – atmospheric perspective, I think they call it – or an obstacle on the line. Maybe that was why we'd stopped?

But no, it was another a shunting procedure, the first we had undergone in a week, and as we began to move again, twenty minutes later, and the thing up ahead began to move also, I realised what it must be: the rear of the train. The rear of the train, only half a mile away from the front. The addition of further carriages had brought it into view.

Another shunting was carried out the next day, and the day after that, the details of the rearmost carriage becoming more discernible as further coaches were added, and by the end of that week – my third on board – I could see that it too had a bellows appendage and a door in the middle. It was evident, from being able to observe the shunting procedure from the front of the train, that coaches were being added somewhere to its middle, and not to the rear, as I had previously assumed. I hadn't noticed any sidings with rolling stock standing idle, ready to be drawn onto the main track, at any point of the journey, though I hadn't been as observant as I might, an oversight I now vowed to correct. After all, now that I had reached the front of the train, all there was to do was look out. Far from feeling sad that my journey had come to an end, I looked forward to making a detailed record of the surrounding landscape.

It was on the fifth morning, after the addition of considerably more coaches than the day before, that I saw an occupant in the rear carriage up ahead. There was definitely someone there. I could see them moving about. On the sixth morning, when the rear of the train was just a hundred metres or so from the front, I thought I recognised him, and on the seventh when I waved, and he waved back, he appeared to recognise me.

VII

FORE & AFT

808

I STILL KEEP a record of the days - or rather, the days keep a record of me. As soon as I open my eyes, I know where I am on the seven-note scale. Of all human inventions, the marking of time, the division of eternity into various allotments, is surely the most durable. I go so far as to call it inviolable. It's a testament to their robustness that the days continue to flaunt their character, even when is there little to distinguish one from another. Friday still feels like Friday, Saturday like Saturday. It is fitting that I end this today, for today is Tuesday, and it was Tuesday when I set out, six weeks ago.

Thirty metres are all that remain between front and rear now: the equivalent of a single Standard Class carriage. I can see Mark Ramsden clearly enough to know that it is he and not some other man waving at me from the window. To see the blank dial of that face become suddenly so familiar was a welcome revelation, yet not wholly unexpected given the synchronicity that has characterised our working relationship to date. That it should perpetuate itself here, on the 8:08, can be no great surprise to either man.

What will happen when we come together, neither of us can know. I wonder how Ramsden and myself will play it when the two ends interlock and the 8:08 is complete. We will both stand, I imagine, perhaps even salute one another, at least straighten our caps, make ourselves presentable. We will both want to mark it in some way, I should think, each doing his best to co-ordinate with the other man, opening the doors at the same time and meeting in the middle of the tiny vestibule formed by the hoods on our cabs.

It is here, in this snug interstice, that the formalities will be conducted. I've decided to present Ramsden with a gift. My folio is all I have. I have laboured to complete the account in time for the insertion of the final coach, notwithstanding my suspicion that the train itself has been postponing that moment until the last words are set down. Perhaps it's unwise to hope for anything in return, but I'd be very surprised if Ramsden did not offer an account of his own adventures on the other side of that original Coach B. Is it too much to ask, is it too much to hope that my colleague has compiled a report of equal rigour, a chronicle of the events that brought him to his latitude, as I was brought to mine? Yes, Ramsden will learn of how I was hurled onto my trajectory, and I shall learn of how he stumbled into his. Ramsden will read of how I broke bread with various men and women, partook of their sundry recreations, sat with nine grown men dressed as planets and discussed cinema, imbibed something that may or may not be an illicit substance, subjecting myself to an experiment that may or may not be a legitimate scientific enterprise, and of which we may suppose Ramsden to be the other human subject. Ramsden will learn that not only have I donned women's clothing, I've felt comfortable in women's clothing; that I've lost my appetite but relocated my libido, only to be propositioned by a man twice my size; that I fell in love with a cat, fell in love with a woman, aided in the recovery of her past life, and live in the hope that its recollection will not eclipse the memory of her saviour when she meets him again, as she will surely do, the second time around.

310

I doubt we'll embrace. A firm handshake will do. Anything more would be indulgent. Anything more would be vulgar. A meeting of palms is more than enough to mark the fusion of front and rear.

I do not need to carry myself aloft to see how this will register on the surrounding terrain. It is already implied, I think, by that staggering intersection in the middle of our circuit, where one part of the train is seen to pass over the other. This tells me all I need to know about what we would see from our notional vantage point. Behold the insignia on my jumper. Behold the number on my cap. Behold the gap in the upper loop, echoing the distance between Ramsden and myself. Distance has always been key to our relationship, and never more so than now. We share an employer but see no reason why the right hand has always to know what the left is doing. We prefer to rely on instinct, and on those occasions when instinct leads to our replicating a task, the results are not uninteresting. I go so far to call them enlightening.

You won't be around to see it, so let me perform for you now, on the page, the union to which you will not be party, the imminent fusion of front and rear, fore and aft, north and south, east and west, left and right, top and bottom, inside and out, let me conjoin the first and last, black and white, beginning and end, allow me to remove from 8:08 what will give us 808. Here, I offer it up as keepsake, a souvenir, as it might be:

:

ACKNOWLEDGEMENTS

I'M GRATEFUL TO Sally O'Reilly for her notes on *The Way to Work*; to Anat Ben David for reading the snippets I sent her; to Professor Adam Smyth at Balliol College Oxford for his generous advice; to Professor Simon Morris at Leeds Beckett University and Nicholas Royle for their charismatic support; to Zinovy Zinik for giving me confidence when I needed it; and to Sharon Kivland at Ma Bibliothèque for coming to my rescue in 2017.

Respect is due to the following artists, whose work is referenced in the text: to the late David Dye, for *Distancing Device* (1970); to Cosey Fanni Tutti, for *Magazine Actions* (1975-80); to Marcel Duchamp for *Why Not Sneeze, Rrose Sélavy* (1921); to Fonda Rae for 'Heobah' (1983); to Nigel Cooke for *Morning is Broken* (2004); and to the taggers 'ELAMENT', 'TWIST' and 'TOXIC' for applying themselves so energetically on the British railway network.

Lastly, thanks to Matthew McDonald and the Stroud spotters for demonstrating that trains can be cool, and to my spiritual guide Panpoons, for showing me the way.

RECENT FICTION FROM SALT

The Watch
by Bibi Berki
ISBN 978-1-78463-237-3

Fox Fires
by Wyl Menmuir
ISBN 978-1-78463-233-5

The Retreat
by Alison Moore
ISBN 978-1-78463-221-2

Elephant
by Paul Pickering
ISBN 978-1-78463-225-0

Every Seventh Wave
by Tom Vowler
ISBN 978-1-78463-239-7

Dreamtime
by Venetia Welby
ISBN 978-1-78463-241-0

NEW FICTION FROM SALT

God's Country
by Kerry Hadley-Pryce
ISBN 978-1-78463-265-6

Seahurst
by S. A. Harris
ISBN 978-1-78463-271-7

Reservoir
by Livi Michael
ISBN 978-1-78463-290-8

Nameless Lake
by Chris Parker
ISBN 978-1-78463-258-8

Dry Cleaning
by Trevor Mark Thomas
ISBN 978-1-78463-282-3

Chimera
by Alice Thompson
ISBN 978-1-78463-254-0

This book has been typeset by
SALT PUBLISHING LIMITED
using Neacademia, a font designed by Sergei Egorov
for the Rosetta Type Foundry in the Czech Republic. It
is manufactured using Holmen Book Cream 70gsm, a
Forest Stewardship Council™ certified paper from the
Hallsta Paper Mill in Sweden. It was printed and bound
by Clays Limited in Bungay, Suffolk, Great Britain.

CROMER
GREAT BRITAIN
MMXXIII